XIDA

PEOPLE

The Eagle Clan

A Chance and Choices Adventure
Book Six

Lisa Gay

Copyright © 2019 Elisabeth Gay
All rights reserved.

ISBN-13: 978-1-945858-13-0

Those Involved in these incidents:

Place of Origin – Dover
Gumdrop– mule purchased by Noah
June – mule purchased by Noah

Place of Origin – Fort Gibson
Colonel Stephen Howland – Commander
Sergeant Matthew McCormick - Master of Supplies
Sergeant Timothy Anders (Tim)
Specialist Gilroy – Trading Post worker
Private Ezra Knuckles
Private Ham Blanders
Private Morgan Finch
Lieutenant Jackson
Lieutenant Olson

Place of Origin – Harmony
Ann Williams – oldest sister – Noah's wife
Stephanie Yates – middle sister – Eli's wife
Sally Williams – youngest sister
Eli Yates – Stephanie's husband
Tom Yates - Eli's father/owner of Yates Mercantile
Helen Yates – Tom's mother
Chris Williams - Ann, Stephanie, and Sally's father
Emma Williams - Ann, Stephanie, and Sally's mother
James Williams – Chris Williams' brother
Smithfield Wyman –livery owner/blacksmith/sheriff
(Smitty)
Mara - Smitty's wife
Earl – the man temporarily running Yates Mercantile
Clara – Earl's wife

Joe – Saloon/Inn Owner

Zachariah Eggleston – a previous travel companion

Minnie Eggleston – Zachariah's wife

Clyde Eggleston - Zachariah's father

Patty Eggleston - Zachariah's mother

Lawrence Gridley – town doctor (Doc)

Nellie Gridley - Doc's wife - nurse

Laura Gridley – Doc's daughter

Horace Devine– a friend, shot while tracking the Butterfield Gang

Betsy Devine– Horace's wife

Eyanosa – Noah's stallion

Blanche Kennedy – Helen Yates' alias

Phillip Kennedy – Tom Yates' alias

Fletcher Kennedy – Eli Yates' alias

Royal Kennedy – James Williams' alias

Sarah Kennedy - Stephanie Yate's alias

Prudence Kennedy - Sally William's alias

Place of Origin – Indian Territory
Cherokee Nation:

Waya- warrior of the Cherokee

Dustu – grandson of Waya and twin of Adahy

Adahy - grandson of Waya and twin of Dustu

Ghigau – Waya's mother-in-law/village leader

Kangee – Cherokee War Woman / village leader

Oukonunaka – lead male warrior of Ghigau's village

Hota- a woman of Ghigau's tribe

Wasa – Hota's husband

Petang – Zitkala's betrothed

Tizhu – Weayaya's betrothed

Zhawe – Dowanhowee's betrothed

Ishtasapa – Mache's betrothed

Washta – a man of Ghigau's village

Shangke - a man of Ghigau's village

Osage Nation:

The'-ha – Kangee's captured spoils-of-war slave

Quapaw Tribe:

Noah Swift Hawk – Ann's husband (Tahatankohana)

Chetan – Noah's father

Bethany – Noah's mother

Luyu – Chetan's mother

Hanataywee – Noah's oldest sister

Ehawee – Noah's next oldest sister

Ke – Noah's brother

Chumani – Noah's youngest sister

Algoma Williams – James Williams' wife

Dowanhowee – James' oldest daughter

Mache - James' second daughter

Mi - James' youngest daughter

Te – James' oldest son

Nanpanta – James' youngest son

Ppahiska – village chief

Mikoishe – Ppahiska's wife

Chaska – Ppahiska's oldest son

Mikakh - Ppahiska's daughter

Kanizhika - Ppahiska's second son

Wakanda – village Mystery Man

Onida – Wakanda's wife

Weayaya - Wakanda's daughter

Mina - village girl in love with Tahatankohana
Tatonga – a man of Noah's village
Metea - wife of Tatonga
Zitkala - Tatonga's oldest daughter
Kimimela – Tatonga's daughter
Takoda - Tatonga's son
Nikiata – Mystery Man in training
Enapay – Nikiata's father
Anpaytoo- Nikiata's mother
Capa – a man of Noah's village
Wichahpi – Capa's wife
Paytah – a man of Noah's village
Ojinjintka – Paytah's wife
Mantu - a man of Noah's village
Nahimana – Mantu's wife
Howahkan – the Mystery Man before Wakanda
Arabella – Noah's former horse

Place of Origin – Little Rock
Daniel Hall – Judge of State of Arkansas
Luke Smith –Noah's alias/doctor
Martin Harrow – livery owner
Robert– stable hand at Harrow's Livery

Place of Origin – Maumelle
Zi – Noah's mare

Place of Origin – Perryville
Sebastian De La Cruz – previous travel companion of
Ann and her family
Lola De La Cruz – Sebastian's wife and a previous
travel companion of Ann and her family

Place of Origin – Pine Bluff

Roscoe Bacon – first owner Bacon's Trading Post

James Bacon – Eli's alias as Roscoe's nephew

Nancy Bacon – Sally's alias as Roscoe's niece

Roscoe's mule:

King

Hector

Eli's Mule:

Ace

Place of Origin – Unknown

Butterfield Gang – Gus, Ben, Roy, and others

Russell French – Traveling Resupply Business owner

Arnold Buzmann-previous partner of Russell/ purchaser of Bacon's Trading Post

Will – Resupply Business worker

Mule team previously owned by Russell French:

Beauty– injured mule, given to Sally (Mule 17)

Dollie – mule with injured eye purchased by Sally

Mule 7 & 8 –injured mules purchased by Sally

Honor– injured mule earned by Dr. Luke Smith

Justice- injured mule earned by Dr. Luke Smith

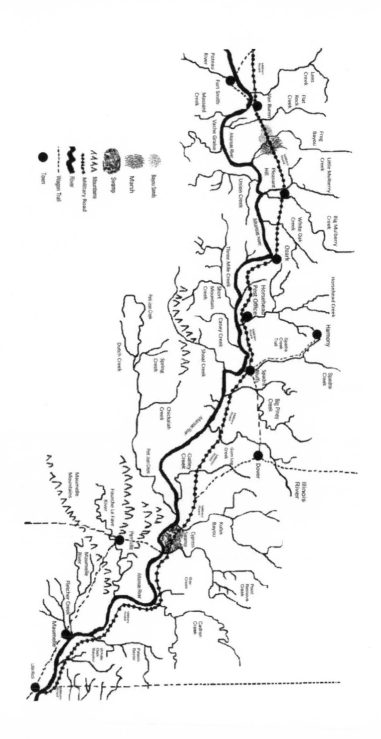

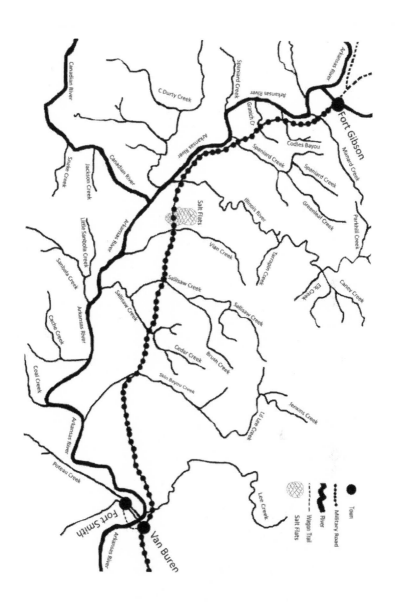

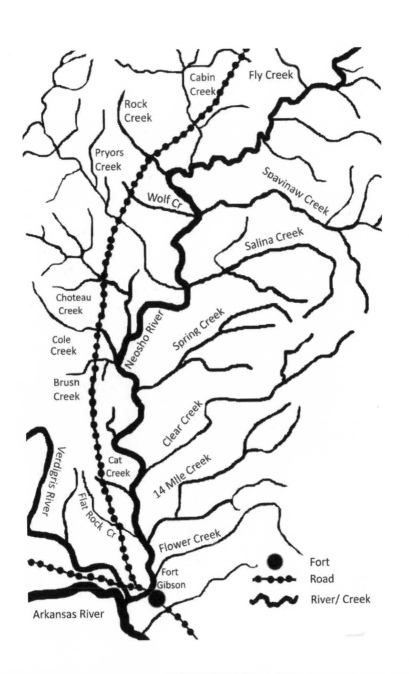

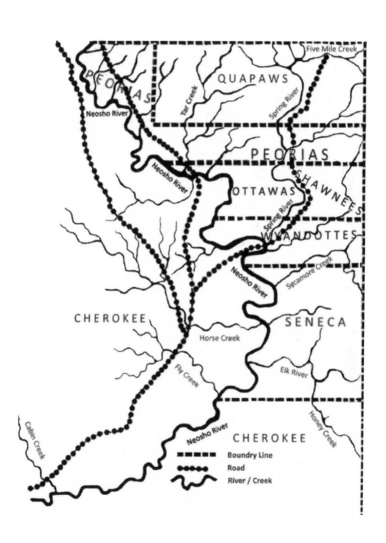

ONE

Noah Swift Hawk put on his deerskin pants, shirt, and moccasins. He hung his long knife at his hip and his bow and quiver over his shoulder. He could hardly wait to see the family into which he had been born. At the same time, he dreaded his homecoming and intensely hoped the person most likely to cause him problems would leave him alone.

The sun had just raised the top of its head over the horizon when the warrior manning the Quapaw village lookout saw the approaching wagons and a long string of animals. One of their people was gone, but this looked like a white man's outfit. The sentry prepared to warn his people to defend the village.

Noah had been gone for over a year. Even so, he thought whoever would be watching should know that he was the man approaching. Still, he didn't want to take any chances with the safety of the people with him. He signaled his village's customary greeting.

The sentry dashed into the village. "Tahatankohana is back!"

On the first day of July in the year of 1840, Noah returned home with his new wife sitting in front of

1

him on his horse. Ann rode with Noah not because they didn't have another horse, but so the people in his village would know her special significance. Noah prayed that would deter the person whose presence he dreaded.

Noah's good friend, sixty-year-old Roscoe Bacon, drove the rear wagon. Ann's fifteen-year-old sister, Sally Williams, piloted the lead wagon. A herd of horses, mules, donkeys, and goats walked between the wagons.

Every villager stood outside. Noah scanned for the only yellow-haired woman who would be in the group. Every day since Noah had left, the woman he most wanted to see had hoped it would be the day Noah would come home. She had waited fourteen months. The woman and Noah locked eyes. "Noah!" She dashed across the village.

Before she got to him, Noah was off his horse. He hugged his mother. "I've missed you so much!"

A second later, Noah's Quapaw father held his oldest child. "Welcome home."

Before Noah could speak, the rest of his family surrounded him. In the Quapaw language, his seven-year-old brother demanded information. "Tell us what happened while you have been gone."

"I will tell you later. First, I have some people I want you to meet."

Noah helped Ann off the horse. He waved Sally and Roscoe over. In English, Noah said, "This is my father, Chetan. His name means 'falcon'. My mother,

Bethany, that's the name of the town where Jesus raised Lazarus from death." Noah hugged each of his family members as he named them. "My grandmother, Luyu, which means 'wild dove'; my sisters, Hanataywee 'faithful', Ehawee 'laughing maiden', Chumani 'dewdrops', and my brother Ke, which means 'turtle'."

Still speaking in English, Noah introduced his new family. "This is my wife Ann Williams, her sister Sally, and our good friend Roscoe Bacon."

Ann had learned how to say the customary Indian greeting. She did so. "Hawe."

Bethany greeted Ann in proper English. "It's very nice to meet you."

A woman, not in the group Noah had identified as his family, called out, "Tahatankohana, I knew you would come home to me!" The woman threw her arms around Noah and attempted to kiss his lips.

Like Ann, she had almost black hair. Hers, however, was very long and braided. She had the braids rolled up and pinned behind her ears.

Ann had cut her hair short only four months earlier during the grieving ceremony for her parents. Both women had strong, well-muscled, beautifully ample female bodies, but the Indian woman's eyes were dark brown, whereas Ann's were the beautiful green that enchanted Noah.

Before the Indian woman was able to kiss him, Noah stepped back and gently pushed her away. Noah knew Ann and Sally would think this woman was his wife or at least a woman he had loved. Because he didn't want to embarrass the woman, Noah whispered, "Mina, stop."

Ever since Noah, the man she knew as Tahatankohana had left, the woman had hoped he would change his mind, come home, and want her. Mina knew by the way the man she loved had ridden into town that the pale-skinned woman was the one he had chosen. She refused to acknowledge her rival's position. Mina didn't give the man she wanted the choice to be gracious. "Do you not want to kiss me again?" she loudly asked as she smirked into Ann's face.

Tahatankohana told Mina in Quapaw, the only language the woman knew, "I never kissed you. You kissed me. I did not want you to kiss me then. I still do not."

The Indian woman informed Tahatankohana. "When you change your mind, I will be here." She again tried to hug him.

Ann hadn't understood what the woman or her husband had said. However, it was obvious that Noah was upset with and by the woman. Still, she didn't want the woman hugging or kissing her husband. She pressed her side against Noah, put her arm around his waist, and blocked Mina. Sally did the same on the other side.

Noah kissed Ann's lips, then turned and smiled into the face of Sally. He drew both women tight. As Tahatankohana, he spoke to Mina in Quapaw. "Meet my wife Ann and my new sister Sally."

The woman glared at Ann and then turned and stalked away.

Ppahiska, the leader of their village, instructed Tahatankohana in their native language. "Get settled in then we will all meet in the community lodge."

In Quapaw, Noah respectfully replied to his chief, "I will come and tell the story of my journey." To his Indian family, in English, so his new family could also understand, he said, "Help us put our animals in the field."

They took the wagons to a hut built of long sticks driven into the ground in the shape of a rectangle and then bent over and joined in an arch at the top. The vertical sticks had horizontal branches and thatch woven through them. The structure then had a layer of bark shingles, which had been covered with mud plaster both inside and outside. It had a thatch roof.

"Are you home to stay?" Bethany asked.

Noah answered, "At least until spring."

Chetan wanted to ensure his son would stay as long as possible. "Then we should take everything inside before we go to the community lodge."

"Yes, we should," Noah agreed.

Ann, Sally, Luyu, Bethany, and Noah's siblings unloaded the wagons while Noah, Chetan, and Roscoe took the animals to an enormous fenced field of tall grass.

At five-foot-eight, Chetan was an average height Indian man with long, dark brown hair and brown eyes. At forty-six, he was still a very physically fit man. He should have been one of the leading men of the village, but a childhood tangle with a puma had made him slightly less of a man. Therefore, Chetan had never been accepted as an equal. Even though he hunted just as well as any of the other men and had as many children, they had relegated him and his family to the bottom.

Roscoe admired the land as they herded the animals into the field where a few horses grazed on the highly nutritious prairie grass. The village was in the northeast of the four hundred and eighty-five acres of land the U.S. Government had assigned to the Quapaw Indians. It was situated on the floodplain between the western edge of the Ozark Plateau on the northeast, Spring River on the west, and Five Mile Creek on the south. The mountains rose sharply, making a natural barrier for the wide flat land of the river's floodplain. The field where the animals grazed was a forty-five-acre wedge of the lowest, flattest part of the land between Five Mile Creek and the cliffs. The lodges clustered together on the higher land next to the mountain.

Chetan opened the gate. "I don't think we'll have a problem with them getting along since these already here are females."

The mares allowed the new herd to join them. Until Noah's horse, Eyanosa, asserted his position as stallion over all of them, the females jostled to establish their place in the larger herd.

TWO

As they carried supplies into her home, Bethany commented to Ann and Sally, "You have a lot of food."

"We just stocked up at Fort Gibson." Ann followed Bethany with another load of food. "You remind me of our other sister, Stephanie. She's also just over five feet with long blonde hair and blue eyes, and she's beautiful just like you."

"Thank you. Chetan thinks I'm beautiful. He loves me being different, but the others say my skin is too pale and that shiny, black hair looks better. I don't care what they think. The only one who matters is my husband. Although, when I look at Chetan's hair flowing over his shoulders, I agree with them wholeheartedly about the hair."

Sally said, "We've found that people tend to not like anything that's different."

"It seems that way to me too," Bethany agreed.

Noah's brother, Ke, carried a large smoked ham. The boy needed food to grow, and his mouth was watering. He brought up the topic of food again. "We haven't had very much food here. Hunting hasn't been good, and all our seeds burned away in a fire."

Ann said, "Then I'm even happier that we're here. We get to be with you, and we have seeds and food to share. When Noah goes back to Fort Gibson, he can get more."

Sally asked, "Do you like goat milk?"

"I've never tried any," Ke answered.

"I'll get some." Sally took the milk buckets and went to the field. "Is it safe for me to go in and milk the goats?" she asked Noah.

Noah didn't want to take any chances. "Everybody needs to get to know these mares. We'll go with you to be sure you're safe."

"Much obliged. I want to get milk for your brother." Sally whispered, "They don't have much food here."

"What's happening?" Noah asked his father in English, so Sally could also understand.

"Nikiata doesn't bring good medicine to the people. Wakanda is getting old. This land is too small. There aren't enough animals in this valley. Last winter, a fire destroyed all our seeds. We don't have money to buy more." Chetan saw a scowl pass over Noah's face. "You're home now. You will bring back good medicine."

"We have enough food to take us across the plains, but we're not going yet, so we'll give it to our village."

"Why did you bring food to cross the plains?"

"I'll explain more at the storytelling, but a man in Little Rock wants to kill Ann and me."

Chetan was surprised. "Why would anybody want to kill you? You're a good man."

"I'll talk some about it at the storytelling. We don't have enough time right now."

Roscoe had been forty when he had been with an exploration team and gone to a storytelling. Even though twenty years had passed, he had not forgotten. He made a suggestion. "Let's take food. How many people?"

"There are fifty-two Xida people."

Roscoe exclaimed, "You didn't tell me your clan is the eagle people! That explains a lot."

Chetan asked, "Explains what?"

"I'll tell everything at the storytelling."

"I'm ready." Sally stood up with two pails of milk. "Noah, who is that woman who hugged you?"

Noah started back to the lodge. "Her name is Mina, even though she has no brothers or sisters, her name means 'oldest daughter'. She's a woman who will not accept that I don't want her. I never did. I've told her over and over. She keeps pushing herself on me."

Noah stepped into the lodge behind Sally. He saw another good friend: the man who had built the farm back in Arkansas and had sent him east. "James, I see you've met Ann. This is Sally."

James said, "Sally, I'm so glad you're here. Ann told me you're my nieces!"

"Uncle James! How wonderful to meet Papa's brother!" Sally exclaimed.

"I'm very sorry about your parents. I only remember Chris as a boy. I hope you and Ann will tell me all about him and Emma."

"I'd love to. Did Ann tell you that your farm was destroyed?"

"Oh, no! I worked hard to build that farm. That's why I wanted to give it to somebody in my family. What happened?"

Sally replied, "It's upset all of us very much. But you'll hear about it when Noah tells his story."

Noah saw the things they would need already set aside. "Let's go over and get ready."

Luyu left with James's wife, Algoma. They told everybody, "Bring sharp knives, eating spoons, forks, pots of hot water to make tea, food bowls, and cups. It will be a long story. Plan to be there all day. Come in fifteen minutes."

In the large, rectangular, open-sided building in the center of all the homes, they covered the ground with five large woolen blankets. They laid out smoked elk, salted goose legs, and the last of the bear meat sausages, as well as cheese, dried apples, apricots, sassafras roots, goat milk, and honey.

As the people of the village arrived, Luyu and Algoma directed them to one of the blankets filled with food. Noah greeted the village that had never wholeheartedly accepted anybody in his family. He offered them food for the story, anyway.

On her husband's blanket at the center of the lodge, Ann served big pieces of meat, cheese, and other food. Noah had told her the proper etiquette. She put apples, and handfuls of apricots, meat, and cheese first into Ppahiska's bowl, then Wakanda's, then Nikiata's, and then the others. In their hot-water pots, she put sassafras roots. Sally, Luyu, Bethany, and Algoma did the same for the other groups.

Noah spoke first in English. "I'll start when I left here on Arabella." He then told his story in his native Indian language. As Tahatankohana told the story, Ppahiska and Wakanda asked questions. Most of the time, Ppahiska asked how followed by Wakanda who asked why.

Ann had some idea where he was when he hit his head, fell to the ground, and then pointed to Ann. Everybody looked at her. Ann wished she could understand, so she could hear the story from Noah's point of view.

Mina watched Ann and Tahatankohana. Tahatankohana never asked her for anything. Ann refilled his water, handed him more tea, or passed him small pieces of food that he could quickly chew and then continue the story. When Tahatankohana looked at Ann, his face filled with affection and happiness. He also looked happy when he spoke about the woman's sisters, the man one of the sisters had married, and the old man.

Mina told herself, *none of them are Indian. They can't truly understand Tahatankohana. Soon he will want a woman who understands how to be an Indian man's wife, and then he will want me.*

Tahatankohana squatted on his knees, so Ppahiska and Wakanda could see the scar on his head and verify that it was real. Ppahiska asked, "Why did she save you when you were bleeding to death in the saloon?"

Tahatankohana turned to Ann, "Ppahiska wants you to explain why you saved me. I'll translate what you say."

"Because you were a person who would die if I didn't," was Ann's simple reply.

Tahatankohana translated. Wakanda nodded his head. "She is a good person to everybody?"

Tahatankohana said, "Yes. She is a very good person to everybody." Noah then told Ann what Wakanda had asked and his reply.

Ann smiled about the compliment that Noah had given her before his entire village. "Thank you for thinking so, my husband, my love." She handed him a refilled cup of sassafras and honey tea.

Ppahiska wanted to know what a woman who would save anybody would say about such praise. "What she say now?"

Noah looked at Ann. He knew she didn't want to be a source of strife in his village. She was serving tea to Mina who sat in the group around him. Noah remembered the night she had served sassafras tea by the fireplace in her family's home. She had been as gracious then as she was now. Noah loved the way she cared for people. He translated her words.

Ppahiska and Wakanda nodded their heads

again. "What happened next?" Ppahiska urged Noah to continue the story.

When Noah told about Sally's experience in the cave, and her subsequent fear of small spaces, a twelve-year-old girl and her ten-year-old brother immediately felt connected by the shared and very powerful force of having had the same terrifying experience. They went over and sat at the blanket where Sally served.

Tahatankohana saw the children change places. He knew they had been lost in a pitch-black cave in the mountains for two days before their father had found and rescued them. He asked the children if he could tell Sally what had happened to them. They gave their permission. Tahatankohana told Sally that he had told of her losing her lantern in the cave and then told her what had happened to the children.

"Ask them if they would be willing to be my friends and sit with me," Sally replied.

Tahatankohana told the children what Sally had asked. They nodded their heads and went to the middle of the blanket. "Can we help her?" the girl asked.

Tahatankohana pointed to the girl and then her brother. "Kimimela and Takoda want to help you. Their names mean butterfly and buffalo horn."

"I would love their help."

He passed the message to the children. Because he liked it, Takoda cut a hunk of bear sausage for everybody while Kimimela poured hot water over the sassafras roots in everybody's cups.

Lisa Gay

Tahatankohana's expression changed to one of anger when he told of the Butterfield Gang burning down Ann's farm because Judge Atwood of Fort Smith had found the gang not guilty of the previous attack on her home. When they had tried to take the guilty to Little Rock, a different judge named Daniel Hall had declared Noah's marriage to Ann illegal, forced him and Ann to rebuild the Cadron Ferry, and then ordered them to separate forever.

Even though Tahatankohana had told of his deep sorrow when he had thought he had lost Ann and her family, Mina thought, *so he is free. He can still come to me.*

Tahatankohana's joy was obvious when he revealed that Ann, her two sisters, and her brother-in-law had walked over a hundred miles during the winter to reunite with him.

Tahatankohana explained that none of them had wanted to part, but he had felt that he needed to get home. They had left Ann's sister, Stephanie, and her husband, Eli, in their hometown to wait for Eli's father, Tom Yates, to return to Harmony. All of them hoped he would get home soon.

He did not reveal that they were putting the village in jeopardy because Judge Daniel Hall would surely have deployed an assassin to discover Noah and Ann's location. He also failed to add to the story that he believed whoever Daniel Hall had sent would have orders to haul the corpses of him and Ann back to Little Rock regardless of how many Indians he had to murder. Nor did he relate during the storytelling that they could not flee farther away from Judge Daniel Hall until the family reunited or that they were in the village because they believed that Indian Territory would be the safest place for him and Ann to hide. Noah prayed that his wait before heading to the western sea would be shorter than the search of Judge Hall's assassin. When the day ended, Tahatankohana's story had too.

Beyond the words, Wakanda had heard that he had made the right decision to train Tahatankohana as a Mystery Man. Tahatankohana had healed people and animals of physical injuries. He had healed his family of psychological pain when their clan totem, the eagle, had caused Tahatankohana to enter the spirit world. Tahatankohana had spoken with the spirits of the ancestors. Wakanda knew a few people who claimed to have entered the spirit world and then returned. Tahatankohana was the only one who had what appeared to be proof that he had done so.

Tahatankohana was also a skinwalker who had been protected from a poisonous dart by the spirit of the bear in whose skin he had walked. He had found people who would oppose injustice and had walked over a hundred miles in the winter to find him because of their love for him. He saw that Tahatankohana was a strong Mystery Man surrounded by a family of strong people who were also skinwalkers and healers. They said they were servants of the God of the Jews and the Christians.

Wakanda had watched Nikiata and Mina as Tahatankohana had told his story. He saw that Nikita knew he was much less of a Mystery Man. He also saw Mina's jealousy of Ann.

THREE

Tahatankohana had brought food and seeds into the village. The reigning village Mystery man wondered. *Will Tahatankohana put his people first and share his food?* He stayed after Ppahiska had dismissed the people. He informed Tahatankohana, "I knew you would be a great Mystery Man."

"But not for this village." Tahatankohana held out tightly twisted tobacco leaves folded over into a large plug. "I need your help. You know the needs of the people. Help us distribute food tomorrow. I offer two twists of tobacco for your service."

Just as I thought. I knew Tahatankohana was supposed to be a Mystery Man. Wakanda took the tobacco. "Let me see the food." They walked to the home of Luyu, Chetan, and Bethany.

As Wakanda sorted and divided the food into piles for each family, Ann picked up a package. "I give this to the village." She handed Wakanda one of their collections of vegetable seeds.

"Ann is giving a gift to the village," translated Tahatankohana.

Wakanda held out the package in his hand. "Tell her I cannot accept. She must give it to Ppahiska, but thank you for wanting to give it to me. Tomorrow, after Ppahiska accepts the gifts, we will give the food and then prepare Mother Earth for the seeds."

Tahatankohana requested more help. "I want to make Roscoe our relative. I can give you more tobacco or something else you would like. I have many medicine plants."

"Do you want to be a grandfather to these people?" Wakanda looked at Roscoe.

Roscoe had not known such a ceremony existed, nor had he known that his friends were going to ask for this, but he knew his answer. "I would love to be a grandfather to these people."

Wakanda turned back to Tahatankohana. "Show me what you offer."

Wakanda's eyes went wide when he saw the extensive supply of plants. He set aside ginger root, black cohosh, Devil's bit, Indian head, sage, mugwort, cloves, crushed walnut husks, and a gallon of whiskey to make extracts. "You decide what you want to give me. Any of these would be fine."

Ann, Sally, and Tahatankohana wrapped together all the items Wakanda had set aside and then added a big package of roasted hickory nuts. Tahatankohana handed the items to the Mystery Man. "Roscoe is worth much more than this."

"Since you do not know when you will leave, we can have the ceremony whenever you are ready."

"We will start to prepare. There is one more thing I need."

"What more do you need from Wakanda?"

"As I said in the storytelling, the bearskin has poison on it. Help me remove the poison. If you will help, again pick what you want in payment."

"The spirits rightly picked you to be Mystery Man. I will tell you as part of your training. You must catch a live bird or a rabbit."

"I will." Tahatankohana had learned to do whatever Wakanda told him. He usually didn't understand why until much later."

Before Wakanda walked out the door, he turned. "Be careful of Nikiata and Mina."

Tahatankohana already knew to do so. "Thank you for the warning."

"Ann, how did you know to offer the seeds to Wakanda first and to do it in private?" asked Luyu.

"Because Noah did," she replied. "I think there is power of one kind and power of another kind and you need to acknowledge each in its own way."

Luyu knew that love and approval were powerful forces and that she held them. Therefore, she always told people when she thought they had done something good. "That was perfect."

Ann hugged Luyu. "Thank you for telling me that I did well."

Chetan wished he and Bethany had realized sooner that there were different kinds of power. They might not have endured so many years of disrespect. "It's good you already know that."

"Why is your Medicine man named Wakanda?" Sally asked.

"It's more correct to say Wakanda is a Mystery Man. His name means possess magical power. He got that name when he became ours."

Tahatankohana's sister, Hanataywee, stood among the piles of food. "Yesterday I wondered where we would get enough food to stay alive. Now, there's not enough room because of all the food."

"We'll sleep in the wagons." Tahatankohana excused them, so everybody could get to bed. "It's been a long day. We'll see you in the morning."

FOUR

Tahatankohana heard a whisper outside the wagon. "Noah."

The faint morning light filtered into the wagon as Noah slipped out of Ann's arms. Ann pulled him back for a kiss. "Yesterday, your mother had to share you all day. Go be with her."

Bethany heard what her daughter-in-law had said, and it made her happy. Mother and son walked to the animals. "I've missed you. You were gone so long, but I heard your story. I know you got home as soon as God let you."

"I missed you too, but I'm glad I went. I didn't think I would ever find a woman to love me like you love father, but I did."

"I'm happy for both of you. Even though these people have made it hard for us, Chetan and I have found very much happiness with each other.

"When we leave, we can take the whole family."

"I would go, but you'll have to ask your father. I'll only go if your father goes."

"Thank you for being such a loving wife to father, mother to me, and daughter to grandmother. You taught me what to look for in a woman."

As they looked at the animals Noah had brought home, Bethany commented, "You're very rich."

"Only four of these are mine, but I do have two more that I left with Stephanie and Eli to bring my wagon. They were named Gumdrop and June when I bought them. Sally owns four mules. Roscoe owns ten mules, ten donkeys, two goats, and both these wagons." Before arriving at the village, they had agreed to say nothing to anybody about money, jewelry, or clothes. Noah did not mention them.

"Roscoe may be richer, but you're rich too."

"None of it matters except my family."

"Which animals are yours?" Bethany asked.

Noah's two horses stood together. "This is Eyanosa. We haven't named the mare. Ann wants to name her something that goes with Eyanosa."

"I'm very sad about Arabella." Bethany walked with Noah to the patchwork mules that had been their own group long before they had become a small part of their current herd. They usually stayed together.

"Ann named our mules Honor and Justice."

Bethany ran her finger along the scar on Honor's side. "This is where you fixed them."

"Sally fixed these. I'll show you the one I worked on. It's a wonder the mule is alive. Sally named her Beauty." They walked a few steps to the mule, still protecting another of Sally's mules, which she had named Dollie.

"Poor animal. You're right. It is a miracle. You

should name your mare Arabella. It means beautiful, and Eyanosa means fat and tall. Those go together as opposites."

"Arabella was a specific horse, and it would make me too sad to always be reminded of how she died."

"What about Zi? That means thin like hair." Bethany had seen the animals and spent time alone with her son. "Let's ask Ann. We should get back. Ppahiska and Wakanda will be coming over."

As they passed the wagon, Noah told those in it. "Come to the house."

When the family was together, Chetan proceeded in the proper way for his low position. He went to Wakanda. "Please ask Ppahiska to come to my lodge, so we can offer a gift for the village."

"We will not be long." Wakanda ushered Chetan out the door. "Go home and wait."

Wakanda went to the village leader's lodge. He asked for permission to speak with Ppahiska.

"What do you need?" Ppahiska asked.

"Luyu asks for you to come to her home. Her family has gifts for the village."

Ppahiska knew Wakanda usually knew more about what was happening in their village than he did. "What do they have?"

Wakanda hoped Ppahiska would not force him to reveal anything. "If you go, they can present the gift."

Ppahiska looked into Wakanda's eyes. "Should my family come?"

"Not at first. But they should be ready to come if you accept."

Ppahiska slipped on his moccasins and followed. At Luyu's house, Wakanda called out, "Ppahiska comes now."

The two men entered Luyu's lodge. Ppahiska saw the piles of food. He had never seen so much food all at one time. "What is this?"

As the oldest male, Chetan was the family leader. He offered the gift. "Chetan's family offers this food and this package of vegetable seeds as a gift to the Xida people if Ppahiska will accept."

Ppahiska took the large package. Inside, were many smaller packages with English words marked on them. "What do they say?"

Chetan was proud that he could read English to the village leader. "Tobacco, corn, pumpkin, October beans, butternut squash, crookneck squash, carrots, cantaloupes, radishes, wheat, sunflowers, cotton—"

"Enough." Ppahiska stopped him before he had read half the packages. He looked in the sacks of flour, cornmeal, bran, and dried vegetables on the floor. He also saw cheeses, baskets of eggs, jars of honey, and other corked jugs. He opened one. A strong, pungent odor wafted out of the jug. He turned his head aside and wrinkled his nose. "Vinegar."

Chetan spoke. "If you accept, people will have to bring two containers to get the vinegar and honey."

Ppahiska stopped looking. There were as many

piles as families in his village. "I accept." He turned to Wakanda. "Is it ready for the families to receive?"

"It is," Wakanda replied.

"Chetan, you give a very good gift. It will be part of our history that the family of Chetan saved this village. Bring what you are giving to my family." Ppahiska turned to Wakanda. "Bring one family at a time to receive their gift." He didn't have to remind Wakanda of the order.

Every person of Chetan's family, even three-year-old Chumani, picked up food to carry. For the first time, they could go inside the dwelling of their chief. As Chetan's family moved the food allocated to the village chief, Wakanda, his wife, and daughters carried away his portion. Wakanda then went to the home of Enapay. "Ppahiska accepted a gift for the village and requested that it be distributed. Bring two small water jugs."

Nikiata, the official apprentice Mystery Man, and his parents followed Wakanda. Before Nikiata saw the large amount of food still in Chetan's lodge, a big portion of the provisions sat in the homes of Ppahiska and Wakanda.

Chetan gave instructions, "Take one jug to Bethany and one to Luyu."

Nikiata's mother held out a small jug. Luyu told Ann, "This is Anpaytoo. Her name means radiant. Her husband is Enapay, which means roars bravely in the face of danger. He got that name when he fought a cougar with only a knife."

"Hawe." Ann glanced at the scars on the man as she poured honey. "Then you are very strong and brave and, Anpaytoo, you are a beautiful example of your name. I'm honored to meet both of you."

Ann sees the good in a person and shares with them what she sees. I like the woman. Luyu translated Ann's comment then whispered to her grandson, "Tahatankohana, you did well." *Just like when Chetan found Bethany.*

Anpaytoo stepped over to Bethany and received their portion of vinegar from Sally. Everybody then picked up some of Nikiata's food. Enapay expressed his gratitude. "The gift is very good."

After Wakanda saw Chetan's family return to their home, he arrived with Mina. Mina was high in the social structure. She didn't want to acknowledge the man at the bottom. Tahatankohana was different. Everybody in the village knew it. "Tahatankohana, do you give this gift?"

It was not respectful for the son to take credit. The gift came from Chetan because Chetan made the son who was Tahatankohana. Without the father, there would be no son, and Mina knew that. Tahatankohana refused to let Mina slight his father. "The gift is from Chetan."

Mina begrudgingly looked at Chetan. "Thank you."

"We will help you carry it to your home."

They did the same for each family. The last family was James and Algoma with their sons, Te and Nanpanta, their youngest daughter, Mi, and their oldest daughters, Dowanhowee and Mache, who were twenty and eighteen. Like Chetan's daughters, they were unmarried for the same reason. The population of Quapaw people was small. The men tried to preserve their people and did not marry except with a pureblooded Quapaw woman. James's family took their portion without help.

Chetan's family was at the bottom. They waited for Wakanda to tell them they could take what he had allocated to them. After the family of James had departed, Wakanda said, "What's left is for your family." As he went out the door, Wakanda added, "Tahatankohana you did well. Just like when Chetan brought home Bethany."

What remained was not enough for eleven people for a month. The night before, when Wakanda had divided the food, they had known the allocation didn't leave them enough. None of them had rebuked their Mystery man. They had understood why the allocation wasn't fair. They had been eating well. The people in the village hadn't, and Tahatankohana could purchase more. Wakanda left without seeing even a tiny look of bitterness. *They are different. I will find out why.*

FIVE

Ppahiska waited until everybody had sufficient time to prepare and eat a good breakfast then called the village together. "I accepted a second gift for the village. Now, we will have plenty of food. Wakanda will assign each family what they will plant and tend."

Wakanda gave each family the packages of seeds they would have to labor hard to plant and tend. When everybody had their assignments, they went to the fields of rich, deep dirt left behind every time Five Mile Creek and Spring River flooded. The soil around their village had always yielded large harvests of crops. The people dug into soft, fertile, Mother Earth with antelope shoulder hoes.

On the northeastern side, the field was bounded by a narrow strip of woods below the mountain cliff where the village nestled in its shadow. On the western side, Spring River flowed. At the southern edge, Five Mile Creek protected their land. Twenty acres surrounded the point of the mountain west of the animal pasture that ran east on the north side of Five Mile Creek and south of the Boston Mountains.

Through his father, Tahatankohana had also

given their second set of seeds to divide between the other three villages. Ppahiska sent his two sons, Chaska and Kanizhika to take them to the other villages.

Tahatankohana didn't work beside Ann. Instead, he worked with his father. He wanted to talk with him about something on his mind.

Mina purposely planted close to Ann. In Quapaw, she told Ann, "You are not the wife of Tahatankohana. You are not married by white people customs, and he has not married you as an Indian either. When he realizes he wants me, he will leave you."

Ann didn't know what Mina said. She could tell by her tone and the look on her face that it wasn't something nice. She chose to smile and continued planting.

Even though they couldn't talk to each other, Kimimela and Takoda asked to plant with Sally. Their father, Tatonga, told them they had to help their own family. Sally saw that the children were upset. "What happened?" she asked.

Bethany explained what the children had wanted and what their father told them.

Sally asked, "Would it be acceptable if I worked with them for part of the day, then came back over to help our family?"

Bethany asked Tatonga if Sally could work with the children for a while then leave to help her own family.

"I agree to let her come. Tell her thank you for doing this." Bethany told Sally she could go with the children. Sally took each child by a hand and walked to the field. She picked up the pole with an antelope shoulder lashed on and put it into the soil. It wasn't long before she realized how much harder the work was than guiding Samson to pull an iron plow, even with the lack of the extremely tough roots of Arkansas grass.

After explaining his plan, Tahatankohana and his father walked to Ann. "My wife, father and I are going to the river. I have an idea about something that could help the village. We won't be gone long."

"All right, my husband. I love you." The two men went to tell Bethany the same thing.

Mina saw Tahatankohana walk away without Ann. "You see. He already does not want you with him," taunted Mina. The whole day, Mina said the same thing over, and over, and over. Ann continued to smile and ignore her. Mina knew Ann didn't understand the language. Still, it upset Mina that she consistently failed to irritate her rival.

Chetan looked at the thriving population of mussels in Spring River. "They're in there, but the water is too fast to get them loose and keep ahold of them. The water is slower in the creek. We should look over there."

In both waterways, the mussel bed stretched from one end of the land assigned to their village to the other end and then beyond. Tahatankohana

Xida People

believed his plan could work. "We'll figure out how to get them. Right now, we'll load as many shells from the heap behind the village as we can fit into the wagons. They buy them down at Fort Gibson. The white people make them into buttons. We can harvest more, eat the meat, and sell the shells with what we already have. We can also sell any pearls we find."

Chetan knew his son couldn't wait long to go and buy more food. "This week we can load what's here into the wagons. We should ask Wakanda if Nikiata could be the village representative for the sale."

"Good idea. Let's get the fields planted first."

At the end of the day, after the people had stopped their work, Chetan and Tahatankohana walked back to the village with Wakanda. Chetan explained their plan.

"The plan is good." Wakanda instructed Chetan, "You ask Nikiata if he will negotiate for the village."

After his father left, Tahatankohana told Wakanda something else they had contemplated. "If we ask everybody for their ideas about how to harvest large amounts of mussels, it will be the plan of everybody and not just ours."

Wakanda directed him, "The people already had a big stirrup today. Wait a few days to ask." Then he said, "I saw you caught a pigeon. Bring it, the bear fur, and the dart. It is time."

Tahatankohana left Wakanda and walked to his

hut. Mina saw that he was alone and joined him. "That woman you brought here is a mouse. She does not even stand up for herself. I am a strong woman. People do what I tell them. You said you are not married to her. You can still come to me."

"I did not say I did not marry Ann. I said the white people said our marriage was not legal. That does not matter anyway. I will never want you. You are a bully. That is why people do what you tell them, not because they want to. Ann is not a mouse. She is the strongest woman I have ever known. She is much stronger than you will ever be. I do not want a bully for a wife. I want a woman who is meek."

"She is your little servant girl with no mind of her own."

"You do not know Ann to even speak about her, so stop. I love Ann, and there are so many things about you I do not like that I will never want you."

Mina informed Tahatankohana of what she believed was the truth. "You just think you love her and that you do not want me, but you will." She walked away.

Tahatankohana breathed out a breath of exasperation. He wished she would leave him alone.

SIX

Tahatankohana gathered the cage with the pigeon and the rolled up bear fur with the dart still in the jar. Behind the backs of everybody else in the village, he went to learn how to stop a poison.

Wakanda explained, "This was intended to go into your body by the dart. It is probably not poison. Most likely, this is venom.

"Does it make a difference what it is?"

Wakanda wetted a thin but long stick. "It does. Poison from plants can go through the skin or through your stomach. Venom has to get into your blood. One way for the Mystery Man to get respect is to drink the venom of a snake. You have to be sure you have no cuts or sores in your mouth or on your lips. Then you can drink it, and it will not hurt you. You can rub it on your skin, but you have to be sure you have no cuts, not even tiny cuts. It is still very dangerous because you may not realize your skin is cut."

"I will probably never have to do such a thing. How can we find out what this is?"

Wakanda rubbed the stick across the dart in the jar. "You never know what life will ask. I did this to become Mystery Man."

"How did you become our Mystery Man?"

Wakanda put his hand into the cage, tightly grasped the bird, and brought it out of the cage. He related his story. "Howahkan, of the mysterious voice, was the Mystery Man. He trained Hu and me. I was named Wazika then, only a small bird. Hu was called fish. Howahkan believed the Mystery Man should take his place by power. He told us that he would not be the one to decide. The Great Spirit agreed with him. One day, Howahkan danced the war dance against the Chickasaw. Their scouts lay outside the village. They saw him dancing, pierced him with their arrows, and killed him. Our people could not attack them without a Mystery Man. The Chickasaw thought they had won, but we could not let them. Hu and I had to prove which of us should be Mystery Man."

Wakanda held the pigeon and drew its feathers back with his thumb. "I remembered what Howahkan had taught us about the difference between poison and venom." As Wakanda continued speaking, he rubbed the substance on the skin of the bird. "Poison goes through the skin."

He allowed one wing of the bird to get free but held the bird tightly as it furiously flapped. He watched the pigeon for several minutes. "This is not poison. Poison goes through the skin. Venom will only kill if it gets through the skin and into your blood. As I said, you can drink it. I caught a bird and a cottonmouth snake to show my power.

"Hu chose to show power by killing a panther with only a knife. He carried the carcass home. Blood ran from gouges on his chest and arms as he held the panther before the people. 'Look,' he jeered, 'Wazika caught a bird and a snake. I killed a panther. Judge who has power.'

"I said, 'Hu is very strong and brave. Now watch.' I made the snake bite into a deerskin and spray its venom into a bowl. I cut off the snake's head with its teeth still in the deerskin. I threw its body to the ground. It writhed while I removed the deerskin then put a twig into the venom and pricked the bird with it. It died quickly. I threw the lifeless bird beside the finally still body of the snake then picked up the bowl and slurped down the venom. Everybody gasped in horror. When I did not die, they pronounced me Mystery Man. They changed my name to Wakanda, 'possesses magical powers.' Hu they named Enapay, 'goes out bravely.'"

Wakanda pricked the bird with the stick. It flapped briefly then lay still in his hand. Wakanda dropped the carcass to the ground. "This is venom."

"Very impressive!" Tahatankohana exclaimed. He realized that the dramatics were as important as the story and the explanation.

Very sub-climactically, Wakanda went on, "We neutralize the venom with ground charcoal." Wakanda had guessed what the substance would be and held out a large chunk of cold charcoal. "Grind this into a fine powder."

When Tahatankohana had smashed the charcoal

sufficiently, Wakanda said, "Pour it into water and stir it. Dig three deep pits. Lay this part of the skin in the pit then pour the charcoal water over it. Carefully swish it around with a long stick and let it stay until the sun has moved four fingers. Turn it over and put it into the second pit. Pour another batch of charcoal water over the back. Let it stay one finger of the sun while you bury the first pit. Move the hide into the third pit, fill it with charcoal water, and then bury the skin in the pit. Bury the second pit too. Two days later, put on elk skin gloves and dig up the skin then drag it to the creek. Secure it in the creek and let the water flow through it for a week. Take it out then rub a long slender stick over the whole fur and test it again with a very small animal like the bird. Let the fur dry then test it again."

"That much. It must be strong poison."

"Not poison. Venom. If you do not do all this, you will be afraid to use it. I thought you just saw the importance of perception."

Tahatankohana didn't want to do work that he didn't need to do, and he trusted Wakanda. "How much do I really need to do?"

"I am not sure. Do it all. Then we will both be sure it is safe."

"I will." He thanked the bird for its sacrifice, so he could heal his bear fur. He buried the bird then carried home the fur, the dart in the jar, and the large jug of charcoal powder. He explained the bear-fur-cleaning plan to his family.

SEVEN

Roscoe wanted to be sure the fur and Noah were safe. "I'll dig deep pits then I'll help plant."

"Thank you. We'll dig them together." It was very late in the planting season. All the men, women, and children wanted the seeds planted as quickly as possible. They hoed diligently.

When Tahatankohana and Roscoe had dug the pits and had the fur soaking, they worked in their assigned fields turning the soil. When the time had passed for the first washing, the two men went back and moved to step two of the fur cleaning. They made sure they didn't splash the infected water as they filled the first hole.

Once again, they helped prepare the ground until it was time for the next step. Noah and Roscoe carefully move the fur into the third pit and then buried the two open pits. The remainder of the day they tilled the soil with the rest of the village.

Two days later, as if Tahatankohana had forgotten, Roscoe said, "It's time to get the bear fur."

Tahatankohana walked to the pit. "I'll be glad to use the fur again."

Because their hands were raw from hoeing,

Roscoe warned him, "Put on your waterproof gloves, and be careful how you touch the fur." They carried the heavy fur to the creek, dropped it into the net they had built, and left it in the creek.

At the end of the week, his family followed Tahatankohana to the creek. Wakanda joined them on the way. With his hands inside the gutta-percha pouch that Sally had bought in Little Rock, Tahatankohana pulled out the fur. Roscoe and Chetan worked heavy poles to help with the weight. To be sure they didn't splash any residual venom onto the people gathered around, they carefully lowered the fur.

"Here." Ann handed her husband the birdcage.

He rubbed a thin stick over the bear fur and then stabbed it slightly into a scissor-tailed flycatcher, which chirped, flapped, and careened around the cage but continued to live. He rubbed the stick on the fur again and poked the bird that was unable to get out of the way inside the cage. After several rounds of rubbing the stick over the front and back of the fur, then pricking the flycatcher, Tahatankohana had tested every inch of the hide. He, Chetan, Roscoe, and Wakanda carried the fur to the village and stretched it out to dry in billows of smoke.

The whole village watched as Tahatankohana spoke. "You have given me back my bear fur. Thank you for your service." He let the living bird he had needfully tortured fly away. Later, he set up a trap to capture another.

EIGHT

The last day of planting, the women went alone to the fields. The men went to the community building to devise a plan to harvest and sell as many mussel shells as they could. Just as he had done when he had been a child, even though Chetan had already spoken with him, and he knew they would be discussing the trip to sell the shells, Nikiata hadn't fit the meeting into his schedule. The rest of the men contemplated and planned.

In the fields, Mina continued to harass Ann. Even though Ann didn't know what Mina was saying, she had heard the same words so many times that she could repeat the phrases. She continued to ignore the woman.

Mina's failure to upset Ann produced rising irritation. Today, Mina started her same taunt, "You are not Tahatankohana's wife. When he realizes I am the one he wants, he will leave you." Ann smiled and ignored her, but her resistance had worn thin.

No matter where Ann went, somebody made things hard for her. Her back ached from bending over to plant seeds with hand tools. She stood up, put her hands behind her back, and stretched as she once again ignored Mina and the foul words coming out of the woman's mouth.

Mina walked to Ann and grabbed the hair necklace Ann always wore. As Mina sliced the necklace off Ann's body, the blade carved a gash across Ann's collarbone.

At first, Ann was shocked. She had never thought the woman would actually attack her. A cloud of anger swept through Ann's mind. She held it in check as she prepared to defend herself with the hoe in her hands.

Not sure what they should do, the other women in the field looked at the two women about to battle. They all knew something was brewing and that it would not lead to anything good. Sally took off running.

Mina threw down the necklace then ground it into the dirt with her foot. The necklace that Mina had just disrespected was a symbol of Ann's dead parents from the mourning ceremony. Ann was tired of putting up with horrible behavior. She hit Mina squarely across the side of her head with the hoe handle.

Attempting to again cut Ann's blood-covered chest, Mina swung the knife.

Ann told herself, *I am not here to injure anybody in Noah's village.* She knocked Mina's arm aside and poked at her belly with the end of the hoe's handle. Blood flowed from Ann's neck down her arm and over the hoe.

Mina again attempted to thrust the knife into Ann's heart.

This time Ann hit Mina's arm full force. Ann's blood flung from her arm across Mina's face and spattered the women standing nearby. The hoe broke as the knife flew from Mina's hand.

Mina ran for the knife then lunged at her adversary.

There wasn't any doubt of Mina's intentions in anybody's mind. Mina was trying to kill Ann. All the women were close enough to see what was happening. They could have intervened, but they didn't. Again, Ann knocked the knife from Mina's hand then dropped the broken hoe and raked her nails down Mina's cheeks, gouging eight lines into her attacker's flesh.

Mina pulled away. Blood streamed from her cheeks. She became mindlessly infuriated, flew at Ann, and punched her squarely in the stomach.

Ann twisted to the side, turned back, and pounded her fists into Mina's back then yanked hair from Mina's head.

Mina pulled Ann's hair in retaliation. Both women smeared and flung blood and hair across each other, across the women watching, and onto the soil.

NINE

Sally jetted into the village, screaming, "Noah!"

No one had called him Noah since he had returned home. "She's killing her!" Sally's voice was clearly one of panic. "Come now!"

"Who's killing who?" Noah ran after Sally.

"Mina's killing Ann."

Noah ran like the wind. If he was too late, he would never forgive himself, and he would kill Mina on the spot. He remembered that the spirits of Chris and Emma Williams had told him to stop the woman to save their first grandchild. *I have to stop Mina. Ann must be pregnant.*

TEN

In the field, Mina tripped Ann, jumped on her stomach with both knees and pummeled Ann's face.

Ann put up her arms to protect herself. She used her legs to grab Mina over the head and pull her backward. They rolled across the dirt. Ann ripped more hair from Mina's head then saw the knife in the dirt. They rolled within reach. Ann's fingers circled the knife handle. She knew Mina intended to take the fight to the end and was prepared to do what Mina had forced her to do.

Noah saw Ann kneeling over Mina. Both hands rose. In them, she held a knife. *The woman I have to stop is Ann. If she kills Mina, Wakanda or Nikiata will kill her in return.*

Fully intending to plunge the knife into Mina's heart and stop the woman's insanity, Ann's arms started down.

"Don't kill her," Noah screamed.

Ann stopped.

Mina smugly said in Quapaw. "I told you he would realize he loves me and not you."

Ann didn't know what Mina had said, but she saw the look on Mina's bleeding face. She wanted to make her stop; permanently. It would have been so easy for Mina's skin to open as the knife pierced it, but Noah had told her to stop. Since the men were there, Ann assumed the fight was over. She got off Mina, dropped the knife in the dirt, and then walked toward Tahatankohana.

Mina picked up the knife, took aim at Ann's back, and flung it.

As if a miscarriage of gravity had occurred, the instrument that would have been Ann's death sailed sideways into the field, accompanied by an arrow. Nikiata stood at the edge of the woods, bow in hand, with another already nocked arrow. He knew the same thing Tahatankohana knew. If Mina killed Ann, Tahatankohana would kill Mina, even if it cost his own life.

Mina walked to the knife, picked it up, and again took aim. The weapon dropped when an arrow went through her wrist.

Do not touch it, Nikiata thought. If she tried a third time, the Mystery Man was required to execute the sentence. Everybody was watching. There would be no way to avoid it. Ann wasn't even an available target. Tahatankohana had her safely behind him.

Mina saw that the man she thought she desperately loved had again chosen the woman he had brought into the village. She took a step toward the dagger.

Nikiata dropped his bow and dashed across the field as Mina stooped. He grabbed her by the hair before she could touch the knife. Then, with the arrow still in her wrist, he dragged her across the field, thrashing and screaming, "Kill me."

In the field, Ann dropped to the ground to look for her necklace. Tahatankohana asked the question filling his mind. "Are you pregnant?"

"Yes," she confessed.

"When? Why didn't you tell me?"

"I think it was the night we dyed ourselves at Fletcher Creek. I didn't tell you because you don't want me to be pregnant. We've been trying to keep this from happening. I was afraid you'd be mad."

Noah looked at his wife crawling on the ground with two blacken and swollen eyes, a split lip, missing patches of hair and a slashed shoulder dripping blood into the dirt. "Is the baby alright?"

Ann focused on her body instead of finding the necklace. She felt her thigh. Immediately in a panic, she cried out, "No, I feel blood on my legs!"

Noah scooped his wife into his arms. "One of you make medicine. We need to keep Ann from losing the baby."

As he, Sally, and Roscoe ran to the village, Wakanda called out, "We could use blackhaw and false unicorn."

Roscoe added his suggestions, "And wild yam and vitex."

"And shepherd's purse," Sally concluded.

Noah explained to his wife, "I didn't want it to be hard for us to travel. I would never be mad about a child we've made." He ordered his child, "Hold on. Do not let go. Your grandparents said I could save their first-born grandchild. You better listen to them. Do not leave us. We love you."

Ann feelings grew even stronger by her husband's comment to their child. "I love you, Noah."

ELEVEN

Nikiata dragged Mina through the woods until she calmed. "Will you listen to me?"

"Yes," Mina told him.

He stopped, let go of her hair then sat beside her and cradled her in his arms. "You have to let him go. He does not love you. Whether or not he has Ann, he has told you many times that he does not and will never love you."

"But I love him more than anybody. He should love me back."

Nikiata knew loving a person did not make them love you back. "You cannot make a person love you. You have to let him go." Nikiata looked at Mina's arm. He hated that he'd hurt her. To protect Mina he'd had to keep her from killing Ann. He had shot the arrow exactly where it would do the least damage. He hadn't severed any major vein, and he hadn't damaged the cartilage or the bones. He held the arrow firmly in his hand then broke off the end. He pushed the short piece of the shaft through, wrapped her arm, and then gently wiped the blood from Mina's face.

As he cared for her, she told Nikiata, "I wish you

had killed me." Mina had been high in their social order. Chetan's family was at the bottom. A member of his family had bested her. "I am defeated. Nobody will listen to me."

"You do not need to order everybody around anyway." Nikiata rocked her in his arms.

"You defied our tradition when you did not kill me." She pointed out what she thought was going to be a problem for Nikiata.

"You are worth the chance, and I took you away before you touched the knife the third time." Nikiata held Mina until she felt able to face the consequences she didn't know might be her death. Nikiata helped her up then walked back to the village beside her.

TWELVE

In the village, Tahatankohana laid Ann on their palette in Luyu's lodge. He got his medical supplies and washed her injuries. "I need to stitch this, but I don't want to give you any sedative. It may be all it takes to kill the baby."

"Does it have to be stitched?" Ann hoped it didn't.

"Yes," he told her.

"Then do it."

Sally offered what she could. "Squeeze this." She placed her hand in the hand of her sister. Roscoe took her other hand.

Bethany gave her a soft, thick cloth. "And bite down on this."

Feeling every painful stick in his own heart, Noah stitched the gash across his wife's collarbone. "I'm sorry that I'm hurting you." When done, he bandaged then held her. "I wish I hadn't brought you here. I knew Mina would be trouble."

When the tea was ready, Sally brought it to Ann. "God, please make this work."

Their family was in the house to support Ann and Tahatankohana. Ppahiska and Wakanda had to be there to verify if the baby was lost. Roscoe gave Ann a second cup of the tea. After several minutes, she still bled. Tahatankohana commanded, "Wakanda, get the sweat lodge ready."

"They're open to everybody. Are you sure?" asked Bethany.

"Anybody who wants to be there can join us. Tahatankohana did not ask for permission. He told everybody what was going to happen. "Nikiata and Mina must be there."

Wakanda left to start the fire to heat the grandfather rocks. James, Roscoe, and Chetan went with him to help. When the fire blazed over the rocks, Wakanda left the other men to tend it while he went to his home to prepare. Tahatankohana's sisters Hanataywee and Ehawee spread the word so the people could prepare their prayers if they wanted to participate. Tahatankohana prepared too. Bethany, Sally, and Luyu stayed with Ann while they tied small pieces of cloth around herbs.

When Wakanda was ready, he went back to the fire with a rolled-up fur and the grandmother medicine bag. He told James and Chetan, "Go make your prayers."

Bethany prayed fervently that Ann and her son would not have the same heartache of losing a baby like she and Chetan had endured. Ann was still bleeding, but Bethany hadn't seen the baby leave. She knew exactly what a miscarried baby looked like. She and Chetan had buried five before she had been able to keep a baby and had given birth to Tahatankohana. Bethany could not keep herself from thinking about her past.

***

She had been Chetan's wife only a short time when they had lost the first baby. Every time she had lost a baby, the other women told her she wasn't a woman and Chetan wasn't a man. She had desperately wanted to make Chetan a baby, but when she lost their fifth child, she could not face losing another. She had left Chetan's bed. He had let her grieve for months before he asked her to come back to his bed.

She wouldn't.

Chetan rode away, hurt and angry. They hadn't seen him for days. Luyu spoke with the daughter-in-law she had taken into her heart. "Chetan lost his babies too, and now you are making him also lose his wife."

Bethany prayed, "God, Jehovah, bring Chetan back to me. I want him to know I love him. If I have to lose a hundred more babies, I will." Every night she slept in the bed she had deserted and hoped that he would come home and find her there, so she could share her love with him again.

Chetan hadn't known where he was going when he had left their lodge. He had ended up at the farmhouse where he had found Bethany. He went into the abandoned home and remembered that day.

He'd been looking for game when he had come

across the house and had heard somebody crying. He had gotten off his horse and then peeked through a window. Inside, a young, blonde-haired girl's head rested on her arms splayed across the tabletop. He glanced around the area. Two low hills of rocks rose from the ground not far from the cabin. He searched everywhere. Nobody else was there. He knocked on the door.

The girl's father had thought he would always be there to provide for his family and therefore, didn't need to teach his daughter how to survive. Then he and Bethany's mother had died. Bethany had eaten what was there. Unable to provide more for herself, she had not eaten for several days. She thought it could not get worse, and a fast death might be better than the slow one she was living. She opened the door.

There stood a young man with a strong body, a handsome face, long black hair, and dressed only in a loincloth and moccasins. Four long scars crossed his body diagonally from just above his left hip down across his right thigh. His brown eyes looked at her. He continued to stand in the doorway. She pointed to her mouth and worked her jaws as if eating.

He understood. She was a young girl alone who needed food. He was a young man who had lost half his manhood when attacked by a puma as a child. It had been four years since he had become old enough to marry. Now nineteen, no woman had consented to be his wife. He might not be able to make children.

Without children, they would not have anybody to take care of them when they were old. He believed he would live his life without a wife. *I will ask.* He pointed to her lower parts.

There wasn't anything important where he was pointing. The girl had no idea what the gesture implied.

Before he went to his horse, he again pointed to his eyes then what he wanted. He came back with food, pointed to his eyes, and then her crotch.

If he wanted to look, she didn't care. She nodded her head, yes.

He gave her bread and deer jerky and then drew water from the well. After she had eaten the last crumb, he had unfastened the long row of buttons on her dress and taken off her pantaloons. He laid her on the bed and looked at what he had never before seen and probably would never see again.

When he touched her softly, she looked too. She hadn't known those parts were there. The man held her tenderly and kissed her sweetly. She liked that, and she liked giving her lower parts to him. Most importantly, Bethany knew if the man left her there, she had no way to get food. She knew the man had felt intense pleasure. She pointed to her mouth and her other parts and then motioned for him to take her with him.

He agreed.

A smile lit up her face. She hurried to get clothes. She looked at him to see if she could take them.

He nodded, yes.

She picked up a book and looked for approval.

He shook his head no.

She put it down then picked up a tintype of a man and woman.

He assumed they must be her parents, so he said yes.

She wrapped the picture and clothes together. She had followed him out of the house.

Chetan got on his horse and pulled her up in front of him, facing forward.

So she could hold him, Bethany had turned around and wrapped her legs and arms around him. Her parents had never touched her, and she had never seen them touch or kiss each other. She kissed her handsome savior again then laid her head against his chest.

Chetan had known that the girl liked him and that she was happy to go with him. He had been pleased to have been invited to take her. He would have a wife, and she would have a husband to take care of her.

As Chetan had sat there remembering, he thought about the book she had wanted. In the three years Bethany had lived with him and his mother, she had learned to speak Quapaw, and they had learned to speak and read English. He found the book and read the first page. It was part of the story she told about how Wakan Tanka, the Great Mystery, and the Great Spirit had created the earth. He flipped to another page and read, "If you love the Lord your God with all your mind and heart and soul, He will give you what you ask for in the name of His Son."

He heard Bethany pray to her God every night and day. All the time, really. Many times, he had heard her tell God, "Thank you for bringing Chetan to save and love me."

He decided to pray. "God of my wife, I will love you with all my heart, with all my mind, and with all my soul. Give me back the love of Bethany." He took the book she had wanted and left. Two days later, he arrived home in the middle of the night, expecting to find his bed empty. He thought he would give the book to Bethany in the morning then maybe she would love him again. He went to his bed and found her there.

When her husband came into their home, Bethany woke. She took Chetan into her arms. "I love you. I do not want to live without you. Share your love with me."

When Luyu heard them, she knew everything would be all right. She loved Bethany as much as she loved Chetan. The girl had been a child who had needed a mother when Chetan had brought her home, and she had immediately loved the mother Chetan had given her. Luyu had allowed Bethany to be the child she was as well as the wife of her son.

That night, they had made Tahatankohana. Chetan had given Bethany the Bible in the morning. "I brought this home for you. I thought it would make you love me again."

"I never stopped loving you, but thank you for getting the Bible. This means a lot to me. I'm very happy to have it."

***

They had never lost another baby. Chetan had turned his heart, mind, and soul over to the God of the Bible. He had read the Bible many times. To Chetan, God was Wakan Tanka, the Creator of the Universe that he had always known. He believed the Bible explained his God.

THIRTEEN

Today, Chetan and Bethany wrapped the sage that was theirs in small pieces of cloth as they said the prayers they wanted to send to the Great Spirit. They prayed for their son's baby to live, thanked God for all their children, thanked God for bringing Tahatankohana home, for giving them new family, and for restoring life to the village.

Hanataywee explained to Sally and Roscoe what they were doing, so they could make prayer ties if they wanted.

Tahatankohana dressed Ann in her coyote fur and the necklace of claws and fangs she had made. He put on the dry bearskin that had not undergone the final test. Sally wore her coyote skin and shrew bone necklace. Tahatankohana asked Roscoe to wear the headdress of eagle feathers that he had made. He asked Bethany to wear the goose wing collar and Chetan to wear the remaining coyote skin.

Tahatankohana handed his medicine bag to Roscoe then carried Ann into the lodge. He laid her on the fur of the elk they had killed together at Pine Bluff. He sat in the position of Mystery Man facing the door. He asked Chetan to sit in the northeast position, Roscoe to sit in the east to bring the spirit of the thunderbirds, Bethany in the southeast, James in the south, Algoma in the southwest, Sally in the northwest, and Luyu in the north.

Bethany put the basket for the prayer ties beside the entrance and the basket of sacred herbs beside her son.

Tahatankohana placed the ancient eagle talon he had brought from Pine Bluff into the smudge bowl made by Stephanie. He put that small bowl in the large bowl of herbs and then brought out the two parts of the Calumet he and Ann had made at Pine Bluff. He placed them on opposite sides of the larger bowl. He then placed the ceremonial knife Eli had made between the two halves of the pipe.

Wakanda entered wearing a bison skin. He was surprised to see Tahatankohana in the position of Mystery Man and equally surprised that James sat in the south as fire tender. If the people joined them in the ceremony and if James, Sally, Roscoe, Algoma, Luyu, Bethany, and Chetan, who were also in positions of power, fulfilled the tasks before them, they would be Xida and no longer at the bottom of their social structure.

Tahatankohana saw Wakanda pause. "Great power will be required to hold the west. Will you stand in the gate to the spirit world?" He asked this because he didn't want Wakanda to be offended and because, if his plan was going to succeed, he needed a strong Mystery Man at the gate to the spirit world.

Wakanda believed Tahatankohana only planned to put on a show just as he had taught him. "I'll stand before the spirit world." He sat in the west.

As soon as they arrived back in the village, Ppahiska ordered Nikiata to assure that Mina went into the sweat lodge. Ppahiska entered. He sat in the middle opposite Tahatankohana on the other side of the fire pit.

Mina came into the sweat lodge next. Tahatankohana told her, "Lie in front of Ppahiska." She was the person who may have killed his child. He would make her face the truth about herself before she left the world. If the baby died, the village leader would execute her as a murderer.

Mina hadn't wanted to kill Tahatankohana's baby. She hadn't known Ann was pregnant. She lay opposite Ann on the other side of the rock pit. Tahatankohana removed the ceremonial knife from the basket and handed it to Ppahiska.

Nikiata came in. Tahatankohana told him, "You will be Mystery Man one day." *You need to learn how to bring good medicine and healing. This will be a lesson a Mystery Man rarely has the opportunity to teach an apprentice.* "Today, I need two Mystery men to perform a difficult task. Sit in the west with Wakanda." Tahatankohana continued, "We are here to request the life of this baby. Be strong and fearless, so we can prevail."

Wakanda thought that was an unusual thing to say, and it was strange for him to have spoken to those in the positions of power before the people had entered. "James, allow the people to enter the universe."

James opened the door. Until they were all inside, the people dropped their prayer ties into the basket and then circled clockwise along the outer edge of the sweat lodge around the bear, bison, goose, eagle, and coyotes at the center. When the last person was inside, James closed the door. Darkness engulfed the people who had entered the universe. None of them knew that Tahatankohana and Wakanda were about to change everything or that nobody would be the same when they left the sweat lodge.

Tahatankohana put a handful of the sacred herbs onto the hot rocks in the central pit. The fragrance floated into the air. He put a second handful on the rocks to cleanse not only the air but also the people. Unknown to anybody, Wakanda leaned forward in the darkness and threw some of what he had brought into the bowl of herbs and onto the rocks.

Tahatankohana prayed. "Father God in Heaven above, look down on us, accept our praises, and grant our requests. Cleanse us of impurities. Thank you for placing us in families and communities. Show the people of this village how to live and work together to benefit the whole. Bring glory and honor to yourself. Earth below, sustain us. Join with the rain and sun sent by the Father. Give us crops and animals for food. Give us animals to join us in labor and life." He put water on the rocks. Steam joined the fragrance in the air.

Wakanda tossed another handful of peyote onto the rocks. Hallucinogenic smoke rose into the air.

Tahatankohana continued. "North, bring us honesty and truth. Open the eyes, ears, hearts, and minds of every person here." He put another ladle of water on the red-hot rocks.

Wakanda added more peyote behind him.

"East, give knowledge of the way. Bring the thunderbirds to guide us into the spirit world." Tahatankohana requested, "Give us the life of this baby."

Wakanda realized what Tahatankohana was planning. He had seen this attempted when he was young. The spirit of that man had never returned. He had joined the soul of the wife he had wanted to bring back from the spirit world. Wakanda commanded his apprentice, "Don't try this."

Tahatankohana heard Wakanda. He knew it was dangerous, but he had already been to the Spirit World when he had frozen in the river at Pine Bluff when saving the eagles. Ann had brought him back to the world of the living. He tried to choke back the emotions displaying in his voice, "South, bring healing to the tiny being growing inside this woman. They mean more to me than anything on this planet." He ladled water onto the rocks. Peyote billowed into the air on the steam.

Wakanda didn't put anything on the rocks. He

wished he hadn't added the hallucinogenic cactus to the herbs in Tahatankohana's bowl or put any on the hot rocks.

"West, I ask for help from the Great Spirit. If this baby has gone to the spirit world, guide me to its soul and give us back the spirit of my child. Give strength to Wakanda and Nikiata. Enable them to hold back the evil spirits that will try to come into this world when we open the door. Holy Spirit, guide us, protect us, and protect the world. Show Yourself to Wakanda and Nikiata as The Truth You are. Give them wisdom and discernment, so they do not let any spirit pass except You and those You bring home."

Tahatankohana put more water on the rocks then took the two halves of the Calumet and held them up. "Creatures of the sky, creatures that walk on the ground, creatures below the surface, and creatures of the water, give your strength to the male power and the female power that are joined to make this pipe and were also joined to make this child."

He joined the two halves of the pipe, filled the bowl with the ingredients in front of him then took the red glowing stick off the hot rocks and used it to light the peyote and other plants in the pipe. He inhaled the first puff then handed the pipe to Ann.

"Father God, save this child, bring glory to Yourself, and show Your power. Let every person here know it was You who did this." Ann inhaled a puff before she gave the pipe back to her husband.

Tahatankohana passed the pipe to Wakanda then placed his hands over the place where his child was fighting to regain its connection to its source of life inside Ann's womb.

They were this far already. Wakanda knew he might be the one to lose his spirit, but he was also the one who had trained Tahatankohana. "Make me strong; allow me to discern the true nature of the spirits. Protect our own spirits, minds, and hearts." He inhaled what he knew included the substance he had added. He decided to complete everybody's original plan. He leaned over. "This will strengthen the baby's attachment." He gave Ann the tea that should do what he had said. As he did so, he dropped the remainder of the peyote on the rocks so that everybody in the sweat lodge would experience the same effects as those who smoked the pipe.

Nikiata took the pipe. *Wakanda told Tahatankohana not to try. Tahatankohana is going to do something dangerous. I do not want to be a part of this. I see no way to avoid it.* "God that Tahatankohana worships, help me do whatever I need to do." He passed the pipe to who should have been Luyu.

In the darkness, Sally received the pipe, inhaled the smoke, and then spoke. "Let your will be done, Holy Father."

Tahatankohana heard Sally speak. Only the people at the four corners should have smoked the pipe, but it had already happened. *Maybe we need everybody to complete the task.*

Sally passed the pipe to Luyu, who said, "Spirits of my five grandchildren, if this child's spirit tries to join you, send it home to its body." She handed the pipe to her son.

Chetan's heart cried with sorrow over another loss not only to him but also to his wife. He didn't know if she could undergo the loss of another child even if it was a grandchild. His son and daughter-in-law, his mother and all of Ann's family, would lose a member of their family. "You took away five of my children don't take my grandchild too." He smoked the pipe then sent it on to Roscoe.

"Father above, don't take this baby into the earth below. Let the child of the eagles rise to soar just as the eagles do." He took his puff then gave the pipe created at his home in Pine Bluff to the grandmother of the child they wished to save.

Bethany felt the same as her husband. After twenty-four years, the full pain of losing a child again flooded over her. She smoked the pipe. "Don't let this happen again," was all she had the ability to say before giving the pipe to James.

James didn't want to lose the continuation of his brother. "God of the Jews and Christians, allow the first grandchild of my brother to live." He puffed a few times, added the smoke of the pipe to the air then passed it on to his wife.

"You've given us the birth family of James. Don't take any of them away." She smoked and then handed the Calumet to Ppahiska.

"Great Spirit, send healing in all the ways it is needed in this village." The village leader took his turn smoking than handed the pipe to Mina.

"Don't allow this innocent baby to lose its life. Instead, let there be scars on my cheeks to forever remind me of the evil I've done." A puff of smoke went into her lungs then joined the smoke in the air. She passed the pipe back to the man she wished would love her.

Tahatankohana threw another handful of the sacred herbs onto the cooling rocks. They only sizzled, but the hallucinogenic smoke was already thick in the air. "Get two more rocks."

James opened the door. The smoke cleared slightly when he brought in a rock from the fire burning outside the lodge then went back out to get the second one. He put it in the pit then pulled closed the door and once more shrouded them in darkness. The red glowing rocks set the herbs ablaze and refilled the small space with peyote smoke. The people didn't realize that they could barely think.

"Nikiata, add the prayers of the people to the fire."

"We offer these praises as sweet incense in your nostrils. Hear our praises and grant our requests." Nikiata poured the small packages of herbs that were the prayers of the people onto the heat of the grandfather rocks. As the packages burned, the prayers rose to God on the smoke.

Tahatankohana asked Ann, "My wife, how are you and our baby?"

"I think it's too late. I'm bleeding too much."

"Wakanda and Nikiata don't let any spirit but the Holy Spirit come through the open door. Roscoe, call the thunderbirds to take me into the spirit world."

Ann realized what her husband was about to do. "Noah, don't do it."

Tahatankohana handed the smudge bowl to Roscoe then drank the liquid in a small bottle. He lay beside Ann and kissed her lips. "Ann, my wife, my love, bring me back once again."

"Get our child and come back to me, my husband," were the last words Tahatankohana heard in the land of the living.

Wakanda commanded, "We have to finish what has started, or we will not get him back." He poured all that remained in the sacred basket into the fire. The smoke of the aromatic herbs Noah had brought and the last of the peyote that Wakanda had added swirled into the air.

Nikiata had been told about this ceremony. He had never believed that he would perform the rite, but he did remember what he was supposed to do. He added more water to the rocks and filled the lodge with mist. "Roscoe, call the thunderbirds if you can."

Roscoe had no idea what to do. He dropped his hand into the bowl and felt the ancient talon. He held it up. "Thunderbirds, carry the spirit of Noah Swift Hawk to the spirit of his child then bring him back to his body."

The steam swirled into a vapor eagle that swooped into the lodge from the east. Roscoe put the talon on Tahatankohana. The misty eagle landed where the talisman summoned. Its talons sunk into Tahatankohana. The people who sat inside the lodge saw the image and felt the moving air, perhaps of flapping wings.

Bethany saw the claws of the eagle rip the spirit of her son from his body. "Open the spirit door!"

Wakanda and Nikiata joined hands. Wakanda called out, "Holy Spirit, Tahatankohana asked for You to guide him. Be his spirit guide, help us to recognize You and not let any other spirit enter our world."

Nikiata scooped more water on the hot stones. An explosion rocked the lodge and sent projectiles of stone into the dirt of the pit. Tendrils of light appeared to flow from the people in the inner circle and join over the pit where the light shimmered. The eagle soared through the portal into the spirit world. The draft of its flight pulled out the spirits of Wakanda and Nikiata and deposited them in the door of light where spirits tried to escape into the world of the living.

The two mystery men knocked the spirits back to the place they belonged, they stomped them as they tried to crawl past as small bugs, and they swatted them from the air when they tried to fly through the gate as tiny flies or large vultures. None of the spirits found success as they attempted to be free of their confinement.

Brute force was not the way. The spirits changed their tactics. In the shape of a man, one approached Nikiata. "I'm the spirit you're seeking. Let me go to my body in the woman."

Nikiata remembered that Tahatankohana had said the Holy Spirit was The Truth. This one did not feel true. Nikiata refused, "No, you cannot pass."

With their minds saturated with peyote smoke, the people sat in the sweat lodge and peered through the smoke. They saw the bodies of Wakanda and Nikiata slumped over between them and the light in the center of the lodge. They could not see the spirits beating against the men as they blocked the gate. Sally, however, did see a spirit penetrate the barrier. On the side of the world, it came up from the ground as a tiny worm then began to grow.

Sally cried out the alarm. "One got through." Her spirit knew to protect. It left behind the body it inhibited, jerked the deceiving being from the world, and threw it back into the place where it belonged. With the men, she held back the evil, desperately trying to escape into the world. Sally, however, looked into the world of the living while Wakanda and Nikiata looked into the spirit world. Together, they fought to give Tahatankohana the time he needed to search for the soul of his child then find his way back to his body. Nikiata noticed a spirit that didn't beat at him but then quickly re-entangled with the spirits that did. In the fierce battle with the spirits that assaulted him, he forgot about the spirit that patiently waited.

FOURTEEN

The eagle released Tahatankohana in the world of the spirits. Tahatankohana called out, "My child, where are you?"

"I'm your child," a spirit told him.

Tahatankohana did not feel himself or Ann in the being. He denied ownership. "I don't believe you." The spirit vanished. Spirit after spirit insisted they were the one for whom he searched. He worried. *What if I make a mistake? Maybe I denied my child. I need you, Ann. Help me."*

Time ticked. The people in the sweat lodge watched the shimmering light above the pit draw streams of power from the inner circle of people while the bodies of Wakanda, Nikiata, Sally, and Tahatankohana lay unconscious. They had all seen the mist remove the spirit from the body of Tahatankohana and then disappear into the light.

"He's been gone too long," Ann stated. She picked up the bottle. Only a drop remained inside. She dripped it onto her tongue.

Above Tahatankohana, green eyes formed. "My husband."

He called out to the eyes. "I can't find our child. Help me."

"See through my eyes, my love." As if he looked through eagle eyes, the green eyes helped him see clearly. He searched both far and wide.

"No spirit from us is here. I'll come back." Lost in the spirit world, Tahatankohana circled. "I don't know which way is home. Bring me back to you, my wife." He followed the eyes until he saw the light and then Wakanda, Nikiata, and Sally.

Tahatankohana requested passage, "Let me through."

As Wakanda had guarded the passage, many spirits had insisted they were Tahatankohana. "I don't believe you," Wakanda replied.

Tahatankohana said, "Look for The Truth, Wakanda. Spirit of Truth, take our spirits back to the world of the living."

The Holy Spirit of Truth who had been quietly waiting spoke into their hearts. "I only enter through a heart willing to receive me. I wait to be invited."

"Reveal yourself to them. Only You can save us."

Nikiata remembered the Spirit of Patience. "There was one who wasn't trying to force its way or to convince me to allow it through?"

Wakanda reminded, "Tahatankohana told us, 'Look for the Spirit of Truth.'"

Sally heard the spirits of the men talking. She wondered why the Holy Spirit wasn't seeing her as a conduit then realized that two souls were being given the opportunity to accept the Lord. "Open your heart to the Spirit of the Savior," she told them.

Tahatankohana, Sally, Ann, Wakanda, and Nikiata agreed together. "I accept The Truth into my heart." The One, who had patiently waited, entered their hearts. The spirits of the five and the tiny new soul carried in the arms of The Truth recognized their homes and returned. As the door closed, everybody heard the shrieking of the fallen, damned, and trapped demons.

Tahatankohana returned to Ann's green eyes that peered intently into his. "Thank you for helping me and for bringing me home."

"I will never desert you, my husband, and I feel the presence of our son back inside."

As if giant wings moved, the air inside the lodge churned. The smoke and mist inside the lodge vanished. Tahatankohana spoke, "My son is Wambleeska, the white eagle. James, open the door."

James pushed aside the door flap. Fresh air and light flowed in. Minds cleared as the people made their way out of the womb of the universe.

Tahatankohana searched. "Where's the talon?"

Ann knew what had happened to it. "You won't find it. The eagle spirit took the talon in payment for its service," then added, "I'm not bleeding anymore, but I'm afraid to stand."

"I'll take you." Tahatankohana carried Ann with her arms wrapped around his neck.

Bethany desperately wanted Ann and her grandchild to be all right. "Lie on your back for at least several days." They all agreed that was the proper course of action. Ann vowed to do exactly that.

FIFTEEN

The next day, the men set up a tightly woven net to trap the mussels they planned to dig from the riverbed. They did not talk about sitting in the womb of the universe with the spirit world open before them. Everybody believed it had happened, including Mina. She went to the field, found the necklace, and then went to speak with Ann.

Luyu opened the door.

With her head hung low, Mina requested, "I want to apologize and to give this to Ann."

Sally, Luyu, Hanataywee, Ehawee, and Bethany stood guard with bows drawn and arrows nocked. Ke held a knife at the ready to make sure Mina didn't try to hurt his aunt again. Mina held out the hair necklace that she had cut from Ann's body then ground into the dirt. "I am sorry I disrespected your parents. I did not know what the necklace is."

Bethany translated. Ann answered, "I understand why you want him. I do too. He's a very desirable man."

Ann knew the second hair braid Mina offered was made of Mina's hair because she stood before Ann with short hair. "Tahatankohana does not want me. He thinks I am a horrible person. He is right, and now I have these scars. No one will ever love me now."

Bethany repeated to Ann. She then told Mina Ann's reply. "I think the person who has loved you all along still loves you."

"Who is that?" Mina thought, *nobody loves me.*

Ann stated what she believed. "Nikiata loves you."

"We are friends since childhood. Besides, we are both from this village."

Everybody had to provide for their own family with limited resources. They all knew that Nikiata hunted for Mina even though he had no obligation to do so. Bethany made her own comment. "Mina, I think you need to ask Nikiata about that."

Mina was a single woman with no family. She, like everybody else, was required to marry outside the village. She had nobody to marry except Tahatankohana or James. She wasn't willing to be a second wife for an old man, and Algoma was one of the few women she couldn't manage to manipulate. Mina looked at Luyu.

"Ask him," Luyu instructed her.

Nikiata had always been kind and had provided for her ever since her parents had drowned in the fast waters of Spring River. She thought that was because he thought of her as a sister, but Ann, Bethany, and Luyu were implying that he didn't. Bethany told Ann what they had suggested to Mina.

Mina looked at Ann. *Ann overpowered me and could have killed me. The power of her love has completely captivated Tahatankohana. With her personality, she has people she has known only a short time fiercely protecting her. Her spiritual power has twice brought Tahatankohana back from the spirit world. I saw her do it yesterday.* "Now, I understand the difference between mouse and meek."

Bethany repeated in English for Ann.

"What?" Ann had no idea what Mina was talking about.

"A person can be very powerful but keep her power subdued and under control. I see you have many kinds of power."

When her mother-in-law told her what Mina said, Ann had no idea where the comment had come from. "What is she talking about?"

"Tahatankohana told me you are the most powerful woman he has ever known but that you are meek. He said that is what he wants, not a bully like me. I thought meek meant somebody who was nothing herself. Somebody he could dominate."

Bethany translated again.

"All right," was all Ann said.

"Tahatankohana wants you. It is you he loves. It does not matter why. I will not bother you anymore. You are too powerful. Please keep the necklace of my hair as a reminder that I have submitted to you."

"I don't want you to be submitted to me. Live your life. Just stop bothering me and Tahatankohana, and go talk with Nikiata."

Bethany told Mina what Ann said.

"I will." Mina didn't understand why Ann didn't want her to be her servant. She went to think about that and to wait for Nikiata to come home.

Ann knew her need. She asked her family for help. "Teach me how to speak your language."

"Me too," Sally requested.

They all agreed to teach the girls. Ke pointed at Ann's tummy then acted as if he was holding a baby. "Shizhika."

"Even though they aren't nice, you already know a few phrases. Let me explain each part." Bethany sat down beside her daughter-in-law.

SIXTEEN

As Bethany started the process the same way she had learned, an argument erupted at the creek. Tatonga stated his thoughts about the division of the harvest. "The only fair way is for every man, woman, and child to get an equal share for food and have an equal chance of finding a pearl."

Nikiata replied, "Absolutely not. You have eight people in your family, and no matter which person finds a pearl, you get it. Mina has only herself. It would not be fair."

Tatonga disagreed, "I have more people to feed. She cannot possibly eat that many mussels."

Ppahiska told them what they would do. "Each family will get an equal share of mussels to cook and open. Smaller families will have to work harder, or if they do not want to work so much, they can choose to give them to another family. When they are all cooked and opened, then the meat will be divided by the individual person."

Nikiata spoke up again. "If I have to work three times as hard to open my share, I should get a larger portion than one portion."

"You speak correctly. We will divide the meat

proportionally by the number of people in a family, the amount of food each person needs, and the amount of work." Ppahiska thought he had settled the matter.

"What will be the proportion?" Wakanda knew they should completely define the matter.

Tahatankohana, doing math with a stick in the dirt made a suggestion. "If we get three thousand mussels and divide it between our ten families, each family will cook and open three hundred. Then, if we divide three thousand by fifty-one, each gets just over fifty-eight. After that, we add them all up by the family. From Wakanda, we take one hundred and give fifty to Mina, twenty-five to Nikiata, and twenty-five to Capa. Next, we take seventy-six from Tatonga and give thirty-eight of them to Paytah and thirty-eight to Mantu. Last, we take fifty from my family to give forty to Ppahiska and ten to James. Therefore, every family has an equal chance to find pearls. However, the division of the food is by need and by the amount of work per person.

"Wakanda would have four hundred and eight mussels. Tatonga you would get three hundred and eighty-eight. Father gets three hundred and fifty-six. James would have three hundred and forty-eight. Ppahiska gets three hundred and thirty. Paytah and Mantu would each end up with two hundred and seventy. Nikiata and Capa would both have one hundred and ninety-nine, and Mina would have one hundred and eight. Of course, it will all be adjusted slightly by the exact number of mussels we harvest."

The rest of the tribe was astounded. Ppahiska spoke for them as they pulled another net full of mussels out to the creek. "I have no idea how you came up with those numbers, but they sound right."

"You must have understood Eli's accounting method better than me," Roscoe told him.

Tahatankohana started to explain. Tatonga was the one who had been the most concerned. Even he didn't want to figure out the numbers. "Never mind. I agree with the plan."

They dumped the mussels into the wagon and took the net back to the creek. They had the wagon full after several rounds of digging in the creek bed and catching the dislodged mussels in the net.

The men arrived back in the village with so many mussels they decided to take bushels of them and forget about counting. The women already had vats, tubs, or whatever they had that would hold freshwater set out beside their lodges.

Mina wanted to talk with Nikiata about how he might feel about her, but she didn't know how to start the conversation. She didn't know anything about the argument on the division of the mussels or that it was a result of Nikiata looking after her interests.

Nikiata heard her sigh as she looked at the huge stack of mussels. "Mina, do you want to join my family? I will help you with yours and work on our share too."

She kept her head hung, "I am not worthy of

your help. I am the bottom. You are the next Mystery Man."

"I want to help you. We will bring everything to my lodge."

"Thank you." Mina felt humbled. Nikiata didn't have to help her. Not only was he willing to help her, she hadn't had to beg or bully. He offered to help of his own choice.

Mina behaved like a completely different woman as she and Nikiata carried her share to his lodge. Nikiata noticed that Mina wasn't interacting with him as she usually did. She was acting like a woman interested in a man. *After years of pursuit of Tahatankohana, maybe Mina has finally given up.*

Mina stood at the door of Nikiata's home. His parents welcomed her. She had been there many times before. They knew that their son always helped her and was her friend. Together they put loosely woven baskets over large pots of boiling water then filled them with mussels. Mina asked about one of the things Bethany and Luyu had suggested. "Were my parents from this village?"

Nikiata's mother, Anpaytoo, told her, "Of course they were."

That didn't make sense. Maybe Tahatankohana's family had deceived her. "How long has your family lived here?" Mina asked.

Mina had never before inquired if their families were from the same village. Nikiata wondered. He told her, "Everybody is the first here. We are from the village on the north side of the Arkansas River. Your parents were first to come here from one of the southern villages. Chetan came here from up by the mountains. Right now, none of us are from the same clan."

Mina opened the basket lid to see if the mussels had opened. She looked at Nikiata out of the corner of her eyes. "They need a few more minutes. I will go home to get jars and salt. I wonder if we can eat some now."

Nikiata followed Mina. "I can help you."

They walked into Mina's home and retrieved the items she wanted. He wondered if things were changing. They took the jars and salt to his home.

When they entered the house, Anpaytoo informed them, "I took them off and started more."

"I want to eat some too. Put these in a bowl with fermented honey. I will go to talk to Ppahiska." Nikiata left them.

Mina checked her batch for pearls. Anpaytoo and Enapay checked theirs. Neither found any. They put the meat into the large bowl of fermented honey and the shells into an empty basket.

Nikiata came back into the lodge. "It does not matter if we eat some. Everybody has so many that nobody cares."

Anpaytoo and Mina poured dried vegetables and rice into boiling water. Later, they would add them to the mussels and honey. Nikiata wanted to find out what was happening. As Mina scraped salt into jars, Nikiata sat close enough that her shoulder could touch his if she wanted.

Mina leaned against his shoulder. He stopped scraping and turned to look at her. She looked back into his eyes with the same question she saw in his. "I need to go back to my house," she said.

"I will help you." As they walked across the village, Nikiata again stated, "So I guess anybody could get together with anybody since everybody is from a separate place."

"Would you want to get together with anybody?" Mina asked.

"There is somebody I have thought about for a long time."

"Maybe she thought about you too but did not know there was any chance for anything but friendship." Mina barely touched the side of Nikiata's hand as they walked. He took her hand in his as he went with her into her home. Mina pressed his hand to the side of her face "I did not know any of this. Does this matter to you?"

"No." He pulled her toward him. "I have talked with you too much to be fooled by your act or the scars on your cheeks. I know what is in your heart."

"What do you see in my heart?"

"A person who deserves to be loved." Nikiata found Mina's lips.

After the kiss she had waited years for somebody to give her, Mina asked, "Why did you never tell me this before?"

"You have always been in love with Tahatankohana."

"I was in love with the idea of loving him. When I wake up in the morning, I always look forward to seeing you. When I go to sleep at night, it is you I think about."

"Then forget about the past and choose the love we can have now."

"I choose the love we do have now."

Nikiata kissed her again then pointed out that they should get back to the task of shucking, "Right now we need to cook mussels."

"I know, but kiss me once more before we go."

Nikiata kissed her again. "If I kiss you more, we will not leave at all." He led her out of the house back to his lodge.

Enapay, told them, "Your turn to do the next two batches," then saw his son looking at Mina with a very different smile.

"Eat these." Anpaytoo handed her son a bowl with mussels, vegetables, rice, and fermented honey then watched him and Mina eat together from the same bowl.

As they ate, Anpaytoo looked at Nikiata. She looked at Mina, then her husband, Enapay. Enapay shrugged his shoulders. Anpaytoo had known for a very long time that her son loved Mina and that he hunted so much because it helped him to not think about her. She hoped they had finally found each other.

The four of them ate then worked together for hours. It was late in the night when Nikiata's parents lay down to sleep and left the two young people to finish.

"This basket has the biggest mussel ever." Mina placed the last batch into the stream.

"That one might have a pearl. It had a long time to make one," Nikiata agreed.

They watched with anticipation. Except for the big one, which refused to open, the others all opened and exposed their shiny insides. Mina dumped them into the tray, then plopped the big grandfather back into the basket and the steam.

"We are going to force you to open," Nikiata informed the mussel that desperately tried to hold onto life. They scraped the meat from the other shells into the jars of brine. Mina leaned against Nikiata. She closed her eyes to rest for just a minute while they waited for the monster to open. In a moment, with Mina asleep in his arms, Nikiata's eyes closed too.

Mina woke very early and found her head on Nikiata's shoulder. His arm was around her. She didn't know what she would say to him when he woke. She carefully slipped out of his embrace. Nikiata felt her moving. He kept his eyes closed. If she wanted to sneak away, he was letting her. He didn't want to do anything to make her uncomfortable or prevent her from coming to him.

Mina glanced at the basket. The fire was out, and

the water long ago boiled away, but they had accomplished their task. The mussel had finally succumbed to the steam. In its last seconds of life when it wasn't able to hold itself closed, it had revealed the irritation it had spent decades trying to relieve. Like a flower, the open pearly white shells filled the woven reed basket. Nestled in the center, sat a teardrop of barely, golden white. She put her hand beside the pearl. It was the size of the last section of her little finger.

Mina spoke loud enough for the other three in the lodge to hear. "Grandfather Mussel has given his gift."

They hurried to look. "It is beautiful," Anpaytoo exclaimed.

Enapay said, "We are very rich now."

Mina looked at Nikiata, silent and frowning. "What is wrong?"

He looked at Mina. "Let me talk with you in your lodge."

"All right." They left the pearl sitting in the mussel that had been its home for many years.

"I want to marry you, but you wanted to leave this morning when you thought I was not awake. I think you are not sure if you want me. Now, you will think I want you for that pearl. I want you to own the pearl and never give me any part of it whether or not you decide to marry me."

"That was the most beautiful marriage proposal I could have ever imagined. I see your heart. I want you, I love you, and I want to marry you right now before you go to Fort Gibson, but only on one condition. We must be one family with your parents and everything together, including that pearl."

"Then we will take everything you have to my lodge, or bring everything to your lodge, but after I come back from Fort Gibson. Then we will become one family."

"I will come to your lodge as your wife." Mina embraced and kissed Nikiata.

"Let us tell my parents."

They went back to Nikiata's lodge. "Father, Mother, I want to bring Mina into our family as my wife. I asked her to marry me, and she agreed."

Anpaytoo hugged her soon-to-be-daughter-in-law. "Welcome to our family, Mina. I have waited a long time, hoping to say that to you."

"I add you to my family with happiness," Enapay also embraced her.

"I never knew you wanted me to be your daughter!" Happiness flowed from Mina's eyes, as she again became part of a family.

Nikiata said, "Are you unhappy?"

"I have never been happier. You give me love and a place to belong, and your parents give me love too."

The new mussel shells glittered with their potential to provide for the village. The people loaded them along with the old but still pearly shells that had accumulated in a pile ever since the people had settled in the wedge of land assigned to them.

With the money from the shells, they planned to buy what they needed as a village. To trade individually, each family had at least one representative to carry the pearls they had found in the past or the previous night.

For the first time, just like the other men who said goodbye to the people they left waiting for them to come home, Nikiata held the woman he loved in his arms and kissed her goodbye.

It was not close enough to the first of the month to need to look for Eli, Stephanie, and Tom at Fort Gibson. Therefore, in case Judge Hall had already deployed his assassin, Tahatankohana did not risk going to a place where somebody might discover him. He volunteered to protect Ann, the other women, and the children and remain one of those who waited in the village.

Safely hiding with her husband, Ann lay on her back as their baby reattached inside her womb. Sally sat beside her and cut white buckskin into the parts they needed to make a set of clothes for Roscoe.

SEVENTEEN

The men planned to hunt and forage along the road to Fort Gibson. Roscoe remembered where they had seen rabbits and a prairie dog colony as well as the places where sunfish and crappie had been plentiful in the river. They knew Tahatankohana would find a way to hunt close to the village and that the women would forage. Still, they left everything with their families.

The first day the men traveled across the lands of the Peoria, Modoc, and Wyandotte then the Seneca Indians. Roscoe asked Chetan, "Will you find out if Wakanda will teach me what he knows about plants? If he will, will you help us talk?"

"I'd be glad to translate. I'll ask." Chetan waited until he could speak with Wakanda privately because he thought this kind of training might be Mystery man training. Therefore, it was likely that Wakanda wouldn't be willing.

Wakanda surprised him. "I will teach him but only about plants. I will ask Nikiata if he wants to learn with us."

"I will get him." Chetan hurried to Roscoe. "Come on. He's going to teach you about plants. Nikiata may join us."

"Wonderful!" Roscoe exclaimed.

The two men joined Wakanda who was already speaking with Nikiata. Nikiata wasn't sure what spirits really were. However, since he'd stood with Wakanda guarding the spirit door, he knew they were real. He knew he had to learn how to deal with spirits and everything else Wakanda could teach him. As the four walked, Wakanda named the plants. He explained what they could be used for, the kind of places they were found, and the things that would positively identify them.

Roscoe carried his paper binder. Chetan translated. If Wakanda spoke about a small plant, they dug one up. At its page, he wrote where he had found the specimen he pressed into the binder. If anything was too large, Roscoe only drew a picture.

Wakanda commented about Roscoe's book. "This helps you remember much at one time. I had to learn slowly because I had to repeat over and over until I remembered."

"Yes, but if I lose this, it's gone. That is why I will also review it. Right now, I want to find out everything I can before we leave. I will probably never again have a chance to learn from someone who knows so much."

Roscoe understands the value of what I share. Wakanda told Chetan, "Tell him he does well."

Roscoe, Chetan, and Nikiata learned about plants, Roscoe started learning Quapaw, Wakanda and Nikiata began learning English, and a friendship grew between the four men.

EIGHTEEN

In the village, Sally got her binder, paper, and pencils to section out the land. She searched for anything useful and documented what she found. She added the new pages to those she had already made about the fields they had planted. Sally asked Hanataywee to ask Kimimela and Takoda if they wanted to join her. They did, and so did Hanataywee and Ehawee. She gave them all their own set of papers, binders, and pencils. Sally, Hanataywee, and Ehawee told each other about the plants they saw. As they wrote the information on their papers, they also gave Sally lessons in speaking Quapaw.

NINETEEN

On the second day, Ppahiska and the men entered the vast portion of the prairie assigned to the Cherokee. With Cherokee scouts tracking buffalo, they spent that night beside the road. Together they gathered wild asparagus, burdock, cattails, purslane, watercress, and wood sorrel to supplement the many crappies they took from the river.

When the two groups parted in the morning, Chetan noted the direction of travel of the Cherokee men who had said they were tracking the buffalo. "Back in Arkansas, we went into Osage land to hunt antelope. Maybe we could hunt buffalo in this land on the way home."

Ppahiska agreed, "If we do find some, we must take away what we kill quickly."

TWENTY

Back home, when Sally, Hanataywee, Ehawee, Kimimela, and Takoda started out of the village in the morning, James' daughters Dowanhowee and Mache, Ppahiska's daughter, Mikakh, Wakanda's daughter, Weayaya, and Tatonga's daughter, Zitkala, asked if they could join. "Of course," replied Sally, "I'll get everybody a binder, paper, and pencils."

Hanataywee explained to Sally, "There is no written Quapaw language. Mikakh, Weayaya, and Zitkala don't need those things."

They took turns telling each other what they knew about the plants in the sections they mapped. When they saw Sally sketching, the Quapaw girls changed their minds because they could draw the plants. They used the same letters and numbers to mark the sections. Even though they didn't know the meaning of the marks, they realized they would help them remember where to go.

Sally studied what her friends told her, absorbed the vast plant knowledge of the Indian women, and worked hard at learning Quapaw. Mikakh, Weayaya, and Zitkala also learned about new plants, mapping, and the English language. Hanataywee, Ehawee,

Dowanhowee, and Mache also learned about translating. Like the men, they enjoyed what they were doing and being together. They did, however, do exactly as Tahatankohana had told them and did not go beyond the land between the mountains, Spring River and Five Mile Creek.

TWENTY ONE

As a young boy, Tahatankohana had discovered a way up the cliff behind the lodges. He had climbed to the plateau many times, and he loved doing it. There was no large game in their little section of land, so he went up and looked for animal signs. He found deer tracks. Before the sun rose the following day, he waited at the spring. When a whitetail deer came to drink, he admired its sleek, beautiful body in the dim light of dawn, asked for permission to take the animal then put an arrow into the heart of the large stag.

While he skinned the animal, Tahatankohana thanked the animal for giving its life to feed the people in his village. After he cut off its legs and head, which he suspended in a tree, he tied the rest of the body to his back and carried it to the cliff edge.

Ke waited below. He heard Tahatankohana's whistle, answered back with his own then saw a deer body coming down suspended on a long rope. As it approached the ground, he positioned the hide attached between the two long sticks of a travois. He untied the line and then whistled that his brother could retrieve the rope. Ke picked up one end of the sticks. The other ends of the sticks dragged through the dirt as he pulled the deer home.

By the time Tahatankohana was back with two legs, Ke was back with the travois. Tahatankohana made a third trip while Ke took the legs to their lodge where Luyu and Bethany not only worked on the torso but also cooked a portion of the long muscle that ran down the deer's back.

Tahatankohana carried the last two legs and the head to the rope. After the parts were on the valley floor, Tahatankohana whistled that he was going back to the spring to wait for dusk and try to get another.

Ke again went into the lodge, "Brother will get another. He won't be home until after dark."

Ann tried not to feel afraid. *If Noah thinks he can climb down the cliff in the dark, then he can.* "Thank you for helping him, Ke."

Ke informed his sister-in-law. "It's nothing to pull the travois. Tahatankohana is the one to thank."

"He deserves our praise, but you're very strong. You got the parts here, so your brother doesn't have to climb up and down the cliff to bring it all down. Your mother and grandmother can't keep walking to the cliff to get the pieces and cut it up too. Your help is very important."

Bethany told her second son, "And we need your help again, Ke."

"You see. They need what you can do."

Bethany and Luyu had the first portion of meat

ready. "Please take this to Ppahiska's family and then bring back the basket."

"I'm glad to do my part." Ke repeated what he'd heard Sally say many times, "Together we are as strong as eagles." He took the basket to their leader's lodge. As each family's portion was ready, Ke delivered the meat in the proper order down to James's family.

Normally, they would give the choice parts to Ppahiska and Wakanda. Today, however, they kept the stomach contents and the tongue for Tahatankohana because he had provided the meat. When Ke brought the deer meat to Algoma's door and told her that his brother had killed a stag, she went to Luyu's house. "I've come to help."

"Welcome, Algoma," Luyu told her. They worked together on the first deer. As they roasted the back strap, Bethany prepared the put aside treats for her son to eat when he got home.

Sally, Hanataywee, and Ehawee came into the lodge with purple-skinned Wapato tubers, Sunchokes, and large baskets of watercress to wash and eat.

At dusk, because he was sure his brother would have another deer, Ke took the travois back to the cliff. Ke heard the whistle that meant more was on its way. *I knew he would get another.*

They got all the parts down then Tahatankohana let the rope drop. He went back to the crack in the cliff face and climbed down. When he entered the

Lisa Gay

lodge, Bethany hugged him. "Well done, my son. Sit down." She served him the two delicacies with delicious watercress, Sunchokes, and Wapato tubers.

The next day, all the women in the village went to Luyu's lodge to help cut up the second deer and, of course, to get a portion. By afternoon, the village was a cloud of smoke as strips of deer meat hung beside smoky fires. After they had hung the last of the meat, the girls again went searching, documenting, and gathering. Not only did they enjoy searching and gathering, but they were also glad to breathe the smoke-free air in a patch of purple Indian Head flowers. Sally lay back and admired the beauty of the flowers. She heard Weayaya chastising her friend. "Zitkala, you took too much."

Kimimela defended her sister. "We need a lot of it."

"Here take what I have if you need so much. We have to leave enough for more to grow."

Zitkala took all the plants offered. "Thank you. Your father says our mother needs this for her stomach."

Weayaya immediately changed her mind. "I did not know that. We will look for more." All of them went in search for more Indian Head for Zitkala and Kimimela's mother, Metea.

Sally saw another patch of the purple petaled flower with a large button of brown spikes in the center. She called out in Quapaw, "I found more."

Every day, they explored then went home at

night and told their families what they had learned and discovered. They were all surprised at how much they had found using Sally's very thorough systematic approach. When Sally was home during the evenings, she worked beside Ann to make a shirt, pants, and moccasins from the white buckskin.

All the family, especially Bethany, Luyu, and Ke talked with Ann not only to teach her the Quapaw language but also because they enjoyed talking with her. Ann wanted to learn, and it gave her something to occupy her mind as she lay very still, guarding her baby's life.

Some days Sally spent time with her Uncle James, Algoma, and her cousins Dowanhowee, Mache, Mi, Te, and Nanpanta. Sally told stories about her parents and growing up on the farm that James and Algoma had built. James told her about growing up with her father, Chris, and their other two brothers as well as about his life on the farm by Harmony, moving to Indian Territory, and also about their lives there.

TWENTY TWO

Six days after the men left home, they stood inside Fort Gibson. Ppahiska went directly to Colonel Howland to request permission to trade. Ppahiska knew no English, and the Colonel had limited knowledge of Quapaw, but they managed to communicate enough for the Colonel to understand what the man wanted. It was rare for any Quapaw to come all the way to the fort. The colonel wanted to promote good relations with all the Indian groups, so he gave written permission to trade whatever they had brought.

While they waited for Ppahiska to return, Roscoe looked around. He saw no evidence of shells currently in the fort, but he remembered seeing some on his previous visit. Roscoe believed that confirmed that they traded shells.

At the wagons, Roscoe asked Chetan to translate. "I want Nikiata to know the proper amount to accept for the shells."

Chetan explained what Roscoe advised, "Do not agree to less than one hundred and twenty-five dollars but start much higher and let him bring you down. If he will not give you that much, do not sell. Walk out. We will take them to Fort Smith."

Chetan translated the negotiations. The Master of Supplies, Sergeant Matthew McCormick, started low. "I'll give you one hundred dollars for them."

Nikiata immediately said, "One hundred twenty-five."

"One hundred per wagon," Chetan countered with his own offer.

"I can't get that much for them from the button buyers. I'll give you sixty-two dollars for each wagon."

Chetan told Nikiata, "The man said, 'One hundred ten dollars.'"

Nikiata repeated his previous offer, which Chetan translated as, "One hundred and seventy-five dollars for all the shells, and we unload them."

"One hundred sixty-five and you unload."

"Agreed. Where do you want them?" Chetan accepted for Nikiata.

Sergeant McCormick led them to a storage shed, unlocked the padlock, and then opened the door. "Put them in there." He sat in the shade and drank lemonade while the Indian men shoveled shells.

Roscoe was not about to leave any evidence that Noah and Ann were in the vicinity. Sergeant McCormick would surely remember him, so he went to the store and bought what his family needed while the master of the store was gone.

Roscoe told the clerk, Specialist Gilroy, "Please write the prices beside everything on this list."

Since they now lived in the village, where they

could hunt and harvest from the land, Roscoe didn't buy the same things they had the last time. As a private gathered the items on Roscoe's list, Roscoe pretended to consider purchasing other items that he knew were on Ppahiska's list. He asked about their prices and wrote the information on his list.

Roscoe was very pleased when he saw lemons and limes. "I'll buy as many as you'll sell me."

Roscoe believed Sergeant McCormick would try to recoup the money he had paid for the shells. When he left the store, he knew the standard asking prices of most of the items in the store. He planned to pass the knowledge on to Ppahiska and then remain out of the attention of the soldiers for the remainder of their stay. He packed his purchases in the front partition of the wagon built to keep their supplies separated when his goats and miniature donkeys rode in the back half. He then sat in the empty animal section and waited.

When the last shell was in the shed, the sergeant locked the door with his padlock. They went back to the store. Nikiata held out his hand. The shopkeeper handed him the one hundred and sixty-five dollars he had agreed to pay. As planned, Nikiata took the money and left. James stayed in the store.

When together at the wagons, Roscoe gave the price list to Chetan, who told Ppahiska the names and prices of everything on the list.

James joined them with a spinning wheel and a large loom carried by four soldiers who Specialist

Gilroy had assigned to deliver the purchase. Ppahiska asked James in Quapaw. "What are these?"

James put his hand on the spinning wheel and replied in the same language. "This is a spinning wheel. It makes yarn and thread." He put his hand on the loom. "This is a loom. It weaves the thread into cloth."

"How did you buy these?" Ppahiska believed they must have cost a lot, and he knew James didn't have more than a few pearls.

"Ann and Sally are grateful that Algoma and I gave my brother, Chris, the farm. They insisted that I take the money and buy these."

"All our people should be able to make these things."

James agreed. "We will let others use them. The spinning wheel will be easy to share, but the loom can only make one cloth until it is complete. Algoma will teach the women how."

"Do they have more to sell?"

"When I left they had another spinning wheel and a smaller loom. If you buy them, don't mention my name, the names of the girls, or Noah, or anything about any of us."

"Why?"

"Because Judge Daniel Hall might have sent somebody to find Tahatankohana and Ann, and we don't want that kind of person in our village."

"They would hurt us too?"

"If nobody knows we have anything to do with them, nobody will come to our village."

"Tahatankohana should not have come home."

Chetan was at the bottom, and he shouldn't have opposed the opinion of Ppahiska. He did anyway. "My son has done many good things for the village. We would not have food, plants in the ground, or be here buying anything if he had not come home."

"You are right. The best way to spend the money we have because he did come home is to get the other spinning wheel and loom. Then we will trade thread, yarn, cloth, shells, and pearls. We also need a wagon to carry what we sell and buy. I will tell the others to keep this secret."

Ppahiska handed Roscoe's list to James. "We do not need this paper." *James is part of this village. It doesn't matter if the soldiers know that. He can translate for our people.* "James, come with us. You too, Chetan. Talk to the man in the store and get us good prices."

Thinking it was safer to divide their resources between trips, none of the people from their village had brought all the pearls they owned. If robbed, they would not lose everything in one fell swoop. They still had as much in the village as they traded today. They all planned to come again just before winter with the rest of the shells.

The people bought different combinations of items. They loaded up with blankets, rifles, ammunition, whetstones, and steel knives. Some of them purchased chickens, goats, or pigs. All of them selected flour, spices, coffee, cornmeal, bran flakes, dried compressed vegetable cubes, and tobacco.

Remembering what Chetan had given them at Tahatankohana's storytelling, many of the men bought smoked ham and smoked beef. Rice, beans, and cracked corn, along with lots of sweet and white potatoes were also on several lists of wanted items.

After seeing the cast iron skillets, dutch ovens, and the sheet metal oven Tahatankohana had brought into the village, most of the wives had sent their husbands with orders to try to get some along with corked jars and glass bottles of matches.

James explained the uses of the more durable items like metal hoes and shovels and seed planters, which the group decided should be purchased with the village money along with saws, iron axes, and construction tools.

As the Indians loaded their purchases, two soldiers walked past. They assumed no Indian could understand their conversation. "There's no way we can remove that rock."

"We could if we had dynamite."

"But we don't, and there's not any within five hundred miles."

Chetan knew his son had brought dynamite into the village. He found Roscoe. "Those soldiers said they need dynamite, and they think there's not any around."

Roscoe instructed him, "Ask to speak with Colonel Howland. Find out how much he needs and what he'll pay for it."

Colonel Howland struggled to speak to Chetan in Quapaw. "What do you want to discuss?"

In very good English, Chetan explained, "I am Chetan. I can get dynamite. How much do you need? How much will you pay for it?"

"You speak English very well."

"Yes. I had somebody teach me."

"That was a very wise thing to do. I need two crates with at least twenty sticks each, blasting caps, and fuses. I'll pay three hundred dollars for each crate with its caps and fuses."

"I'll bring it on the first day of August for a delivery fee, or you can come and get it."

"We need it as soon as possible. I'll send some men to get it now."

"I'll go talk with my people. I'll come back soon." Chetan left to first discuss the terms with Roscoe then the other men.

Roscoe said, "That's a good deal. We should keep the money for when we're going west."

Ppahiska's answer was, "A military escort would be safer. Ask the colonel to provide rations for everybody for seven days."

Chetan returned to Colonel Howland. He added what he thought was wise. "They said, 'yes' but the money has to be paid in either gold or silver coins. You have to provide rations for all of us for seven days and also rations for your men for an extra seven days to get back to the fort."

Colonel Howland accepted the offer. He had expected to go much higher, and a few rations were no problem. "How many people?"

"Thirteen of us and however many men you send."

"Agreed, it's a seven-day trip, so leave today."

Chetan went to his people and told them, "We have to leave today."

Roscoe informed them, "It's just as well. They won't let any of you stay inside the fort after dark. You might as well be outside with a military escort."

Ppahiska consented, "We go as soon as I get back from the bakery. I want to try that thing Tahatankohana called 'éclair.'"

Chetan went back to the colonel to confirm the agreement. Roscoe couldn't go to the bakery because the baker would recognize him from the incident with Ann and Sally when they had first visited the fort. The soldier in the bakery knew Sally's real name and would know they were still close if he was seen in the fort. He also didn't want to associate the bad feeling the soldiers had toward him with the people of this village. Roscoe, therefore, spoke to James. "Ask Ppahiska if he will buy me four loaves of bread, six danishes, and three éclairs."

James passed on the request. Ppahiska held out his hand. "Buy me the same."

James told Roscoe what Ppahiska said. Roscoe handed over the necessary money. All the men, except Roscoe, went to get these things called 'danish' and 'éclair.'

The colonel released six hundred dollars in gold coins to Sergeant Timothy Anders. He ordered him to select three other men and then get the dynamite. He authorized them to take four horses, one wagon, and rations for all seventeen men for seven days to go to the village and seven more days of rations for the soldiers to get back to the fort.

When the military detail came beside Roscoe's wagons, they found twelve men eating éclairs. The soldiers watched with hungry eyes. Hiding inside one of the wagons, Roscoe breathed a sigh of relief. None of the men was a soldier they had encountered during his previous visit with Noah, Ann, and Sally. He popped his head out of the wagon. "We should all start the journey with the same pastry." He handed one of the men a bit piece. "Get four more."

When the soldier was back, he handed each of the other three an éclair. His was already gone, so he climbed into the wagon. Sergeant Anders called out, "Forward Ho!" They rode out of the fort as his fellow soldiers enjoyed a very rare treat.

Roscoe watched the soldiers lick their fingers. *Goodwill is always a good plan.*

TWENTY THREE

As a military excursion, they crossed toll-free on the ferry to the west side of the Neosho River. That was their first added benefit. Since it was past noon when they started, they traveled only six miles before setting up camp beside the river.

Ppahiska, his sons Chaska and Kanizhika, the other men of the village, and Roscoe waded through the plants in the narrow sliver of marsh at the edge of the river.

They gathered watercress and cattails and speared blue suckers. When they had enough for seventeen people, they returned to the camp. Chetan shook the yellow pollen from every head of the harvested cattails onto a cloth then poured the majority of it into a small pouch. He removed the long, sharp leaves, so he could cut up the solid stem bottoms. He squirreled the bag of pollen into his medicine bag but left everything else for communal use.

While Chetan was again in the river, the others made a stew with the fish, along with the peeled and chopped cattail rhizomes and young stalks. Just before they served the stew, they added the watercress, the remaining pollen, and the gel created by ripping off the cattail leaves. The broth thickened. Roscoe recorded how they had prepared and used the ingredients.

Chetan gathered more of the prize he wanted to give to Bethany. He came out of the marsh, a yellow creature. Pollen covered his long hair, clung to his eyelashes, and coated his skin as a congealed paste of pollen and sweat.

Wakanda commanded, "We do not want to be pollinated. Clean off in the water swamp man."

Chetan kept the pollen he scraped off his body then obliged like a good plant spirit directed by a Mystery Man. He found a place with clear water and transformed back into the red man who had first entered the marsh.

"What about the rations we brought?" Sergeant Anders asked.

James explained the options as he thought they should be since his Indian friends didn't understand the question. "Give us the rations we would have eaten for this meal. You can eat yours or give them to us and eat what we prepared."

"Ham, give them their shares and mine. I'd rather eat that stew then more salt horse."

Morgan and Ezra told him, "Give them mine too." Ham and James put all seventeen portions assigned for the meal into the village's wagon that Ppahiska bought at the fort. In Quapaw, James told the other men from his village what they had done.

The morning meal consisted of eggs from the chickens the village men had bought, and army rations of bacon, sugar, milk, and butter. Roscoe shared a loaf of his bread and some of his ground coffee. They used all the army rations allocated for the meal and all the eggs the chickens had lain. Together, Chetan, Roscoe, James, Ppahiska, and his two sons secretly ate danishes.

The land on the west side of the Neosho River was an open prairie of low, grass-covered hills that allowed them to see for miles. As they traveled, they shot prairie chickens by bullet or arrow when flocks took flight.

At mid-day, they let the animals graze for two hours while they roasted the birds to go with the army rations of dried peas cooked into soup with a small amount of salt pork.

Ppahiska had two Danishes left. Roscoe gave him one of his because dividing two Danishes between three people was more geometry than any man should have to perform, except maybe Eli. Ppahiska ate them with his sons while the others slept. Chetan privately shared his last Danish with James the next morning. Roscoe ate his final sweet pastry, also out of view of those who did not have any.

At mid-day on the third day, they stopped at the solid sea of white that was the salt flats. Fine salt particles puffed into the air as their new axes pounded the hard surface. As a haze, a cloud of salt hung suspended in the air around them. Even with a bandana over their mouths, they breathed in too much salt. It crusted their bodies and sucked the moisture away. When they had each chopped a large hunk of salt out of the salt flats, all seventeen men were exhausted and dehydrated. Fully dressed, they plunged into the slow-moving clear water of the Neosho River, washed the salt off their bodies and out of their clothes, then drank all the water they had previously boiled and stored. Upstream just far enough to reach edible grass for the animals, they stopped for the day.

The following days, they and the animals drank large amounts of water as they crossed creeks and searched the plains for game. They cooked a mixture of the food they scavenged from the land and the rations the army had provided. In the afternoon of the fifth day, they saw what they had hoped to find: a herd of buffalo. Thousands grazed on the plains beyond one of the low hills. Chetan, Nikiata, Chaska, and Enapay quickly jumped on unharnessed horses.

"Keep a sharp lookout for any Cherokee," Ppahiska reminded them.

If they were caught taking buffalo, the Cherokee would consider them stealing, and the Cherokee did not deal kindly with thieves.

Nikiata was the best hunter. They followed his slow, downwind approach. When they were between a large portion of the herd and the road, Nikiata signaled.

Screaming and waving wildly, Nikiata and Chaska charged the giant beasts of the plains. A group of buffalo broke from the herd and fled to the south. When they had run them far enough, Chetan and Enapay turned them back to the north on a path parallel to the wagons. The sound was deafening as thousands of pounds of scared stampeding buffalo thundered toward the men waiting to kill them. A cloud of dry dirt kicked up by pounding hooves filled the air as the buffalo ran toward their doom.

"Now," Private Knuckles screamed then shot the buffalo leading the stampede.

Bullets and arrows flew at the animals the men could barely see through the thick dust. Buffalo crashed to the ground. Others veered, ran into each other, and desperately tried, with their short legs, to jump over the fallen. Many successfully made the leap.

In front of the beast approaching Sergeant Tim Anders, a buffalo rose from the ground. Buffalo bodies collided. The rebound sent one skidding. Tim shot it between the eyes. He was sure he would be crushed into the wagon anyway. With no control from its brain, the buffalo's front legs buckled. Tim attempted to get out of the way. He jumped backward, lost his footing, and went down in front of the massive animal. He put his hands over his head. "God, forgive me."

The beast's massive nose slammed Tim, knocked the breath out of him, and rolled him under the wagon. That animal lay dead with a bullet in its brain while the guilty animal escaped. When he could breathe again, Tim examined himself. *Ugg! I sure hurt. My entire back must be bruised.* He stayed under the wagon while the rest of the herd thundered past.

The dust cleared. Nikiata counted only nine dead buffalo. One thing he had learned from Wakanda was that the Mystery man should keep peace in the village. That would only happen if each family had a buffalo. Nine meant Mina would not get one. He chased the herd back toward the road where it would be easier to gather another carcass then shot the tenth animal. He let the rest of the animals escape with the larger group that went over the hill and then out of sight.

Ppahiska immediately directed his oldest son, Chaska, "Ride the wind to the village. Bring back all the people, all the animals, and every travois."

The sixteen men who stayed behind started the slaughter. At least one ton each, the only way to transport the carcasses would be to cut them up. Together, they rolled the four smallest buffalo onto their stomachs, pulled the front legs straight ahead and the back legs out behind.

Chetan, Roscoe, Sergeant Tim Anders, and Private Ham Blanders set to work on the buffalo that had slammed Tim. Along the spine, they slit the skin from its horns to the tail. From the slit on its back, being careful so they could tan it later, they cut down each leg and flayed the skin off.

James, Paytah, Private Morgan Finch, and Private Ezra Knuckles set to work on the buffalo Ezra shot. Mantu and Tatonga, with the help of Ppahiska and his second son, Kanizhika, skinned the bison killed by Tatonga. Capa and Paytah worked with Wakanda, to butcher Wakanda's buffalo.

They worked diligently to not leave any evidence. As they butchered, they put the pieces into the wagons. They cut tongues out and tails off. Being careful to protect the long sinew, they detached the two back muscles from the backbone. At the front end, they cut the skinless head off at the base of the skull. Keeping the neck meat and the vertebrae in one chunk, they cut off the neck where it joined the body.

Next, to preserve the bones for making tools and to harvest the marrow, they hacked the legs off above the top of the long bones. With their new axes, they chopped the spinal bones of the back off in one piece. Once that was out of the way, they halved the rib cage and loaded the pieces into the wagon.

The exposed insides were then attainable. They removed the lungs, heart, liver, stomach, bladder, kidneys, and intestines. They split the back end of the carcass and moved the pieces into a wagon. Last, they pushed the fluids off the skin, shook the dirt off the furry side, folded the hide up, and put it under the wagon seat away from the blood that dripped from between the boards of the two wagons not coated with pitch.

Just over an hour from the time the animals had died, the four groups had their buffalo ready to transport. Ppahiska, Kanizhika, Wakanda, Enapay, and the soldiers resumed their journey with four skinned and cut up bison, along with the chickens, pigs, and goats. They left behind the rest of the men with unharnessed mules, the remaining dead buffalo, and four giant pools of blood.

Two hours later, the wagons crossed the Neosho River out of Cherokee land. Safely out of view, they unloaded the partially butchered buffalo and all the supplies they had purchased at Fort Gibson. Sergeant Anders let them take the military wagon and mules. He and his men stayed on the east side of the Neosho River. He thought it would be best for the United States Army if they did not take sides in this matter. The people of this Quapaw village needed the food, but they had illegally taken buffalo from Cherokee land.

Kanizhika left his father and the four soldiers. He and Enapay went back to the buffalo and people they had left in a dangerous situation. When they got back, Nikiata, Chetan, James, Capa, Tatonga, Paytah, and Mantu had the next four buffalo skinned and cut into pieces. The large bull Chetan had killed must have weighed four thousand pounds. Therefore, they left it for last. To keep the weight down to three thousand pounds in each wagon, they loaded four large butchered buffalo without their heads.

They replaced the tired team with the mules that

had rested for the last four hours. When the wagons left, almost six hours had elapsed since they had killed the animals. Nikiata, Chetan, Roscoe, James, Paytah, and Mantu waited with the remaining buffalo and the four heads. The men started on the last two buffalo. They knew the longer they remained, the more likely it was that they'd be discovered. They also knew it would be four hours before the wagons returned.

TWENTY FOUR

At Five Mile Creek, Chaska signaled the sentry then entered the village. "Emergency! Ten bison to prepare. We leave immediately."

This was vital work. Everything they needed to butcher and bring home the buffalo was quickly packed. Tahatankohana helped Chaska. "Ann cannot go. I have to stay here to protect her."

Chaska led the animals out of the field. "We know."

Tahatankohana didn't allow the goats to follow the herd through the gate. Billy, Roscoe's male goat, protested. "Meh-eh-eh. Meh-eh-eh." Tahatankohana stayed in the field to calm him. Ann lay on her back in Luyu's lodge, sewing beads onto the white buckskin shirt.

Far to the south, the wagons arrived at the river crossing for the second time. They dropped off the headless buffalo. Only Capa and Tatonga returned to the west with the wagons. Everybody else remained east of the Neosho River to butcher the eight buffalo with which the Quapaw had safely absconded. The people in Cherokee land continued to cut up the two carcasses that had not yet been hauled to safety.

The mules had an easy trip back to the west, pulling empty wagons. Ten hours after they had shot the buffalo, the men loaded the last two butchered animals and the four heads. They replaced the second set of animals with the four animals that had remained in the west and hoped they wouldn't need to make a quick getaway with tired animals.

Mantu started the mules toward the Neosho Crossing for the third time. "I think we did it."

Even though the land was mostly flat with only low rolling hills, after nineteen hours of pulling very heavy loads, only a half-hour up the road, some of the animals were too tired to go on. Roscoe insisted they stop, "We'll kill them if we don't let them rest."

Capa urged them on. "We will be the dead ones if we stop. We have been here much too long."

"We should act as if we do not have the buffalo. It is night. We will stop like any other traveler." Chetan laid buffalo chips for a fire.

Capa informed him, "You can stay if you want. I leave now."

"Me too," Tatonga added.

Paytah looked at Mantu. "We go with you."

"Do what you want." Nikiata helped unharness the mules. He knew it was stupid to kill such a valuable resource, and he was glad the others would soon be gone. He wanted to talk to the remaining men. Ever since the sweat lodge ritual, he thought he felt the Spirit in his heart.

In the light of the full moon, twenty mules ate

117

nutritious prairie grass and rested while the men removed sinew from the long backbone muscles. Nikiata asked, "What is this spirit that came through our hearts?"

Chetan explained, "He is what made the universe. There is a book named Bible. It tells the story of everything. It tells us, in the beginning, there was nothing but the being named God. We call Him Wakan Tanka. He created the universe together with the Great Mystery, who is the Word named Jesus, and The Great Spirit, who is The One you asked into your heart. They created the earth inside the universe. In the beginning, only water was here. Wakan Tanka moved over the water and commanded that there be light. The sun that rises every morning formed. Then Wakan Tanka separated the light from the dark, and that is how the day and the night started.

"On the second day of creation, they divided the waters above from the water below. He named the air above the earth, 'sky' and the water below 'sea.'

"On the third day, Wakan Tanka brought the land out of the lower waters and made all the plants on Mother Earth.

"On the fourth day, He made the moon and stars to help us know the seasons and the times.

"The fifth day, He put every kind of bird and flying thing into the sky and made giant monsters and the other creatures to live in the sea and the rivers. Wakan Tanka told them to have babies and to fill the sky and the sea.

"The sixth day, Wakan Tanka made all the animals for the land. Everything was good, but He wanted to make something even better. Something like Himself that would rule over everything on Mother Earth. He made a man and a woman. He told them what they could eat and what the creatures on the earth could eat. He instructed the man and woman to take care of the plants and animals, and He told them to have children, and to fill the earth. The whole universe and everything in it was complete. Wakan Tanka thought it was very good.

"On the seventh day, Wakan Tanka rested. He blessed that day and said that it should always be a day to rest."

"We know The Great Spirit and Wakan Tanka. What is Jesus?" Nikiata asked.

James let Chetan tell him because he didn't want Nikiata to think God was only for the white man. He hoped Chetan would explain in a way that Nikiata would understand that God was the God of everybody. "Everything comes from Wakan Tanka. He only speaks The Truth. When He speaks, the True Words become real. That is how He created the universe. He spoke the Words, and the earth became real.

"A long time later, when the time was right, Wakan Tanka spoke again, and His words became a perfect human. He was completely Wakan Tanka, and He was completely a human man. He came here for a reason. Wakan Tanka had told the first two humans they could eat anything except one thing. He told them if they did eat that food that they would die.

"A creature named Lucifer made the woman think she could be like Wakan Tanka and know good and evil if she ate it. She did. The man stood there with her and let her do it then he ate some too. They no longer had the ability to live forever. The Great Spirit sent them out of the garden into the world. Now, we all have to work hard to live.

"Later, their first son killed his brother. Over time, human hearts became very wicked. The people would not do anything the way God told them. When the Father looked at humans, He saw all the bad things they did piled high. He could not be friends with them anymore, even though that was what He wanted.

"God is always just. He will not let people get away with doing wrong. The penalty for going against the Father had to be enforced. The problem was that a perfect human had to give what God required to forgive them. No human could do it because every person was bad. We still are. That was when Wakan Tanka made His words into the Great Mystery. He was the perfect human man named Jesus.

"Jesus lived His whole life without going against Wakan Tanka's commands. When the people who lived back then killed The Great Mystery, He took all the bad things of everybody who ever lived or would live, including all of us, and paid the price so the people can get back to Wakan Tanka. That was why The Great Mystery came. After the people killed The Great Mystery, Wakan Tanka made Him come alive again and took Him to the center of the Universe at the other end of the Milky Way.

"Wakan Tanka and The Great Mystery sent the last part to the earth. The last part is The Great Spirit. The Great Spirit is the Spirit of Wakan Tanka's son: The Great Mystery. The Great Spirit is what came into our hearts."

"So why did I have to ask Him to come into my heart? Why doesn't He just go there and help me do things the right way?"

"I hope I don't offend you, but I think you have feelings for Mina." So Nikiata would answer his question himself, Chetan asked, "You never tried to force her to care about you, why not?"

"Because if I have to force her to love me, that is no good. I would not want her, but if she gives her love freely, that is real, and I want it."

"Exactly, God waits for a person to choose to want Him. When it is real, He goes to them."

"I asked Him into my heart, but I did not know what I was accepting. Does it count?"

James answered this time, "I think He knows what is in the heart of a person. He can work from the place a person gives whether it is large or small, a well thought out decision, or one not really understood."

"I keep thinking about that Spirit. Sometimes I think I feel it here." He tapped his chest. "And here." He tapped his head. "I want to know if it is in me or not."

Chetan asked Nikiata the most important question. "Do you want Him? Now that you know what you ask, you can again ask Him to be in your heart."

"I want to think about it. I will be Mystery Man. I do not know how it will fit."

"What do you think about the way Tahatankohana fits them together?"

"He is not a Mystery Man."

Chetan, James, and Roscoe thought Tahatankohana was, but they didn't refute Nikiata's statement. Chetan told him, "You can think about it. Wakan Tanka will help you decide."

For a time, the men worked without talking. They knew the Spirit was moving in the thoughts of Nikiata because He was doing the same with them.

Still in Cherokee land with stolen buffalo, the men let the fire burn out but continued what they were doing. They got the two necks out of the wagon and cut the big hunks of meat away from the bones then put the parts back into the wagon.

Afterward, they cut the flank muscles from the belly and cut the long muscles into strips. Chetan thought about the men who had left them on the prairie with the pilfered buffalo. *If they didn't have any troubles, they should be with the others now. Bethany will be worried.*

TWENTY FIVE

Chetan was right. Shortly before Capa, Tatonga, Paytah, and Mantu arrived, the whole village, except Ann and Tahatankohana, had arrived at the buffalo camp on the east side of the Neosho River.

"Where are the wagons and the others?" Bethany asked.

Sergeant Anders walked to the white-skinned woman with very blond hair. "Hello, ma'am. I'm Sergeant Timothy Anders. Are you passing through? Would you like an escort to Fort Gibson?"

"I'm pleased to meet you, Sergeant Anders. I am not passing through. This is where I live very happily with my husband, Chetan."

"I guess that explains why he can speak English." The Sergeant made a mental note to talk with the woman alone. He wanted to be sure that she was not a captive.

Capa answered Bethany, "They stopped. Roscoe said they had to let the mules rest or some of them would die."

"You left them?" Ppahiska questioned.

Capa defended his choice, "There was no reason to stay there. Chetan said they would be fine. He said the Cherokee never bother travelers on the road."

Wakanda stated a fact Capa should have known, "Unless the wet blood of the buffalo calls to the Cherokee from the dirt. They are the only ones close enough to have spilled that blood."

"Take fresh animals and get them," Ppahiska commanded the four men.

Without a word Tatonga, Paytah, and Mantu rounded up sixteen animals, including the two horses.

"They are fine," Capa insisted.

Ppahiska felt irritated. However, as a good leader, he knew Capa was afraid and needed to overcome his fear. "You will take the animals to them by yourself."

Capa said, "I will get them but only because Nikiata is there."

Bethany wanted to slap the man. "My family matters. You act like a scared woman. You stay here. I will go." She jumped on Eyanosa and led the other fifteen animals behind her.

"You're not going without me," Sally followed on her mule, Beauty.

The two women went down the path out of view without Luyu, who knew one of them needed to be there for Ke and Chumani.

What will people think if I say I want to go? Would they even let me? But what if Nikiata is hurt? Mina slipped away unnoticed. *Besides, if there is trouble, it will be better if we are not together.*

"I will too." Chaska hurried after Sally.

When he joined the women, Sally asked him in Quapaw. "What does Chaska mean?"

He gave her a long answer in his language. Bethany translated into English. "Oldest son."

Ppahiska commanded Capa, "Go."

Capa didn't attempt to join the three who had already gone. He followed far enough behind to not be associated. Mina followed behind him.

As the sun's light came over the edge of the world, Nikiata silently once again asked The Great Spirit to live in his heart and to guide him. This time, he understood; no matter what people called Him, there is only One Truth, and that was who he was accepting.

TWENTY SIX

Nikiata, Chetan, Roscoe, and James put the last of the buffalo parts in the wagons and pulled the pucker skins closed. The smell of bloody meat was strong. They weren't likely to outrun a band of Cherokee warriors with the wagons, so the men mounted the four fastest mules and prepared to scatter the others if necessary. Nikiata saw something up the road. "Many horses are coming."

Chetan looked through his spyglass. "Yellow hair. My wife brings fresh animals."

Bethany, Sally, and Chaska saw the wagons ahead and the mules grazing in the field. Just beyond the low hill on their right, Chaska looked west. "The buffalo are back." Chaska put a telescope to his eye. Close to the herd, tiny buffalo crept across the ground. "Stop," Chaska ordered.

Bethany pulled back on the reins. "Why?"

"If we scare the herd, the hunters will not make their kills. Some of them may be injured or killed. That will make it even worse when they see we have taken some of their buffalo. Maybe if they know we stopped to help them, they will allow us to have the buffalo. Maybe they will think we only have two animals."

Another low hill on Nikiata's side of the gap blocked their view of the area where they saw the others looking. They crept to the crest of the hill and looked over the top. The plain beyond was a black sea of tens of thousands of bison accompanied by men under hides, pretending to be buffalo calves. Just as the Cherokee were out of view behind the hill, the wagons weren't in view of the men stalking the bison.

Roscoe asked, "Should we help or should we remain out of the fray?"

Nikiata answered, "They said the buffalo have not been east all year. Like us, their people need meat."

"We should help. I do not think they would be upset if we wait until after they make all their kills then shoot some for them with our new rifles." James went back to the wagons for ammo belts.

Chaska also thought that the men sneaking into the herd needed assistance. He looked at Sally. "You do not know how to shoot. Stay out of the way."

"I know how to shoot!" Sally felt slightly offended, especially since Chaska still had a look of disbelief on his face. She remembered how Eli had quickly reloaded and then shot again when he had first come to work for them at the farm. The same way Eli had, Sally planned to show Chaska what she could do. She got her rifle, powder, wadding, and lead balls ready.

Capa realized what was happening. He quickly

joined Chaska and the women. "I finally caught up with you."

Chaska knew Capa had followed them the whole way and purposely hadn't joined them but said, "Good we can use your help. Get your weapon ready. Follow my lead."

With much relief that Nikiata was safe, Mina successfully stayed out of everybody's detection as she crept to the top of the rise. She lay on the ridge and peered through the tall wildflowers and grass.

Twenty people under buffalo skins slowly crept closer to the herd. In position at the edge of the herd of giant buffalo, the tiny buffalo threw off their skins and plunged spears into the beasts they had deceived into allowing them close enough to take their lives.

The animals that didn't drop instantaneously ran only a few yards before tumbling to the ground. The bison survivors close to the stricken bolted but soon settled back into the comfort of their companions. The animals in the immediate vicinity, however, remained edgy.

When the deceivers had gotten into position a second time, thrown off their skins, and speared their intended victims, a bigger portion of the close by buffalo escaped into the larger herd. A wave of panic spread. As the beasts fled, the men on the plain continued the attack with arrows. Unaware of an impending second onslaught, some of the animals carried away arrows in their bodies, as they charged toward the gap.

To assure their success, Nikiata held up his hand. When the buffalo were close enough, he flung down his hand to signal the people beside him and those across the gap. He also signaled the one he didn't know he was directing. As Nikiata's hand found the trigger, Chaska called out, "Now," to those around him.

Eight people rode forward into the gap between the hills and shot the buffalo being funneled to their doom by the hills to their sides and the crush of the animals behind them.

Sally saw a beautiful yellow beast. Her rifle had a long range and a lot of power. When the target was still far away, she fired. The giant animal went down with Sally's bullet in its heart. Other buffalo hit the ground with Quapaw bullets in their bodies. They all reloaded and shot again. Sally dispatched a buffalo with every shot. Her companions did the same. Mina shot a barrage of arrows continually at the buffalo she thought was small enough for her arrows to penetrate to its heart or lungs from her distance.

The Cherokee saw buffalo dropping and the puffs of smoke rising from behind the hill. As if directed by the divine, the buffalo changed course and ran back toward the Cherokee men who ran together for protection as they speared the beasts frantically attempting to find a safe place.

The herd split. They charged to the north and to the south away from the menace before, behind, and in the midst of them. Buffalo dropped as long as any were close enough for an arrow or spear to reach a vital organ. It was not long before the gigantic herd ran out of range.

Chaska didn't know how the Cherokee men would react to white women. "Take the mules. Get inside a wagon. Hide there unless we tell you to come out."

Bethany and Sally galloped to the wagons with sixteen animals then jumped off Eyanosa and Beauty. With lightning speed, they removed the bridles and lead ropes from all their animals, and let them join their herd in the field.

The overwhelming smell of blood gagged the women as they climbed into the fly-infested wagon and then hid behind a mountain of raw meat. Swarms of flies classified Sally and Bethany as an alternative landing and feeding zone and took full advantage of their available flesh. Trying to keep the irritating pests away from her face, Bethany swatted the insects.

As she attempted to be free of the tiny pests, Sally informed Bethany, "I hope nobody comes near. Waving our hands will give us away. There's no other way to avoid these horrible creatures."

With their women secured safely behind mounds of butchered buffalo, the six men rode triumphantly into view then sat on their mules and waited for the Cherokee men to signal acceptance. A few of the Cherokee men realized their benefactors were the Quapaw men they had camped with several days before. They signaled for them to approach.

Nikiata knew they needed to acknowledge that the animals belonged to the Cherokee. He immediately stated their position in regards to the ownership of the dead animals. "We killed the buffalo for our neighbors." Now, if the Cherokee wanted to share, it would be their choice.

Oukonunaka, the leader of the Cherokee hunting party, looked around. Even though only a tiny fraction of the entire number of animals in the herd lay dead, it looked as if there had been a massive slaughter. At the most, his people might have killed fifty. More than a hundred carcasses littered the plains. "We accept your help. Each of you take one you killed."

"Can we get our people to help us?" Chaska asked.

"One of you go. Bring back only women. We go for our women too."

Chetan wanted to safely secret away the two women of his family and the buffalo meat already in the wagons. "I take the wagons and get them."

At the wagon, he wrapped his arms around Bethany. He knew how blessed he was. Not only did he have a wife, but the woman was a wonderful wife. She had risked her life to bring him mules when she thought he needed them. He wallowed in the devotion of the woman he loved. "Thank you for bringing the animals to us."

Nikiata joined Chetan and the women at the wagons. "We will start while you go."

Chaska climbed into the wagon. "I pick the yellow one Sally shot, so she can have it." He passed out the axes, knives, and tarps.

"Pick the biggest for the other five," Chetan suggested.

Nikiata assured him, "We will," then went to find out who had been shooting the arrows from behind the other hill.

The rest of the men harnessed the sixteen fresh animals. Chetan departed leading all their other mules, donkeys, and horses behind him.

Nikiata stole up the hill so slowly that the woman lying still in the grass didn't notice his approach. When he was close enough to see the object of his hunt, his heart filled with joy. Mina had come to rescue him just as Chetan's women had. He spoke softly. "Mina!"

"Nikiata, I never should have doubted that the best hunter on Mother Earth would be safe."

They lay hidden in the garden of flowers and grass lain across the low hill of the prairie. He expressed what was in his heart. "You came into a dangerous place when you thought I needed help. You asked me what I saw inside you. I saw the woman who would love enough to do such a thing."

"I could not live without you." Passion filled Mina's heart. Hidden in the garden God had laid out for them, Nikiata finally shared the freely given love he had dreamed about for years.

TWENTY SEVEN

When the wagons were out of view, so they could travel faster, they tied a lead rope to the harness of one set of mules, put them in the middle, and then each drove one of the other wagons. They left the road and headed diagonally across the plain to the Neosho River crossing at Spring River.

They arrived at their camp an hour and a half after leaving the field of dead buffalo. Chetan explained what had happened with the second buffalo hunt. "Probably they think we would take more by force if we brought men. Only women can help butcher."

Ppahiska spoke. "That is acceptable. We could not all go. We need to take these buffalo home."

Dowanhowee turned to her mother, Algoma. "Mache and I could go help father. You could go home with the rest of the family to finish working on this one."

"You can go if other people do."

"I'm going back. I want my yellow buffalo," Sally informed them.

Luyu said, "I will go."

"Hanataywee and I could go with grandmother and help father with his second buffalo." Ehawee loved her mother, but she hoped she would meet a Cherokee man who would not know her mother and would decide how he felt about her before he found out Bethany was a white woman.

"Algoma, may Ke and Chumani go home with you?" Bethany asked.

"Of course," she replied.

Ehawee thought, *now there's no chance.*

Wichahpi stated her dilemma, "Capa will need help, but I already have one buffalo to work on and a four-year-old daughter."

It will be exciting thought Weayaya, Wakanda's fourteen-year-old daughter. "I will help Capa."

Wakanda asked, "Chetan, will you protect her?"

"I certainly will," Chetan assured him.

"May I go, father?" Mikakh, Ppahiska's oldest daughter, requested. "Weayaya and Sally are going. I want to go too."

"No. You need to help your family."

Weayaya was disappointed, but she did not question his decision. Not only was Ppahiska her father, but he was also the leader of their village. She knew to obey him.

Zitkala, Tatonga's daughter, said to her father, "I want to go. You already have enough people to help you with your buffalo."

"You should not go without me," Tatonga told her.

"I have as many years as Weayaya."

Tatonga no longer felt that Chetan was at the bottom. Chetan had proven many times that he was a warrior and provider. Tatonga thought, *maybe there should not be a man at the bottom*. "Chetan, can you watch all our girls?"

"I will look after all our women. We all will," Chetan assured him.

"You can go." Tatonga gave his oldest daughter instructions, "Work hard and be obedient."

Sally, Zitkala, Weayaya, Luyu, Bethany, Hanataywee, and Ehawee, along with James' daughters Dowanhowee and Mache packed the tools they needed to butcher buffalo.

Chetan spoke with Ppahiska, "Maybe after you take the wagons, animals, and travoises and get all the buffalo home, you will send them back to get the buffalo we will be butchering."

Ppahiska agreed. "We will bring them in three days."

Privately, Chetan asked Wakanda, "As soon as you get to the village, would you find Tahatankohana and have him set out two crates of dynamite, the blasting caps, and fuses? Tell him to collect six hundred dollars in gold or silver coins."

Wakanda replied, "I will send Kanizhika ahead to tell him."

"That would be very good." Chetan turned to the soldiers. "We didn't eat any military food last night or this morning, and we won't eat any tonight or tomorrow morning. Give us those supplies and what you have for the seventeen of us for the seventh day."

Sergeant Anders challenged Chetan's request. "But you're home. You don't need any for tomorrow."

Chetan restated the agreement he had made, "For two crates of dynamite, the blasting caps, and fuses, Colonel Howland said he would pay six hundred dollars in gold or silver coins plus supplies for seventeen people for seven days and four people for seven more days."

Sergeant Anders had an idea. "In that case, since it's been only six days, we could give you the seventh day of rations for all of us and another day of rations for us four soldiers. Then we could stay and eat with your people for the next two days and leave on the third day."

Chetan passed on what had been suggested.

Ppahiska agreed. "They have been honorable men. They shot two of the buffalo we take home. I allow them to stay with us for two days. They must give the rations now."

After Chetan translated, Sergeant Anders ordered his men, "Give them one day's rations for seventeen and another day's rations for four."

Once finished dividing the rations, the fire in their camp was completely out. With the pilfered buffalo already safely taken out of Cherokee land packed in the wagons or on a travois, they moved north along the east side of Spring River.

Xida People

TWENTY EIGHT

The women and Chetan went west. Five hours after Chetan had left the field of dead buffalo, he arrived back with nine women.

Because the soldiers and other white men at Fort Gibson and Fort Smith pursued the Cherokee women and took many of them away, only a few young women remained in the close by villages. The young unmarried Cherokee men saw that the Quapaw women were as beautiful as they had hoped. They planned to find out if they were unmarried, so they butchered near them. Soon they talked together.

When Chetan had returned to the buffalo camp with their women, a warrior named Waya had noticed Luyu. Even though Waya's wife had died the previous year, he was not looking for, nor did he want another woman. Still, there was something about Luyu that continually drew his attention. At first, Waya thought she was the woman of the white man they called Roscoe. They worked together, and Waya frequently heard them laughing. Waya thought Luyu was very beautiful, and her laughter was enticing. He found himself looking at her repeatedly.

Sally worked on her yellow buffalo with Chaska, Weayaya, and Zitkala. Chaska was impressed by Sally's ability to shoot and wanted to know more about her. Weayaya and Zitkala soon realized Chaska didn't want them there. When Cherokee men started speaking with them, Weayaya and Zitkala went to help butcher other buffalo.

Chaska stayed beside Sally. He didn't give the other men an opportunity to get close. Sally practiced speaking what Quapaw she knew, and Chaska helped her learn. Most of the time, they spoke incorrectly then laughed at their mistakes. Even with their communication problems, they enjoyed each other.

Chetan made sure the Cherokee men knew Bethany was his wife. He didn't stop their daughters from talking with them. If they found a husband among the Cherokee, he would be happy for them. James thought the same about his daughters.

The young Cherokee males swarmed around the unattached Quapaw girls. Chetan had promised he would protect them. He spoke with Oukonunaka. "All the men from our village will defend our women. Make sure your young hunters know they are to behave properly with our women."

On the plains, the Cherokee people, the Quapaw people, Sally, and Roscoe turned buffalo bodies into food that would last through the winter. Everybody skinned carcasses or removed the meat from the bones, cut off horns, hooves, and tails, and pulled teeth from the skulls. They removed sinew from the long back muscles, cleaned out hearts, urine bladders, gall bladders, and stomachs.

They put the contents of the stomach in one bowl and set aside the brains in a different bowl. They smoked the meat and poured the fat they had cooked to a liquid into the cleaned stomachs of the animals. They mixed most of the fat with dried then ground buffalo and berries to make pemmican.

The women also plaited cattail leaves into mats and then used them to keep the body parts out of the dirt and grass. They harvested plants to eat from the river and the plains. The Quapaw women cooked bison tongues and livers the Cherokee men brought them then served them back to those they liked best.

Everybody worked around the clock. Groups of people took turns eating and sleeping then went back into the assembly line. Speed was vital to preserve the meat before heat and insects ruined it.

Nikiata and Mina joined Chetan's family who read and talked about the Bible while they ate. Nikiata wanted to learn about the God he had asked into his life. Chetan or Bethany read the words first in English then translated the verses into Quapaw. Because it took much longer to say everything in both languages and also because they needed to spend as much time as possible working on the buffalo, they read and discussed only a few verses.

Nikiata was afraid that Sally or Roscoe would feel frustrated by the need to translate. He also feared that they would leave the group to discuss the verses without them because they couldn't speak Quapaw. That was not what happened. Sally and also Roscoe wanted to hear what every one of them had to say. Nikiata could tell that they both believed his thoughts were intelligent and interesting.

TWENTY NINE

Kanizhika forded Five Mile Creek. He ran into the village. "Tahatankohana, Chetan says to get out two crates of dynamite, blasting caps, and fuses. He and Roscoe agreed to sell it to Colonel Howland for six hundred dollars."

"How did they know the colonel wants it?" Tahatankohana asked.

"Chetan heard some soldiers talking when they should not have been. Your mother taught him, so he knew what they were saying. He made the deal."

To give Tahatankohana time to remove the dynamite from the rest of his supplies, Wakanda stalled. He stopped to shoot rabbits and quail in the short grasses and to gather wood sorrel in the place they had found it going south. When they finally crossed Five Mile Creek into the village, it was at the very end of the day.

They parked the wagons in the middle of town. Wakanda took the soldiers straight to Tahatankohana. The other men herded the animals, except the chickens, into the pasture. Each family took their buffalo, salt block, and the supplies they had purchased at Fort Gibson into their lodge. Tahatankohana's supplies and buffalo parts remained in the wagons while he conducted the dynamite transfer.

"The crates are dry and unopened. This dynamite may be good." Sergeant Anders ordered, "Men, get the pry bars and open them."

Ezra forced the tops off the wooden crates. Sergeant Anders looked inside. Each box held twenty-four large sticks of dynamite packed in diatomaceous earth. "This is excellent. They'll be much safer to transport in this dirt." Tahatankohana passed two smaller boxes to the men holding pry bars. A soldier pried one open. Sergeant Anders inspected the blasting caps and roll of Bickford fuse. He noticed a woman at the back of the lodge. He surreptitiously inspected her. *They have another white woman, and she's confined to a pallet almost out of view. There are too many white people in this village. Something isn't right.* "All of this is in fine condition. The army will buy them." He counted out six hundred dollars in gold coins.

After he had the crates loaded in his wagon, Sergeant Anders asked. "Is the woman going to help you with the buffalo?"

Ann was beaten up and cut. Tahatankohana didn't want the man to inspect her closely and then think something was wrong. "She was injured and almost lost her baby. She's trying to keep him from leaving. She can't help."

"Are you all right ma'am?" Sergeant Anders called out.

Ann knew she had to alleviate the soldier's

concerns. "I'll be fine. It's my baby I'm worried about. Since I can't help, perhaps you'd like to have some of the buffalo meat, and you'll stay here and help my husband."

"We will." Sergeant Anders agreed. That way, he could verify that the woman was there of her own free will.

Tahatankohana told the soldiers, "Come." They left Ann sewing beads at the bottom edge of something white. Across the village, in Quapaw, Tahatankohana asked Algoma for permission to leave Ke, Chumani, and the soldiers with her. He explained why, then told the soldiers, "I'll come back and get you when I'm ready."

Tahatankohana went to Paytah's lodge. "Since we will be traveling, I want more fat to make pemmican. Will you trade with me?"

Paytah offered, "I will give you half this fat for all the innards and bones of another buffalo."

"I will be back."

Tahatankohana went to Mantu's home. "We will be traveling. I need to make plenty of pemmican. I would like all the innards of your buffalo and all the bones. Will you trade with me?"

Mantu stated his requirements for such a trade, "Take this whole buffalo. Make all the pemmican you can then smoke the rest of the meat. If you do this, I will allow you to keep half the pemmican, everything inside the chest and all the bones. Everything else belongs to me."

"I agree."

After several trips between their homes, most of Mantu's buffalo sat in Tahatankohana's lodge. The hide, hooves, horns, tail, tongue, and head with its brains remained with Mantu. Tahatankohana held the inner parts. "You know that Sergeant Anders and Private Knuckles both killed a buffalo. I ask your permission to let them have buffalo meat to take to the soldiers at the fort. I will ask our families still on the buffalo field to give them meat from there."

"They shot them. They should have meat."

Tahatankohana returned to Paytah's home. "Here are the insides. I will bring the bones after I cut them out."

"Put that on the table. I already divided the fat. Bring the container right back."

Tahatankohana carried away the very large bowl of fat piled high above the rim. He deposited the much-needed ingredient in his home then returned the bowl. He went to all the lodges. From every one of the village men, Tahatankohana requested and received permission to give the soldiers a share of meat at the slaughter field.

Back at the lodge of James, the soldiers helped Algoma and her fourteen-year-old daughter, Mi, cut buffalo meat. Ke and Algoma's twelve-year-old son, Te, tried to contain Chumani and Algoma's four-year-old son, Nanpanta. Algoma opened the door. "Welcome to my lodge."

"All have agreed to let our families give meat to the soldiers when they get back to the buffalo field."

A large amount of the meat was already cut into strips and ready to smoke. Tahatankohana and the soldiers hung it outside on Algoma's racks. I'm ready to take Sergeant Anders, his men, and my family."

"I could stay here and help Algoma butcher," Ham glanced at Mi.

Tahatankohana looked at Algoma. She accepted the offer. "That would be very helpful."

"Behave." The sergeant ordered his soldier. As the other soldiers crossed the village with Tahatankohana, Sergeant Anders chatted. "Colonel Howland will be very happy to have buffalo meat. We've all eaten way too much of that salt preserved fatty beef Sergeant McCormick calls salt horse, and please call me Tim."

"I sure am sick of salt horse," Morgan informed them.

To start the tanning process, Tahatankohana salted his family's buffalo hide. He set it aside, then put together a meal for the soldiers, Ann, Ke, Chumani, and himself. When the time had come for them to eat, to celebrate his first buffalo hunt, Tim retrieved Ham then brought out spruce beer provided by the army to prevent scurvy among the soldiers.

They cut meat while the soldiers and Tahatankohana consumed quite a bit of a day's ration of beer for seventeen people. After hours of work and too much spruce beer, Private Ezra Knuckles asked, "Did that woman over there and the one at the river with the cuts on her face fight over you?"

Tahatankohana looked at him for a few seconds then decided to speak the truth. "Yes, but I didn't want that to happen to either of them. I thought I had made it completely clear that I've chosen the woman here with me."

Young Private Morgan stated, "I've never had even one woman want me."

From the pallet, Ann said, "Give life some time. You'll find a woman who will love you. I waited twenty years before I found my husband."

Tahatankohana added, "And don't settle for just any woman who wants you. Wait for the right one."

"This man is your husband?" Sergeant Anders asked Ann.

Ann remembered what Mina had spent days chanting. Ann knew everybody in the village thought the same thing every white person would feel: that Noah wasn't her husband. She no longer felt truly married, and that bothered her. "I think so."

Tahatankohana heard what Ann said. He also picked up the tone of her voice. He had thought she had been so very silent the last two weeks because she was injured and worried about the baby. He realized something else was on her mind.

As the night wore on, Ann fell asleep. The men worked straight through until late the following day. At the end of the second day, the people in the village had completely butchered all ten of the buffalo they had brought home. After days of hard work without any sleep, everybody was exhausted. As each family finished, they lay down until the whole village slept soundly.

The following day, the people in the village, met in the lodge and decided how to divide the rations belonging to the Quapaw. The cider was already in quart containers. It worked out perfectly for each of the ten families in the village to get four quarts. Each family also got two candles. They used their new glass jars and the beautiful pottery they already owned to get their portions of sugar, rice, cornmeal, molasses, and vinegar.

The rest of the supplies they divided between the thirteen people who went on the trip. Each kept however much butter they had left in the half cup tin they had been given for the trip and their personal small bar of soap. Each of them also got two each of the dried then compressed vegetable and potato cubes.

Because the beans were raw, they hadn't used any of the rationed coffee. As they had traveled home to the village, Roscoe had provided the already roasted and ground coffee that he had bought at the fort. They felt he should be compensated and left ten and a half pounds of green coffee beans with Tahatankohana to give to Roscoe. Because the men had hunted the entire trip, they had used very little of the salted beef. Therefore, each person on the trip also received nine pounds of salt horse.

After the people split the rations owned by the people in the village, Sergeant Anders asked for permission to trade what he had left. The rest of the green coffee beans he swapped with Tahatankohana for a smaller amount of already ground coffee he could use going back to the Fort. He traded another gallon of cider for two gallons of goat milk with Ann. With Tatonga's wife, Metea, he traded twenty-four pounds of hardtack for twelve loaves of freshly baked bread.

He gave eight pounds of salt horse to Nikiata's mother, Anpaytoo, in exchange for eight pounds of smoked mussels. Because she thought the beef would last longer, Capa's wife, Wichahpi, traded four pounds of smoked goose breasts and goose legs for four pounds of salt horse. With the village chief's wife, Mikoishe, Sergeant Anders traded four pounds of salt horse for a large salmon he watched Ppahiska's son, Kanizhika, spear in the river.

That evening, after all the trading, Tahatankohana wrote a letter to his family. He handed it to Sergeant Anders purposely not in an envelope. He wanted the Sergeant to be able to read the message and not realize that they were concealing something. Tahatankohana knew sometimes the best place to hide was in plain view.

"Tim, I need to send Roscoe back to the fort. May he go with you? I'll add enough food for him to get there and back. You can put everything together and share or keep yours separate if you want."

The Sergeant looked at the items: cheese, smoked bear and elk meat, a gallon of mussels in brine, rice, dried pinto beans, ground coffee, sugar, honey, walnuts, and eggs. "He can go with us to the fort, but he'll have to go home without us."

"That would be perfect. Thank you." Tahatankohana was glad. Roscoe wouldn't be alone at least half the trip and maybe not at all if Eli and Stephanie were at Fort Gibson. If his sister-in-law and brother-in-law were ready to go, he thought they should immediately start across the prairie. If they were not, they would have to continue the very dangerous wait through the winter.

During the night, Sergeant Timothy Anders secretly read the letter.

Family,

Sergeant Tim Anders and Ezra Knuckles killed two buffalo for the village. At my request, Tim, Morgan, Ezra, and Ham helped butcher and prepare our buffalo. They also helped Algoma. I have the permission of all the men here to give them some of the buffalo meat. I thought it would be best to keep what we have here and ask you to give them some of what you have there. I'm sure you understand all the reasons why. I don't know how much you have there, but you know the amount we have here.

Roscoe,

Please go to Fort Gibson and pick up the items we want.

Tahatankohana.

After the breakfast for which the Sergeant traded a pint of molasses, the villagers and the soldiers prepared the thirty-eight animals, four wagons and all the travoises to go back to the slaughtered buffalo in Cherokee land. Once ready to go, they poured a swallow or two of the remaining spruce beer into the cups of everybody in the village. Sergeant Anders lifted his cup. "Here's to a successful journey." Tahatankohana translated into Quapaw.

"And friendship," Ppahiska added. Tahatankohana repeated the phrase in English.

In their own languages, they all chanted, "Success and friendship," then gulped an ounce of beer.

When the six men left the village, Tahatankohana went to speak with Ann. Her cup of beer sat beside her unconsumed. Tahatankohana lay on the pallet beside her. He thought he knew what was bothering her. The previous day, he had asked the women still in the village to tell him again what had happened between Mina and Ann. He found out that Mina had repeatedly told Ann that he had not married Ann by white man's laws nor by Indian man's laws. Mina had insisted that everybody knew Tahatankohana hadn't married her because one day he was going to leave Ann to be with Mina.

"My love, will you marry me?" Tahatankohana asked his wife.

"I've already married you," she reminded him.

"I mean. I want to marry you again here in this village in our ways."

"Then we'd be really married."

Noah told her his opinion, "We would be twice really married."

"Yes, my husband, my love. I'll marry you, but we'll either have to do it lying down, or we'll have to wait because I'm still afraid to stand or sit."

"We can wait. I don't want to take any chances either." Noah kissed and caressed Ann. "I really want to make love, but I'm afraid to do that too."

"Hopefully we'll be able to do both before too long." Ann conveyed her desire with another long warm kiss.

THIRTY

Far to the south, the young Cherokee hunter, Dustu, spoke with all the Quapaw women. He even managed to speak with the young white woman for a short minute before Chaska reclaimed her. He thought Hanataywee was the sweetest by far.

Even though Dustu was five years younger than Hanataywee, he was already as tall. Like the other Cherokee braves, the hair on his head was shaved away except one small section of long hair at the top rear, which he tied together to keep out of the way when hunting or working.

Hanataywee watched the muscles in Dustu's arms flex and bulge as he pulled a buffalo into position. *Dustu is very strong.* "Where can I find berries?" Hanataywee asked the men around her.

Dustu quickly answered, "I know where."

Hanataywee was very happy that Dustu had responded. "Would you be willing to show where, and will you help me pick some?"

"Of course." Dustu smiled.

All his teeth are good. Hanataywee left with Dustu to gather berries.

When they approached the raspberry patch,

several prairie chickens flew out of the bushes. Dustu had his bow in hand and two birds dead on the ground in a blink of her eyes. Hanataywee was impressed. "You are very fast."

"That is why I am called spring frog. Just like a frog catches flies, I am so fast I always catch my prey."

"You will be a good husband for some woman."

"Maybe you would want a good hunter even if he was young."

Several Cherokee men had stopped talking to Hanataywee when they had realized she was already twenty. "I do not think the age of a man makes him a good husband or not. Besides, many men think a woman my age is too old."

Dustu thought, *your breasts are much nicer,* but said the other thing he thought. "You have much more sweetness than any of the others." Dustu had purposely taken her to the berry patch with one end just out of view of the field of people. "You have eyes that hold the sky. They are very beautiful."

The Quapaw men had told her she was not pure. "Do you know that my mother is a white woman with blue eyes?" Hanataywee asked.

"I do. Your father also thinks blue eyes are beautiful."

Dustu has a good heart to go with his most handsome body.

"I think your lips must taste as sweet as honey."

"Maybe you would want to find out someday."

"I could find out today."

Hanataywee notified Dustu, "Today, you can only find out if my kisses are sweet."

Dustu took her into his arms. He held her tight, so he could feel her breasts against him. She was the best thing he had ever felt, and he wanted to keep her there. "Hmmm. Very sweet. Much better than honey." She did not move away. He held her for another moment before he reluctantly let her go. They picked every ripe berry in the patch. Dustu noticed Hanataywee looking toward camp. *I want to keep her to myself.* "We should pick more berries. I know another place."

"Tomorrow." Hanataywee walked back to her people.

The day Luyu arrived, she had noticed the tall warrior with a thick crop of long gray hair tied in his skullcap. Even though he was sixty, he was as strong as the other men, and he worked just as hard. He saw her see him looking at her. She stopped cutting meat strips and braided her hair into two long braids then rolled them up and pinned them behind her ears.

I think she is telling me she is not married. All the young women have braids like that, except the two with short hair and the white woman with long yellow hair. She's obviously Chetan's woman. Waya watched Luyu.

Chetan told Bethany, "That man is interested in mother."

Bethany agreed, "And she let him know she's available and look at our daughters talking with those young warriors."

As the people worked by the fires that smoked the strips of buffalo meat, they slow-roasted potatoes and cooked racks of ribs to eat immediately. The women also cooked large quantities of watercress and other greens. Soon, an assembly line of people from both tribes worked together skinning the animals. The next team cut off the back straps and passed them to others who removed the sinew while other people cut the muscles from the bones or cut it into strips. Another group hung the meat on the smoke racks. Groups ate at different intervals then went back to processing. Some rendered fat and heated the ends of the long leg bones. Others broke the hot bones in half the long way down and harvested the beautiful white marrow.

On the second day, Waya found the largest buffalo on the field then asked Luyu if she would help him. Luyu would be with Waya for at least the many hours it took to process the one beast. She immediately consented. She helped him position the animal then knelt beside the buffalo. To show her submission to the leadership of this man, she waited for him to cut the animal's hide along the backbone.

Cherokee women did not do this. They held the authority. Waya wasn't sure what to do. He stood beside the beast and thought. Then he stuck his knife into the back of the buffalo's head and pulled it down the animal's backbone.

Luyu was not a forward woman, so she waited for the man to speak to her. Meanwhile, Waya waited to be asked into a conversation. For many long silent minutes, the two of them cut the hide from the massive carcass. Waya inspected the skin Luyu had very expertly removed. He did not find a single nick, and she had cut away the fat and meat very close to the skin. "You took off the skin very well. It will not need much scraping."

"I am pleased that you think I did good work."

Waya thought *this woman would not be quarrelsome like my last wife.* He knelt beside Luyu. As he moved around, cutting the meat from the buffalo, Waya often managed to touch Luyu's hand or shoulder.

"Why do you have no husband?" he finally asked.

She told him the truth that she had not even told her son. If it mattered to him, she wanted him to know from the beginning. "I believed the white man loved me. I gave him my love then waited for him to come back from trapping in the west. I had his son, and I waited for him. His son grew, and I waited. He never came for me. Then my people came here. He would not know where I went, but he was not coming back for me anyway."

"Which one is your son?" Waya asked.

"Chetan is my son."

"Why does he marry a white woman after a white man treated you shamefully?"

"He does not know anything about his father. Chetan found the girl, and he kept her."

"He stole her?"

"No. He found her starving after her parents had died. She was young. She wanted him to take her, to feed her, and to love her."

"He wanted her too?"

"Yes, he wanted her too."

"You wanted her?"

"She wanted a mother again. She loved me the minute she saw me. I wanted her too."

"Is it a good marriage?"

"Yes."

"You believe they loved each other from the very first time they met?'

"I think there are different ways to love. I think they loved each other one way the first day and they love each other a different way now."

Waya liked this woman. She was wise. "I am called Waya. It means wolf. What are you called?"

"Luyu, wild dove."

"You have the eyes of a dove. They are soft and beautiful."

"And you have the strength and power of the wolf, keeping his family safe and well fed."

Waya thought about that. His first wife would have said he was mean and terrifying. This woman saw what was good about a wolf. "And a wolf also loves his mate devotedly for his whole life."

***

Waya remembered when he was sixteen, married barely a year, and very ill. His wife's mother had told him to hunt antelope. He had gone hunting but had brought home rabbits. His mother-in-law had told him to get antelope. He had not. She hit him. "I have no strength. I will hunt again when I am well," Waya had told her. She beat him with a stick. His wife had not defended him. Instead, she told him to do as he had been told. He had left the home of his wife and her parents and then found his brother. Waya asked him to kill an antelope for him, and he would get him two after he was well. He waited in the woods while his brother shot an antelope. Waya took it to his wife. "I got this for you and your mother." She did not even say thank you. Neither she nor her mother had ever appreciated him. They hit him every time they did not like something.

Waya could have stopped them. For the sake of his daughter, he chose to stay with his wife and live under their authority like all the other men of their people. They had tried hard to break him. In his mind, they never had, and they had known it.

***

Luyu said, "I have heard that about wolves. I have never met one before. It would be nice to get to know about wolves."

Waya replied, "And wild doves." He hoped they would learn about each other as the smoke of the fires filled the air around them.

The third day, Capa waited at the road for Ppahiska and Wakanda to arrive. He knew, on this day, his people would bring the wagons, and none of them knew exactly where they were. He greeted Ppahiska. "Twice I have bravely brought buffalo to our people."

"Yes, you were there when it happened. Take us to our people."

They drove the wagons onto the field of smoking meat. Sergeant Anders gave the letter from Tahatankohana to Chetan. Chetan read it then handed it to his wife, who read it then took it to Roscoe.

"Thank you for delivering the letter." Roscoe threw it into the fire. He was glad to go look for Stephanie and Eli. He was the most logical one to go, and he did not want to butcher buffalo all week. *If God is real and He loves us, He better have brought them and Tom.*

Bethany asked, "Are you going to share the meat with all the soldiers? Will you eat it right away?"

"There are many soldiers. Much of it we will eat right away." Chetan helped load several hundred pounds of raw meat. "Thank you. This is good," Sergeant Anders stated.

"Take this too." Making sure that Ppahiska saw, Capa put a large leg on top of the other meat. James, Chaska, and Nikiata knew the soldiers had shot two of the buffalo in the village. They added three more legs.

"Let's get some smoked meat," Bethany told them.

As they loaded dried meat, the leader of the

Cherokee hunting party came over. Ppahiska greeted him, "I am Ppahiska. These are my people." He swept his hand through the air to identify the Quapaw men and women around him.

"I am Oukonunaka. These are our people." Oukonunaka made a much larger gesture.

"It is good that you share," Ppahiska stated.

"And good that your warriors killed many buffalo for us." Oukonunaka then asked, "Who are these soldiers with you?"

"These men are Sergeant Tim Anders, Private Ezra Knuckles, Private Morgan Finch, and Private Ham Blanders from Fort Gibson. Our men went to Fort Gibson to trade. These soldiers came to our village to finish the trade."

"What do you trade?" Oukonunaka asked.

Sergeant Anders stood there without realizing the man had asked him a question. Chetan stepped in and explained that Oukonunaka wanted to know what he could trade.

Sergeant Anders offered a possibility. "I still have twenty pounds of salted beef bacon. Does he have fresh vegetables?" Chetan passed the answer in universal sign language.

"We will look." Oukonunaka waved his wife over then spoke to her softly. She looked at the meat. It was salty and very fatty: good. The woman returned with other women carrying large baskets of vegetables.

"Is this trade good with the soldiers?" Oukonunaka asked through Chetan.

"Yes. The trade is good. Do you have more vegetable to trade?" the Sergeant inquired after being told what Oukonunaka had asked.

"We have more."

Sergeant Anders looked at Chetan. "Tell him to bring vegetables to the fort if he wants to trade."

Chetan told Oukonunaka, "The Sergeant says the army would like to trade with you for vegetables. If you want to trade, take vegetables to Fort Gibson."

"Tell him we must finish the buffalo then we will come."

Chetan translated to Sergeant Anders.

"Wonderful. I'll tell Colonel Howland."

Oukonunaka's wife took the meat and then made a space in the wagon. As the vegetables poured into the wagon, Chetan noticed three pint-sized bottles hidden under the tarp.

In English, Oukonunaka said, "Goodbye."

Sergeant Anders replied, "We'll be looking for you at the fort."

Chetan walked through the gap beside the full wagon. "Did you give us all the rations assigned for us?"

Sergeant Anders thought he had seen Chetan get a glimpse of the whiskey. He had hoped he wouldn't have to share. Now, he had to, and he also had to make up an excuse as to why he hadn't already done so. "I wanted to give you the last thing alone because it's not a large amount. I know Ppahiska is your village leader, but you made the arrangement." He took out all three bottles of whiskey. "Two of these are your share."

Chetan didn't want the whiskey. What he did want was that the man understood that he couldn't get away with trying to deceive him. However, he allowed the Sergeant to keep his dignity. "Good thinking." He took both bottles then, making sure Sergeant Anders saw him do so, he handed them to Roscoe. "See you again soon, Roscoe. I hope you find what we're looking for."

The Sergeant thought *these are the nicest people. I don't know why everybody thinks so poorly of them. They aren't savages at all.*

As Chetan walked away from the road, he pondered on the recent trading. *A bride price is really just a trade. If those men ask to marry Hanataywee or Ehawee, I will tell them the bride price is permission to hunt on Cherokee land.*

Luyu and Waya heard Chetan telling Bethany his idea. "I think your people should ask what your son suggests. If it is only us hunting, we would be hunting on our own land. He should also ask something that will cost the individual man something valuable."

"Why? We need to be able to get food."

"But the man needs to know in his own heart that he wants the woman enough to give up something else he really wants, and she needs to know it too."

"What if the price is to let our people hunt on

Cherokee land, but that man would not be the one to hunt because he had to move very far to the west?"

"The Cherokee men always go to live with the family of their wives."

Waya hadn't said anything about her ever being his wife, but she wanted him to know about her life, and she wanted to know about his. "If a person had children, he would not want to leave them."

"Not young children who need him, but in that case, he would take them with him because the woman would become their mother. If they were grown, one man might and another man might not."

"It is hard to give up people you love."

"Sometimes, things work out. Look at Nikiata. He would give up everything and cross the entire land to be with Mina, but he does not have to. She already told him she would be his wife, and she asked him for nothing."

Luyu replied, "Sometimes people do ask for a sacrifice. Would you like me to help you with another buffalo?"

"Yes, I would like it."

Eight days after they had shot the buffalo, everybody on the plains knew all the buffalo would be butchered, preserved, and packed for transportation by the end of the day. Therefore, seven Cherokee men and seven Quapaw women buried seven buffalo hearts in the ground to assure that the buffalo herds would continue to thrive and provide food for the fourteen human hearts given and received in love.

Wakanda saw his daughter burying a buffalo heart with a young Cherokee man. He went to speak with Ppahiska.

Shortly after burying the buffalo heart with Hanataywee, Dustu went to Chetan. "I want to ask your bride price for Hanataywee."

Chetan gave him the answer about which he had been thinking, "You must get Oukonunaka to give our people permission to hunt on your land, and you must be willing to walk across the land to the western sea and live there forever. Hanataywee must agree she wants you to be her husband."

"I will walk to the sea and live there, and I will try to get Oukonunaka to give permission, but he may not. It may not be something for him to decide. Is there something else if he will not?"

"No."

Dustu wanted to have Hanataywee, but he doubted that he could accomplish what Chetan asked. He left thinking about how he could complete the required task.

Adahy asked his brother, "What did he say?"

"I think he said no. He gave me a task I cannot complete. He says I have to get Oukonunaka to let his people hunt on Cherokee land."

A few hours later, Adahy went to Chetan. He hoped Chetan approved of him. Unlike his brother, he had spent time talking with Ehawee's family as well as her. "I have come to ask your bride price for Ehawee."

Chetan gave him the same answer. "You must get Oukonunaka to give our people permission to hunt on your land, and you must be willing to walk across the land to the western sea and live there. Ehawee must agree she wants you to be her husband."

"I will go to the western sea, but I do not know if I can get Oukonunaka to allow your village to hunt on our land."

Chetan corrected him, "I said my people, not my village."

"I will try." Adahy walked away.

"What did he say?" Dustu asked.

"He likes me even less. He said I have to get permission for all the Quapaw people to hunt on Cherokee land, and that I have to walk all the way to the western sea and live there."

"I think he said I had to be willing to go not that I have to go, but he did tell me to get permission for his people to hunt here."

Adahy thought about it. "I think he said, 'Be willing to go,' to me too. I want to walk to the west. I wonder what a sea looks like."

After both his grandsons had asked for Chetan's daughters, Waya asked them, "What was the price?"

Dustu told his grandfather the information.

"Are you willing to pay the price?" Waya did not want to force his grandsons to make any choice but their own.

Adahy said, "We would, but it is not fair. Oukonunaka will never agree."

"A task is harder if you do not get all the information you need, and certainly you will fail if you do not even try." Waya gave his grandsons his wisdom. He did nothing more because he wanted them to be the victorious ones.

Adahy suggested to his brother. "Let us ask Ppahiska how many are his people, how often they would want to hunt, and what they will try to find."

They respectfully asked Ppahiska for permission to speak with him. He agreed to hear them. Adahy spoke. "We are to ask Oukonunaka to give your people permission to hunt on our land."

Before Ppahiska could say a word, Dustu asked, "How many are all the Quapaw people, how often would your people hunt, and what would they look for?"

"Why do you want to do this?" Ppahiska asked.

"It is part of the bride price for Hanataywee and Ehawee," Adahy explained.

"Chetan would not change his mind?" Ppahiska asked.

"I told him we could not force Oukonunaka to agree. I asked if there was something else. He said 'No.'"

"We are almost four hundred and forty people. We would hunt all year. We would look for whatever wild plants or animals we can eat. Everybody agrees to something they think will benefit them or their people. You or somebody else knows what Oukonunaka wants."

After the young men left, Ppahiska thought about Chetan. *He could be bitter. We would not let him have a wife. He got one himself. We told him he was not a worthy man, but he has been as worthy of this tribe as the others. He taught his son to think of his people first and still Chetan thinks of his people above his own family. I judged him wrongly.* He went to talk with Chetan. "Why do you make it hard for these men to marry your daughters? Your daughters are old. You should just give them."

"Never! My children are the most valuable thing I have. Nobody can have them who is not worthy. They must pass a very hard test."

"So you do not do this to help your people."

"Of course, I do this for my people. I could have asked them to do something else very hard."

"It is good." Ppahiska went to talk with Oukonunaka.

Oukonunaka, Ppahiska, and Wakanda called all the people together. Ppahiska spoke with them. "If you are one who wants to come to our village to ask for one of our women, you cannot come before this fall. If you still want each other at that time, you have permission to ask the woman to be your wife. If either of you decides you do not want the other, you men will go home to your Cherokee tribe. If you marry, you will live with the family of your new wife."

Dustu heard the words of the Quapaw chief. *That will give us time to find out what Oukonunaka will trade to let the Quapaw hunt on this land.*

Waya considered. *I know what Chetan will say if I ask. I know the task and Luyu can decide for herself,* but then he thought, *it would be more honoring to my wild dove and her family if I ask.* He strode over to the man who was the age his son-in-law would have been. "I ask for Luyu. If you consent to give her, what is her bride price?"

Waya saw the surprise on Chetan's face. Chetan thought Luyu would decide for herself, but he felt honored that the man had asked him and also glad that he had. Chetan wanted to make sure the task assigned to Dustu and Adahy was in their hands only. "You must be willing to walk to the western sea and to live there forever, you must not help your grandsons with their task for my daughters, and Luyu must choose to have you as her husband."

The hard task surprised Waya. He wanted Dustu and Adahy to marry the women they wanted, and he wanted to keep his grandsons in his daily life. Luyu had told him it was very hard to give up people you love. He knew it was true. He didn't want to give up his grandsons, but he wanted Luyu too. Now he couldn't do anything to help make either happen.

The buffalo camp was taken down. The Quapaw men started home with all their women, their animals of burden, and their wagons loaded full with most of six buffalo. The women believed that their Cherokee men would come to their village in the fall. None of the women knew the bride prices that had been given to the Cherokee men.

Tatonga hadn't been at the buffalo camp, so Petang, the young man hoping for his daughter, went to his home thinking he would take horses as the bride price for Zitkala. On the way home, Zitkala asked Ppahiska to let her be the one to tell her father.

Ppahiska informed her he would tell her father what had happened as soon as they got to the village. Ppahiska thought about how his oldest son had kept everybody at the buffalo camp away from Sally. Now, as they went home, Chaska walked beside her.

One day Chaska would be the leader of their village. He had to marry a Quapaw woman. Ppahiska didn't want to upset his son, Sally, or her family. Chetan's family had improved life in the village. He didn't want to repay them with meanness. As they left the land of their bison poaching and their bison sharing, everybody was somber. All lost in their own thoughts; they traveled like a funeral procession for the dead buffalo.

The soldiers and Roscoe arrived at the fort the same day the Indians disbanded the buffalo camp. All the goat milk, along with some of the raw buffalo, most of the vegetables, and all the food they had gotten in the village was gone. They still had plenty of raw buffalo, all the smoked buffalo, smoked goose, and smoked mussels. All the cheese and honey filled the haversacks of Sergeant Anders and his men. They put the bags of commandeered supplies in their quarters then presented the dynamite, blasting caps, fuses, and the wagon piled high with buffalo meat and an example of vegetables available for trade.

Colonel Howland was very pleased with the outcome. He instructed his attendant, "Tell the quartermaster to give double rations of spirits, coffee, and sugar plus double pay to these men for a week."

Roscoe checked the fort for Eli and Stephanie. They were not there. However, since the next day was the first day of August, he waited. Just before the gates closed the evening of the first, he rode out of the fort.

Since this would be the third time Roscoe would make the trip between Fort Gibson and the northern corner of Indian Territory, he knew where to get plants and small game. He planned to get his food on the way. Therefore, he had no other provisions in his new packsaddle except ground coffee, sugar, fresh bread, éclairs, danishes, and hard compressed dried vegetable and potato cubes half the size of a man's hand that could feed four once swelled up by boiling. Ezra Knuckles had made the purchase for Roscoe in exchange for a dozen danishes.

Roscoe spent the night outside Fort Gibson in case Eli, Stephanie, and Tom came during the night. Before the sun was up on the second day of August, Roscoe rode King to the Neosho River Ferry beside the fort. *Either there is no such being or God hates us. He's keeping this family apart, and He's making the girls miserable and me too.*

THIRTY ONE

Chetan walked into his lodge. Tahatankohana congratulated him, "Very well done, father! We have six hundred more dollars and more supplies."

"Since the dynamite belonged to all of you, Roscoe wants to put the money aside to use when we go west. That would help everybody."

"Does that mean you and mother will go with us?"

"Yes, but I want your sisters to go with us too."

Bethany whispered so none of her daughters could hear what she said, "We made the bride price to move away with us."

With surprise, just as his sisters came into the lodge, Tahatankohana replied, "The bride price?"

"Brother, did you think nobody would ever want us?" Hanataywee asked.

As the family carried in hides, meat, fat, brains, sausage, bones, skulls, and other parts, Tahatankohana tried to smooth away the insult he hadn't meant to imply. "I know any man who becomes your husband is very lucky because both of you are very smart, sweet, and beautiful."

From the back of the lodge, Ann called out to her

family. "I wish I could help. I feel horrible that you're doing all the work while I lie here doing nothing."

Tahatankohana stretched out beside his wife and briefly kissed her lips. "You're doing the most important job. You're making our baby."

Ann told him something he already knew, "I know, but I don't like to be helpless."

Bethany remembered something she had done when she had been lying on her back unsuccessfully trying to keep a baby inside. "You can cut the long hairs from this buffalo hide."

"Please, bring me one. I'll be very happy to help." Ann knew Bethany understood exactly how she felt. Bethany had spent long hours of time talking with Ann while Ann beaded the white buckskin shirt. Ann wished Bethany hadn't lost her babies, but she was glad her mother-in-law didn't think she was trying to get out of helping. Ann very much liked having a mother again and didn't want to disappoint her.

Tahatankohana gently rubbed Ann's belly. "I don't know why I thought we should wait to make a baby. I'm very happy he's growing in there."

Bethany handed Ann a basket, a buffalo hide, and a large bone knife. "I can't wait to hug him."

Ann accepted the items. "You'll be the first to hold him when you help him come into the world this winter."

Bethany gave instructions to her first grandchild, "Little man, when the time is right, come see your grandmother," then she gave instructions to her oldest son, "Stop swooning over your wife and child. You don't have any excuse to not help."

Noah told his wife, "I'll be back later."

"Please do, my husband, quickly and with a pair of scissors."

Sally already held a pair in her hand. "This will make the job much easier and the hair more uniform."

Noah watched Ann cut the long hair the same length as the shorter hair, then, so she didn't lose any of it, she carefully set the hair into the basket. Chetan called out to his son, "Tahatankohana, you're back over there, swooning over your wife again."

"Yes, father, I believe you're right. She is irresistible. Wife, stop tempting me to swoon over you."

"I have the same problem you have. You're also irresistible. I can't keep myself from tempting you to stay by my side."

Bethany saw Chetan roll his handsome brown eyes as Tahatankohana went past to get more buffalo parts. She whispered, "I know two other people who can't resist each other."

"I do too, so don't tire yourself too much," he whispered back.

"You can be completely sure that I won't."

Their son came back into the lodge with more buffalo meat. "Don't let me stop your conversation."

"I'll talk to your mother about it later."

After they had everything inside and had checked on the animals in the pasture, Ann said, "Father, please tell me everything that happened."

Chetan was glad Ann wanted him to be her father and not just the father of her husband. He sat close to her to tell the story. Everybody gathered. Ehawee noticed how easy it was for Ann to cut the buffalo hair.

"I like those. Can I try them for a minute?" Ehawee asked.

"Don't we have extra sewing kits?" Ann asked Sally.

"We have four more." Sally asked the other women of her family, "Do any of you want one?"

"Are you sure you don't mind giving them away?" Luyu asked.

Sally went to their well-organized supplies. She knew exactly where they were because she had used hers to make the white buckskin pants. She got the three extra kits they had and her own.

Even though they knew they could buy another later, Ann moved her lips without speaking to say, "Thank you," to Sally. Ann appreciated her giving up her own sewing kit.

Ehawee looked inside the heavy cowhide wrapper. It held a wood-handled awl, scissors, a thimble, a two-hundred-yard spool of stout cream-colored cotton thread, and folded papers containing heavy metal straight pins, needles of various sizes, and a small package of pearly mussel shell buttons. "This is very good!"

Hanataywee pushed the buttons about in her hand. "These are very pretty. Are they made out of our shells?"

Chetan remembered, "The first time I saw your mother, she had on a dress with a lot of those buttons."

Ehawee told her father, "You can't remember what mother was wearing twenty-six years ago." She only knew that her father had found her mother starving.

"Yes, I can. I remember every button very well. At the time I didn't like the buttons, but I agree they are very beautiful."

"Thank you for the gift." Ehawee kissed both of her new sisters on the cheek.

The other women did the same. While the five women shaped the hair on their buffalo hides, Chetan told his family the story of their trip to Fort Gibson up to the time Bethany, Sally, Mina, Chaska, and Capa had brought the animals to them.

"I don't think they can disrespect you anymore," Bethany told her husband.

"Unfortunately, people will do what they have a mind to do whether it's warranted or not," Ann replied.

Tahatankohana praised his father further, "I hope they show you the respect you deserve. You got a good deal for us, you helped Colonel Howland, you acquired a free military escort home, we all got a share of military rations, and all anybody did was what we would have done anyway."

"And you showed yourself to be a good interpreter and negotiator," Luyu added.

"Family, thank you for your respect and appreciation. It's your opinions that are important."

Ehawee changed the subject, "A man named Waya asked grandmother to be his wife. He even asked father's permission and the bride price."

"Congratulations," Ann told her.

"Who are you to be telling stories? Adahy did the same when he asked for you," Luyu replied.

Still trying to make up for his earlier comment, Tahatankohana remarked, "I'm happy all three of you found somebody, and I'm not surprised at all."

Hanataywee told them more about the men they hoped would join their family. "Dustu's is the twin brother of Adahy. They are the grandsons of Waya."

Ke jumped up and put his hands on his hips. "Wait one minute. Everybody can't leave me."

"Nobody is going to leave you," Luyu assured him.

Bethany brought up a different couple. "Aaaaand," she paused, "Mina and Nikiata are together."

"I'm happy for them and not just because she'll stop bothering us," Tahatankohana couldn't keep himself from emitting a sigh of relief.

THIRTY TWO

Over the next week, the village folks tanned buffalo hides. James, Capa, Enapay, Tatonga, and Mantu wove a net then secured it as a weir to catch fish in Five Mile Creek. All the women and children tended the plants in the fields. Algoma showed any woman who wanted to learn how to use the spinning wheel to spin buffalo fur into yarn. With the full awareness of everybody in the village, together Nikiata and Tahatankohana received training as Mystery Men.

When Roscoe returned, Wakanda allowed him to join them for the portion of time that he shared his knowledge of plants. Because they wanted to know about the Holy Spirit who had entered their hearts during the sweat lodge ceremony, they also spent a part of the time talking about verses they read from the Bible Tahatankohana had brought to the village.

In the family lodge, Luyu sat at the table and ground dried buffalo meat into a pulp. At the hearth, Bethany heated then broke bones and harvested the marrow. Beside her, Sally rendered the fat that Tahatankohana had gathered. Ann lay on her pallet and washed chokecherries and raspberries. She felt the flutters of the baby inside. "I felt him!" she called out. "Come feel him."

Luyu put her hand on Ann's slightly bulging belly.

"There it was again. Did you feel him?"

"No. He's still too small to feel from outside."

"Do you think he's going to be all right now? Maybe I could at least sit up. Even though it does give me plenty of time to sew beads, I'm so tired of lying around."

"I think you can, but you better wait until Tahatankohana gets home. You should speak with him about it first," advised Bethany.

Tears rolled down Ann's face. "I'm so glad to know he's all right, and that he let me know on my sister's birthday. I miss her and Eli very much."

"I hope I get to meet them soon," Bethany added the washed berries to the bone marrow.

Wishfully, Ann stated, "Maybe they'll come next month. I can barely stand being apart, and I'm very afraid we'll be found because we have to keep waiting so close to Arkansas. Now, we also have a child to worry about."

When everybody was home, Ann revealed her good news. "I felt Wambleeska swimming today."

Tahatankohana listened to her belly with his stethoscope. "I can hear a swooshing sound. It must be his heart." He kissed Ann's belly then laid his head against their baby just on the other side of a thin layer of flesh. He looked up at Ann's face and smiled. "I love you and Wambleeska very much, so be very cautious. Sit up only a little and see what happens."

Even though it wasn't necessary, feeling he was protecting them, Tahatankohana helped Ann lean against him then sat in the hot lodge with his arms around her. The heat of sitting close made it uncomfortable, but Ann was more against laying down than against being too hot.

Chetan saw how his son protected Ann. Somehow, it made him think about what might happen when the Cherokee people came. "As soon as we finish making it, we need to take the pemmican to the cave. The Cherokee people can't know we killed so many buffalo."

Bethany extended the thought. "You should tell everybody to do the same."

The next day, Chetan knocked on Wakanda's door. "Before the Cherokee people come, would you call the people together and tell them to hide the evidence that we killed so many buffalo?"

Wakanda didn't have to give it a second thought. "That is wise. Bring your family to the meeting lodge. I will send for the others."

Everybody listened to their Mystery Man. "We should hide some of the buffalo before the Cherokee men come."

Capa expected the worst. "We should take everything to the cave. They may be coming here to rob us not to ask for brides."

Wakanda replied, "I think they come only for the women."

"Still, it is good to put everything in the cave." Mantu added, "Better to be cautious."

Ppahiska agreed, "Move everything except what you need right now."

Their leader had spoken, and they all thought that would be the best thing to do anyway. They took their bags of pemmican, parfleches of dried meat, hides, looms, spinning wheels, and most of the other supplies from their lodges to the cave.

Sally, Kimimela, and Takoda walked to the cave but only handed things to other people who took them inside. Capa snapped at Kimimela and Takoda. "Bring things closer. You make me do all the walking." Kimimela shook her head. Capa glared. "Do what I tell you."

Takoda ran away. Sally wasn't about to let Capa bully the children. She told Capa, "I will bring things closer." She hugged Kimimela. "You pass to me. I take everything to the cave."

"Thank you." Kimimela put a dutch oven into Sally's hands.

So Capa would not have to walk anywhere, Sally stood just outside the cave. Even though she didn't look as her arms moved the pot across the threshold of the cave, her arms tingled. She felt as if bugs were crawling on her, and that she couldn't get enough air.

Capa took his time taking anything from her,

and he barely stretched out his hands. Kimimela watched Sally struggle to pass in one item after another. She knew how Sally felt. She thought Sally was the bravest person she would ever know. Kimimela decided to step closer to the cave to hand the items to Sally. With the last item in her hand, Kimimela walked to the cave and held the bag of buffalo fur just inside the cave entrance.

As they walked back to the village, Sally and Kimimela held hands. They knew they had helped each other take a step toward healing, and they had shared something in their innermost being.

All their lodges looked just as they had the day Tahatankohana had come home. The only addition was the six buffalo they had permission to take.

During the night, Ann woke her husband. "Noah, give me your hand." She lay his hand on the place where their son was announcing that his home was too small.

As he kicked for more room, Noah felt the tiny thump. "There he is!"

Ann gave her opinion about the meaning of Wambleeska's kicking. "He wants us to know he's doing fine."

"I'm glad he let us know. Now, we can stop worrying."

Ann wanted her husband and believed Wambleeska was safe. "Since he's safe, share your love with me." Noah happily complied.

THIRTY THREE

Six days before the end of August, Nikiata left the village on a mission. Wakanda had told him that Tahatankohana and his family planned to adopt Roscoe. A person usually received a secret name when adopted, and it was customary for the mystery man to be paid for the name. If he had a successful vision quest and found Roscoe's new name, Nikiata planned to ask for a copy of Roscoe's plant notes. He started his quest the same day that Tahatankohana, Chetan, Wakanda, and Ppahiska left for Fort Gibson.

Outside the fort, Tahatankohana handed his father their family's list of items to purchase "I don't want to associate myself with this village and cause them any problems. You take the money and go to the store. I'll look for Stephanie and Eli by myself."

"I'll meet you at the stables when we're ready to go." Chetan entered with Wakanda and Ppahiska.

When Tahatankohana finally went inside, he discreetly searched the fort. He didn't find his sister and brother-in-law in any of the places he was able to look. He decided to go to the stable and brush their horses while he waited. He went to the far end of the stable to get a brush. *Thank you, God!* He stroked the nose of Eli's horse. *I doubt they would be in the barracks or with Colonel Howland. The only other place I didn't look was in the store. There is no way I'm going in there. I'll wait here. They'll come to their horse eventually.*

Chetan entered the stable. "This young man agreed to help us carry our supplies."

"Eli!" Noah gave his brother-in-law a tight hug. "I'm so glad you're here!"

"Noah! I have so much to tell you!"

"I see you've met Chetan, my father. These men are Ppahiska, our village leader, and Wakanda, our Mystery Man. We can't stay inside the walls tonight. We're going to set up camp outside the gate and leave in the morning. Where is Stephanie?"

"That's one of the things we need to talk about."

Sudden fear and much concern filled Noah. "Is she all right?"

"Yes. Let's set up camp then I'll tell you everything."

Noah felt extremely upset. If Stephanie had not come with Eli, something was very wrong. He wanted to find out quickly. "Let's go."

They packed everything they had purchased, exited the fort, and then laid their bedrolls at one of the fire pits in the field of grass outside the fort. Noah passed out éclairs as he ordered his brother-in-law, "Tell me what's happening."

"The good news is that Pop got home, and he's going to come west with us. The other good news is that he spent several months with his father, which made them all very happy. Unfortunately, his father was ill and passed away. Grandfather worried more about what would happen to Grandma than he did about his own death. More good news is that they decided Grandma would live with us. My grandfather passed peacefully knowing his son loved him, that he had a grandson, and that his wife would be safe with them. He said he only wished he could have met me and that he could have apologized to Ma for the way he had treated her all those years before."

Ppahiska listened intently to the story that Noah translated for him and Wakanda. "If everything is all good, what is bad?"

Noah told Eli what Ppahiska had asked.

"Nothing is really bad. Grandma wants to go with us. She's healthy and can travel, but it's late already, and we shouldn't be out in the winter. I didn't want you to have to come here every month until spring, and I don't want you to leave thinking we aren't coming."

"So when will you come?" Noah asked.

"We won't know how early we can come until spring arrives."

Chetan repeated the message in Quapaw

"That is true," Wakanda affirmed.

"The other thing is that Stephanie needs Sally to come home."

"Why?"

"I know you're going to be upset. We were

trying to keep this from happening, but Stephanie's going to have a baby."

"That's wonderful. How is everything with her and the baby?"

"Everything is fine. It's just that she's afraid to have the baby without her sisters. She really wants both her sisters, but she knows you and Ann can't come home. She wants to come live with you right now, but I think she should stay home until after the baby is born. We thought you would be upset."

"I guess I should tell you that Ann is pregnant too, but we don't know for sure if everything is all right or if something is wrong."

"What's wrong?"

Noah told the story. The other men added their thoughts and opinions about what had happened.

"When is the baby due to arrive?"

"We think it will be around the end of December."

"Doc said Stephanie is due in February."

"I know Ann and Sally are going to ask, so tell me, did Mara or Minnie have their babies yet?"

"They hadn't when I left, but they may have by now."

Ppahiska thought about this. *If Sally goes away, Chaska cannot marry her, and I will not have to openly refuse.* "I think Sally should go to her sister. Ann has Bethany, Luyu, Hanataywee, Ehawee, and Chumani."

Noah replied, "It's not up to us. Do you want to come to our village, or do you want me to tell them?"

"I want to get home as soon as I can. Please ask Sally to come."

Because Sally was his family, and he wanted her to be safe, Chetan asked, "How will she go there? She needs somebody to go with her."

"I don't know. We'll see what happens." Noah didn't know how it would work or if Sally would even want to go. "Did you tell your father about me speaking with your mother's spirit when I froze in the river and was dead for a few minutes?"

"I told him and Grandma. Pop got up and left the house. We didn't see him for hours. I've never seen Pop act that way. When he came back, I asked him if he was all right. He said he was better than all right. He said it was a huge relief for him to know that Ma had accepted Jesus before she died and that she wasn't in Hell. I'm supposed to say 'thank you' to you until he can tell you himself."

"Tell him I'm very glad everything happened as it did."

Ppahiska wanted to know the continuation of the story Tahatankohana had told them. "What else has happened? How is the farm?"

"The plants grew very well. Zachariah should be harvesting soon. Earl is going to take the store. He will never be able to go back to farming with his leg the way it is. Smitty took those letters and the other things to Fort Smith. He found Clarabelle and gave everything to her. She said she got pregnant the last day she was there. She's going to go back to the house because she conceived their son in love. Remember, before he changed again, she wrote that she had loved him so much that day. She told Smitty she wants her son to have what his father left them."

Noah said, "I'm glad that worked out for her. Did she know which of them let her go?"

Eli passed on the information from Smitty. "She said it was the boy and the one she always thought of as her husband."

Wakanda said, "A person to be many people is a new mystery."

"I think it is a rare condition," Tahatankohana remarked.

Chetan added, "I never met that woman, but Tahatankohana told us the story. I'm happy she has a son, the house, and the things in the upper rooms."

"Who is Tahatankohana?" Eli struggled to say the name.

Ppahiska knew what Eli had asked. "Noah," he informed Eli.

"That's how you say Swift Hawk in your language?" Eli then practiced until he could say the name correctly.

"For now, please only tell Stephanie my name."

"All right. What's happened to you, Ann, Sally, and Roscoe?" Eli was curious for himself, and he knew he needed to relay the news to his wife just as Noah would.

Noah, Eli, Chetan, Ppahiska, and Wakanda spent the night talking then on September 2nd, Eli prayed as Chetan repeated the words in Quapaw. "God, please protect this baby. Don't let Ann and Noah lose him. Let what Chris and Emma told Noah be true. Let it be that Noah saved their first grandchild. Cause the baby to hold on tight and reattach well. I pray that the baby is perfect and will be born healthy. Get all of us home safely. Put it into Sally's heart to come back to Harmony. Be with Minnie, Mara, Stephanie, and Ann when they have their babies. Keep mothers and babies safe. Bless all the men here and all the people in both our villages. Guide us, and live in the hearts of those of us who will accept you. I pray in the name of Jesus. Amen."

The other four men all added, "Amen."

Noah hugged Eli, "Thank you for the prayer."

"Tell Ann we will keep praying for her and Wambleeska." Eli returned the hug.

"I'll tell her, and we'll be praying for you, Stephanie, and your baby."

"Goodbye. Be well," Ppahiska said in English.

Wakanda also spoke a few words in English. "Very nice to meet you." He then left with Ppahiska to round up the sheep they had bought.

Chetan shook Eli's hand. "I'm very glad to meet the brother of my son. I look forward to the time you and the rest of the family join us in our lodge."

"I'm glad I met you too. I also look forward to the time we'll be together as one family."

They waved goodbye then went their separate ways.

THIRTY FOUR

The sheep traveled slowly. Ppahiska, Wakanda, Chetan, and Tahatankohana arrived at the buffalo slaughter field three days after they had expected to get there. Wakanda looked through the spyglass. Instead of buffalo, he saw a large group of people coming across the plain

"Our friends come." They waited for the group to join them.

"Hawe," Ppahiska called out.

His whole village had come with Oukonunaka, who returned the greeting, "Hawe. These men want to ask your permission to meet your other women. Some thought there might be women in your village who were not at the buffalo camp. Our women want to meet all the people in your village, so they can decide if they will let their men marry anybody there."

Ppahiska wasn't letting his daughter marry a man who was not Quapaw any more than he was his sons. He didn't mention his reasons. "The others are too young. We will go to our village together."

As they traveled to the Quapaw village, Chetan did not ask Dustu, Adahy, or Waya if they had succeeded, nor did Oukonunaka mention if they had asked.

Capa looked through the spyglass that Chetan's family had allowed the sentries to use. He saw a large group approaching and ran into the village. "Ppahiska comes with Oukonunaka and his people."

"Did you see Dustu?" Hanataywee asked.

Capa told her, "You will find out soon."

Luyu felt just as excited and nervous as her granddaughters. She and everybody else in the village prepared to receive their guests.

When they had crossed the creek, the people in the village heard the bleating of sheep. Ppahiska and Wakanda deserted the sheep to determine on their own how they would share the field with the other animals. The people went into the village. Seven women looked for their man in the crowd. Their hearts soared when each one saw the man they hoped would come and saw that man's smiling face looking for them.

The group walked up the slight hill to the lodges at the base of the mountain. None of the women knew their bride price. It concerned Luyu, Hanataywee, and Ehawee that their men didn't have much more than themselves. After the greeting, the Cherokee people set up teepees in the grass between the village, Five Mile Creek, Spring River, the planted crops, and the animal field.

Tahatankohana went to speak with Roscoe, Ann, and Sally. "Eli was at Fort Gibson."

"Where are they?" Sally asked.

"It was only Eli. Tom is in Harmony with his mother. They are going with us. Tom's father died, but Tom was able to be with him for a while."

"I'm sorry about Tom's father, but I'm so glad they're coming!" Ann exclaimed.

"Stephanie wants to come here now, but Eli wants her to stay at Harmony because she's going to have a baby. He wants her to have the baby there. She wants Sally to go back to Harmony until spring when the baby is born. Then they'll all come here."

Sally informed them, "I can't go there. I want to be here when you get married again. What about when Wambleeska is born? I stood at the spirit door. How can I not be here? I want to help make the outfit of white buckskin and make Roscoe my relative too. Besides, how would I get there safely?"

"I told him it's up to you. If you do want to go, we'll figure out how to get you there."

Roscoe didn't want Sally in danger. "I'll take you if you decide to go, but I would rather stay here."

Ann asked about their friends, "What about Mara and Minnie? Did they have their babies?"

"They hadn't before Eli left." As the women completed their part of the feast to welcome their Cherokee neighbors, Noah and Chetan told the family everything else they had learned from Eli.

Oukonunaka spoke to Ppahiska and Wakanda. "You need to know our people belong to the women. The women decide if their children can marry. They want to speak to your women. As I told you at the buffalo camp; if they marry, they will live here and belong to your people. The women asked me to tell you this."

Ppahiska said, "We will talk together, then I will tell you what we decide."

Ppahiska and Wakanda walked to the field of animals. Ppahiska conveyed his concern to his Mystery Man. "Our women cannot be the leaders. We could say we agree then talk to the men later. They are young. We can train them how to decide things."

"If their women tell ours that they own the children and decide everything, it will make unhappiness here. If we say they cannot marry, it will make unhappiness. If we tell their women do not tell our women, they will not agree to let their men marry."

"We will not let them marry," Ppahiska kicked a hole in the dirt.

"If we say no, we might become enemies of the Cherokee. Our own women will be very unhappy." Wakanda squatted and smoothed the earth. "If their women are wise, they will understand if we explain this to them."

"Then we will tell them the problem and let them find the answer."

"Agreed. "

Ppahiska went to Oukonunaka, "We will talk to your women now."

The Cherokee matriarchs joined the two leading Quapaw men in Ppahiska's lodge. "You asked to speak with us."

"We want both our villages to have peace. The men here are accustomed to leading. The women follow, but we decide many things together. Oukonunaka says the women decide in your village. There will be unhappiness between the men and women here because they will not know how the family fits together."

Ghigau, the oldest woman spoke. "We thought about this problem already. We will speak with your women to see if they are kind and wise. They should not beat their husbands unless there is no other way. We will see if your women will help our men learn to think like your men. They must not let the men we give you become mean. We will tell your women to be patient as our men learn. Some may always be difficult like Waya. I had to beat him often to get him to do what my daughter wanted."

Here I can protect all my children. Ppahiska stood up. "Wait here. We will return soon." This time, he led Wakanda to the cliffs. "We should let those men come here to be free. We should not give our young men permission to take any of their women, or we will lose them."

Wakanda said, "Agreed."

As they returned, Ppahiska contemplated. *I like Waya. I do not believe he is mean or stubborn. His wife and her mother must have been a misery.* Ppahiska again spoke to the Cherokee women for his village. "We agree. Speak to our women, as you suggest. We will tell them to expect you."

Waya watched the door of Ppahiska. When the women came out, Ghigau gave him the same smug, condescending look she always did. *I will be very happy to be away from her and get my grandsons away from that sour old woman too.*

Ppahiska went to speak with the families of Tatonga, James, and Chetan.

Wakanda passed the information to his family before he started the purification ritual. He left his lodge with a large pottery bowl beautifully decorated with the symbols of the east, south, west, north, earth, sky, water, and fire. Outside he danced as he waved an eagle feather fan over the sage smoldering in the bowl. The smoke removed everything negative from the land of the morning sun. Smoke billowed past the lodges, rolled over the earth and floated into the sky. In every direction, he sent the aroma of sage to purify the air, water, land, and fire and to carry all negativity away from the people deciding the futures of others.

That evening, the mothers of the men wanting to marry went to the homes of the Quapaw women their men wanted. Adahy and Dustu's parents were both dead as well as their grandmother. Their great-grandmother, Ghigau, was still living. She took on the duty. *I will decide if these women can marry my grandsons. I will get rid of Waya no matter what the woman is like.*

Luyu welcomed Ghigau. "Hawe, grandmother. Welcome to my home."

Ghigau thought *this is good. This home belongs to the woman.*

Luyu understood what Ppahiska explained. She had told her family to behave just as they always did. Everybody should know as well as possible exactly what the family was like.

When Ghigau started to speak, Luyu stopped her. She simply told the woman what she believed. "There are good reasons for the women to own their children. Everybody knows who the mother is, but you might not be right about the father. I would never have let Chetan's father take him away, but the man never wanted us, so it didn't matter. A woman always wants her child. She cares more about the family and less about war.

"On the other hand, a man has more strength. He does what he needs to do to protect and provide for his family. The man can think about other things too. Most of the time, the best way is to decide things together. Many times a man will respect another man but not a woman."

Ghigau asked Luyu no questions. Even if she had not planned to be rid of her son-in-law no matter what, she would have approved of Luyu. The woman was intelligent, she had spoken her mind, and she had not patronized her.

Ghigau spoke with Hanataywee then Ehawee. She decided they had gotten old and would let a man dominate them for love. She thought they would never be mean to her grandsons, but it would be hard for Dustu and Adahy because they would have to learn how to run a family.

She spoke with Chetan and Tahatankohana. They were strong men but very respectful, and they loved their woman even though she had no idea why either would want a weak white woman.

She did not bother to speak with Bethany, Ann, or Sally. This did not concern white people. Their opinions and thoughts would not be those of an Indian. The white man she did not even consider beyond the fact that it was not good to have so many white people as part of the family.

She spoke with Ke then Chumani who had only recently started talking. Ghigau believed very young children, would not know to pretend or lie. She left satisfied that she understood the family. She did not tell them anything about the roles of men or women in the village where Waya, Dustu, and Adahy had lived.

Ghigau stepped out of Luyu's lodge into the billows of smoke Wakanda fanned across the village. She saw the bowl formed together with a plate and saw that Wakanda carried the hot bowl with ease because the plate kept the heat from his hand.

In the homes of James and Algoma, Wakanda and Onida, and that of Tatonga and Metea, similar conversations took place. The Cherokee women returned to their teepees and the men who would remain with them until they married.

THIRTY FIVE

Clouds of cedar smoke flowed through the village, rolled into the fields of vegetables, and over the animals in the pasture. It crossed the creek and river and rose into the mountain. The delicious scent purified and pleased Cherokee and Quapaw alike.

The Cherokee women spoke with the men about to leave their families. The Quapaw women talked with their families about receiving and loving the men soon to join their village.

Ghigau spoke first to Waya. "You have permission to ask for Luyu. If Chetan finds you have met his price for his mother, you will have it much easier. If he does not, she is the leading woman of the family, she can decide for herself. If you marry her, you must live in her home."

Waya told the woman who had tormented him for decades but would no longer, "Thank you for giving me permission."

"Adahy and Dustu, you must be very kind to Ehawee and Hanataywee. They are weak women and only want you to love them. I believe they will never beat you, but you will have to learn how to think because they cannot. You also will have to live here. It will be very different, and it may be hard. If you decide you want to come home, you can."

Ghigau had not made an accurate assessment of Hanataywee, Ehawee, or her great-grandsons. It was true that the girls would never think of beating anybody, and they did want the love of a husband. However, they were far from weak, and they knew very well how to think. As well, Dustu and Adahy already knew how to think.

"Thank you, grandmother. We will do as you tell us. We will learn how to decide things."

"The three of you go and talk to Chetan. Waya, you go first."

Waya left immediately. He entered the home of Chetan. Chetan sent the seven women in his family to Mantu's home. Sally took the white pants, the beads, thread, and needles. Just in case she did decide to go to Harmony, she wanted to work as much as possible on the pants before she left.

Waya shut the door behind the women. "I did what you asked. It was very hard. You could ask Dustu and Adahy if I helped them before you decide if I met your request. I will happily walk to the west and live there with Luyu and the rest of this family."

"Thank you for telling me. Go with Roscoe and help him." The two men strolled to the fish weir with baskets and narrow ropes.

"Ke, get Dustu." Chetan's youngest son was very happy that he had been asked to help. He felt that he was one of the men working together to decide on this very important family matter. That was why they were as strong as eagles. Ke ran to Dustu's teepee. "Dustu come with me." Ke walked with Dustu to their lodge. "Hanataywee told me you killed two prairie chickens in less than one second."

"I did."

"Will you help me learn?"

"I would be very happy to help you."

"Then you have my permission to marry my sister."

"Thank you, Ke." Dustu was glad he had passed at least one inspection.

Ke led Dustu into the house. "Here he is, Father."

"I am here to ask for Hanataywee."

"Did you do what I asked you to do?"

"It took us a long time because we asked many people before we found out what Oukonunaka wants. He agreed to let all your people hunt on Cherokee land, but that does not give you real permission. Even though I was successful in doing what you asked, I know that is not what you meant. I will go as far west as you want."

"You said 'we.' Who doesn't that include?"

"My brother Adahy."

Chetan instructed the young man. "Dustu, go with Tahatankohana and help him." He turned to his other son. "Ke, get Adahy."

Tahatankohana and Dustu went off to help the other two men.

Ke looked at Adahy. "You are the same man I just took to my father."

"I am a different person. We are twins."

"How will my sisters know which of you is her husband?"

Adahy bent down. "Look right here. I cut my eyebrow when I was little."

Ke got right up to Adahy's face and examined the tiny scar. "I see."

"I have my hair on this side, and Dustu has his on the other side." Adahy turned around, so Ke could see the position of the cluster of hair in the skullcap at the back of his head.

"Thank you for showing me how to know which one is you. I like you. Come with me. It will be fine with me if you marry my sister."

"I like you too. I hope I get to marry Ehawee." Adahy entered the house with Ke.

Ke informed his father of all the important information he had gathered. "Here is the other one. He really is a different person. You can tell by the scar in his eyebrow, and he has his hair on the right side."

"Thank you, Ke," his father told him.

"Please let me marry Ehawee. We got permission from Oukonunaka for your people to hunt on Cherokee land."

"Who is we?" Chetan asked.

"Dustu and me. We asked grandfather to help, but he refused. We were very mad about that, so we went to our great-grandmother and asked her to make him help. She even hit him with her stick, but he would not help. Maybe you should not let him marry your mother. Grandmother was so mad, just to show grandfather what a horrible person he is, she sent a messenger to every village to get permission to make a treaty with your people to hunt on our land."

I might not give Adahy permission to marry Ehawee. If he disrespects his grandfather, he will be disrespectful to me as well. "Do you believe your grandfather is a horrible person?"

"No. I love my grandfather. I do not understand why he would not help. He always does everything he can for us. Even when Ghigau is mean, even if she hits him, he protects us, and he has never let her hit either of us."

"You should be proud of him. He is a very strong and wise person. Which people should talk together to complete this treaty?"

"Mikoishe should speak with Ghigau."

"Ke take Adahy to the others."

Ke took Adahy to the fish weir. Chetan went to speak with Ppahiska.

Chetan stood outside the door. "Ppahiska, I have a very important message."

"Come in."

Chetan, the lowest, entered the home of Ppahiska, the highest. "The Cherokee make treaties through the women?"

"I know."

"You know that I know you are our leader?"

"Yes."

"Mikoishe should speak with Ghigau and make a treaty for our people to hunt on Cherokee land. This is a very important opportunity. It would be good to respect the way they do things."

"Mikoishe is very smart. She will make a good treaty. I will send her."

Chetan left Ppahiska and went to the creek. When he arrived, Chetan informed the men, "Mikoishe goes to speak with Ghigau. If the treaty is made or not, you all have my permission and blessings to marry into my family as long as the women still want you."

Three smiling faces replied, "Thank you."

The six men of the family worked with Ke and repaired the net holes made by a large branch that had washed down the creek during the last heavy rain. The air was unusually cold against their wet skin as they carried home the fish caught in the weir.

James and Wakanda also gave their permission to the young men wanting to marry their daughters. Weayaya's suitor brought the eight horses Wakanda had set as the price for his daughter. James received a wagon for one daughter and six Indian ponies for the other.

Tatonga had not been at the buffalo camp. He'd had plenty of time to think about his daughter's marriage. He didn't want Zitkala to die giving birth. She was very small like his sister had been. Tatonga thought Zitkala needed more time before she became a wife.

Petang went to Tatonga's lodge. "I come to ask for Zitkala."

"You can marry Zitkala if you give Metea a loom." *It will take him years to find one.*

"I have never heard of this animal. I will get one immediately. What does a loom look like?"

"I will show you." Tatonga took Petang to the lodge of James. "James, I ask to enter your lodge with Petang. I want to show him your loom."

James opened the door. "Welcome to my lodge."

Petang examined the device. "What does it do?"

Algoma explained, "It makes cloth. First, you string the threads through all these holes. That is how wide the cloth will be. You roll them around this stick however long you want to make the cloth. When you press this pedal the threads separate, you run the weaving thread between them with this." She slid the shuttlecock across. "Pull this down tight then press the other pedal. The threads reverse, and then you run the thread back. You keep doing this until you finish the cloth."

"This is a very good thing. I will bring two. One for Metea as bride price for Zitkala and another for Zitkala because I love her. Will you take my word that I will get them?"

"I believe that you will bring two, but you cannot have Zitkala until you do."

"I need to talk with my family. I will speak to you again." Appearing to be sure that he could complete the task, Petang left.

After several minutes, Dowanhowee left the lodge of her father with several sheets of paper. She found Petang and handed him the papers. "You will not find any already made. You must make them. Go there," she pointed to the lodge of Luyu, "and ask Tahatankohana for tools. Tell him Dowanhowee told you to ask."

The young man spoke from outside the lodge. "Petang of the Cherokee asks to speak with Tahatankohana of the Quapaw."

Tahatankohana opened the door. "Welcome to our home."

Petang stepped into the lodge and held out the papers. "Dowanhowee told me to ask you for tools to build this."

Tahatankohana looked them over. "You asked for Zitkala, and this is the price?"

"Yes. One for Metea to have Zitkala as my wife, but I want to make another for Zitkala."

"Where will you get the wood?"

"Do you know where I can get some close to this place?"

"Would you allow me the honor of helping you build this? I also want to make one."

"I will."

"Can you climb a cliff?"

"I have much strength, and I always know where my feet are going."

Tahatankohana went to his wife, who along with every other member of his family, had heard the conversation. Before he said a word, Ann told him, "Enjoy the task, my husband."

He kissed her lips, then returned to their guest. "Come with me." Tahatankohana ushered Petang to his first 'living in the Quapaw village' lesson.

THIRTY SIX

Petang would soon be the only other person who would know the way through the crack to the plateau above the village. Tahatankohana tied the rope to his waist then attached it to Petang. "Hold exactly where I do and put your feet exactly where I put mine. I will show you each step."

"Ready." Petang felt excited. At the buffalo camp, he had heard people talking about this man. Now, they would do something exciting together.

Tahatankohana put his foot into a shallow depression inside a slight crack in the cliff face. He turned and slipped his body sideways into the open space between the two sides of the crack. As he pushed up, he grabbed a protuberance just within reach. "Did you see that?"

"Yes."

"I will go back down. Watch how I do it, so you can try this step, both up then down. " He stepped back in the reverse movement then exited the slit in the cliff.

Petang slipped into the crack. He got one foot in the hollow and his back against the other side of the crack. He rose and got his hand on what was not much more than a bump on the rock.

206

"Well done. Come down, then we will try three steps." Tahatankohana pushed up into the crack then pulled forward with his hand and moved his other foot up against the rock at his back. He wiggled his foot around until he felt it slip onto the top of a crag. Once situated, he pushed forward and up with his foot and then grabbed a small projection of stone. He slipped his fingers into another crack at the same time as he brought his first foot up against the front rock. Once again, he wiggled his foot around until he felt it go into the depression. He stood, wedged in the crack, "Tell me what I just did." Petang recounted the procedure correctly. Tahatankohana descended. "Tell me how I came down."

Petang again explained what he had seen.

"Now, you try it."

Petang performed the first three steps up and down three times with no problems. He did not complain about learning the way Tahatankohana taught him. They did the same with the next three steps. Tahatankohana went up to the sixth step, then back down. Petang did the same.

"How do you feel about your ability to do this?" Tahatankohana inquired.

"If we rest a little, and you let me see each step, I will be able to do it."

"Today, we will go halfway with you following. There is a place to rest and change positions. I will go down first. Then, if you think you can, we will climb all the way tomorrow. Are you ready?"

"I am."

THIRTY SEVEN

In Mikoishe's lodge, Mikoishe haggled with Ghigau. Ghigau had wanted her son-in-law to look bad when she had first started the process of gathering permission for the Quapaw to hunt on their land. Now, she wanted to get something for her people in exchange for the right to hunt. The women talked about different things they could trade. Ghigau didn't see anything these people had that she wanted.

After an hour, Mikakh brought cider, mussels, nuts, and the last of their apricots. She carried them in pottery made by her family.

Ghigau asked, "Where did you get this pitcher and these bowls?"

"We made them," Mikakh informed their guest.

"I saw Wakanda with a smudge bowl earlier."

"Onida made that for him."

Ghigau examined the bowl as she popped an apricot into her mouth. *Their pottery is very nice.*

THIRTY EIGHT

While the two women took a break from trying to get something from the other, Tahatankohana and Petang worked together. They easily climbed the first six steps. Petang followed closely. He watched every move Tahatankohana made as they climbed to the widest section of the crack. Tahatankohana's legs stretched wide between the front and the back wall. "This is the hardest part. You see how far apart my legs are. Get as far up as you can. You have to push all the way up into the narrow section, or you will not reach across to support yourself. You watch, then decide if you want to try."

"Show me."

Tahatankohana pushed backward with his front leg, quickly brought it up and then pushed forward with his back leg. He grabbed for the notch he had chipped into a secure handhold when he was much younger. He pulled himself up and once again wedged himself into the space between the rock walls. "If you want to try, I will go up to the ledge. If you do not make it far enough up, I will have you by the rope."

"Did somebody hold you with a rope when you learned this route?"

"As far as I know, nobody else knows how to go this way. Anybody who goes up there goes the way that takes days. I found this way myself when I was your age, but I will not let you try until I sit on the ledge."

"Then go to the ledge. Let me know when to try." Petang would not be less of a man than Tahatankohana, but he would do exactly what the man told him because he wanted him to continue to help him.

"I am here. I will pull in the slack, so holler, 'Go,' the second you start."

Petang took a deep breath. Adrenalin coursed through his veins. If he did not make it and Tahatankohana could not stop his fall, death waited for him to fall into its arms at the ground far below.

Crouching, Petang called out, "Go!" He didn't want to slam himself into the stone behind him and end his life at the very first move. He reminded himself, *not too hard* then pushed backward with his front leg. *Give it everything.* He used his back leg to spring up. His hand reached for the notch that looked miles away. His momentum slowed. His mind screamed; *I am not going to reach it.* He willed himself to stretch. His fingers latched on. Petang called out with joy. "I did it! Death, you wanted me, but you did not get me."

"I will come back and show you the next few steps to this ledge." Tahatankohana got just above Petang. "See that indentation just to the right of your left foot? Slide your foot over to that spot." When Petang had his foot in the proper place to provide support, Tahatankohana explained what to do next. "Move the foot behind you over to the right about an inch. You actually jumped too high. You have to wiggle your foot down a little. The slot is fairly deep."

"Found it," Petang told him.

"Next, you push up with your back foot and get your left hand right here. See where I am? Move into this position. After you watch the next move, move your right hand here and pull yourself up." Tahatankohana demonstrated what they would do next. Petang followed. Tahatankohana took another move, then paused. Petang did the same. Four maneuvers later, they sat on the ledge and looked down.

"We are very high," Petang informed Tahatankohana.

"From here we can crawl to the top."

"Then let us go on."

"You have to have the energy to get back down."

"We can go up and look for the trees we need. That will give us time to rest."

"No. We rest here. It is harder going down." They dangled their feet over the edge and looked at the village below. They saw a tiny woman leave Ppahiska's lodge and walk to her teepee.

"That must be Ghigau leaving the lodge of your leader. I hope they came to an agreement."

"I do too. How are you doing? How tired are you?"

"Not too tired."

High above the village, Petang watched then mimicked Tahatankohana's movements and followed him down. When Petang stood on the ground, he believed he had arrived none too soon. "Now, I am tired."

"You did a lot of practicing at the beginning. Still, you will be more tired after sawing down a tree."

"We should plan to spend the night up there."

"I will let you know tomorrow."

"Thank you for helping me and showing me the way up. I am excited to go all the way to the top."

"Good. See you tomorrow. Prepare to go for two days in case we do stay overnight." The men parted.

THIRTY NINE

After many hours of talking but coming to no agreement, Ghigau told Mikoishe, "We will stop talking about this for now."

"All right," Mikoishe was weary from hearing the woman repeatedly ask what the Quapaw had that they could give her.

After Ghigau left their lodge, Mikoishe confessed to her husband, "I am glad I do not have to do this all the time. I have no patience for this."

A few minutes later, Tahatankohana walked through the village on his way to his lodge. As he passed Enapay's lodge, he heard Mikoishe talking with Anpaytoo, "Our people need to hunt on the prairie. I do not know what to offer."

At home, Tahatankohana told his father what he had heard. Chetan found Waya. "This land is too small for us. There are enough animals on the prairie for all of us. What do your people need?"

"I will see what I can find out."

Waya got his grandsons alone. "What do you think the women might want in order to let the Quapaw hunt on the prairie?"

"I can listen to what people are saying," Dustu replied.

Adahy put his arm across his brother's shoulder. "I will help gather information."

Just like all the other soon to be grooms, Waya, Dustu, and Adahy remained with their family while Wakanda purified and prepared the land for the weddings.

Ghigau called out, "Dustu, my back hurts again!"

Dustu told his grandmother, "I will get Wakanda." He walked to the Quapaw Mystery Man's lodge. "Ghigau says her back hurts."

"I will come." Wakanda got the grandmother medicine bag that had been passed down from Mystery Man to Mystery Man.

"Grandmother. I have brought Wakanda."

"Tell me what you feel." Wakanda set down the large bag. "Exactly where do you hurt?"

"I hurt here."

"May I touch you?"

"Of course, how else will you figure out what is wrong?" snapped the old woman.

Wakanda felt Ghigau's back. He didn't feel anything abnormal. "Dustu, get goat milk from Tahatankohana."

Dustu went for the milk. He called into Tahatankohana's lodge. "Wakanda says Ghigau needs milk."

"Why?" Tahatankohana asked.

"Ghigau says she has pain right here," Dustu touched his back.

Ann encouraged her husband. "I know you are tired, but you should be the one to take the milk." She poured goat milk from a large container into a small pottery pitcher decorated with the symbol of the universe. She handed it to her husband, who had walked in the door not many minutes before.

Tahatankohana took the pitcher, along with a matching cup, and left with his soon to be brother-in-law and the milk he was sure Wakanda did not need. "Does your grandmother have these pains often?"

"Yes, and they are getting worse." They went to Ghigau's teepee with the milk.

"I brought the milk." Tahatankohana entered.

Wakanda touched Ghigau's back and said aloud, "You have pain on both sides?"

"Yes. I keep having pain. Sometimes one side or the other. Sometimes both sides. It comes and goes. When I hurt, I pass no water. Lately, I cannot get my breath."

Wakanda wanted Tahatankohana to hear the information, so he asked Ghigau questions as he poured milk from the pitcher into the cup. Ghigau took the cup. "What a nice pitcher and cup. It is like the bowl I saw you use when you were smudging. You carried that hot bowl with no problem."

"It works very well. My wife made it for me. I will be right back." Wakanda motioned to Tahatankohana. After they left, Wakanda asked, "What do you think?"

"Let me look in my books, but I think her kidneys are failing."

"Kidneys are not something I know about. Tell me if there is something we can do."

"I will." Tahatankohana went home to research the problem. He spent the night reading his books.

In the morning, Tahatankohana walked across the village with his brother Ke. He told Wakanda what he thought was wrong. Wakanda sent Ke to bring Waya, Dustu, and Adahy to his lodge. Tahatankohana found Petang. "I am sorry. I stayed up all night. We will go tomorrow."

Petang's mother said, "Thank you for helping my son. I will send him with enough food for both of you. How many days?"

Tahatankohana felt tired. He didn't want to climb both ways the same day. "Two."

Petang brought up something he had thought about the previous night. "Some people will never be able to climb to the plateau. Would you allow me to build something to raise and lower a basket?"

"Come to my lodge. I will give you paper and a pencil. Draw the design. Show it to me when you have it ready."

"It is because my brother has feet that are not straight. He can never climb the cliff, but he could go up in a basket."

"Is he young?"

"He has twenty-five summers."

"Then his feet are done growing. If he was still young, I could have helped him."

"Tell me how. Other people in my family have

feet like this. If my children are born this way, I want to make their feet right."

They walked into Tahatankohana's lodge. "It is too long to explain right now. I will tell you later. Draw your idea." He handed Petang, paper, a pencil, and an eraser. "Come back tomorrow."

Ke delivered Waya, Dustu, and Adahy to Wakanda because Wakanda wanted them to know first. "I wish it was not so. Ghigau is dying. She cannot pass the water from her body. Her lungs will slowly fill. In the end, she will drown from her own fluids."

"Is there nothing we can do?"

"You can love her and make her as comfortable as possible. Do you want me to tell her, or do you want to tell her?"

Waya spoke with his grandsons then told Wakanda their choice. "Please come with us." He went first to the home of his future wife and requested to go in. "May Dustu, Adahy, Wakanda, and I come in?"

"Of course." Luyu opened the door.

"Wakanda says Ghigau is dying and has only a few days to live. I would like to take her someplace more comfortable than the teepee."

"You may all come here, or if you would rather be in your own place, we can ask if you can use the empty lodge of Mina."

"It would be wonderful to come here if that is what Ghigau wants."

"If she does, just come back. Bring everything you have."

"Thank you." Waya had thought Luyu was a kind woman. This confirmed what he believed. The four men went to Ghigau's teepee.

Waya spoke first. "I brought Wakanda. He will speak with you." Waya, Dustu, and Adahy stood beside her.

Respectfully Wakanda spoke to the old woman. "Grandmother, I think parts inside are no longer working."

Ghigau reached out and took the hands of her family. "Can I live if they will not work?"

"Not long."

"How long?"

"A week at the most. I am sorry."

Ghigau was most afraid of the unknown. "Explain what will happen." As if it would protect her from what he would say, she squeezed the hands of Waya and Dustu. Adahy's hand lay over Dustu's to add his support.

Wakanda told her what Tahatankohana had explained to him.

Ghigau wanted a few things before she traveled the spirit path along the Milky Way. "I have walked Mother Earth much longer than most. My spirit is ready to join the ancestors, but first I want to see my family get married, and I want to complete the treaty with these people."

"I have already started to purify the land," Wakanda informed her.

"Complete the purification quickly."

Wakanda assured her, "I will," then went to his lodge. *If I wait until sundown, I can cover the land with the smoke of sweetgrass tonight to draw in positive energy from the spirit world.*

Ghigau thought about the old woman in the heavens who would judge her soul. *Will Maya Owichapaha find me worthy? If she does not send me to the right, I will not join Wakan Tanka. Perhaps I will not see the Great Mystery. I need to do something good.* She commanded her family, "Get Mikoishe, and gather all the types of pottery you can find in this village."

Ghigau's men started toward the exit to do her bidding. Ghigau called out, "Waya, wait!"

He stopped. "What can I do for you, mother?"

"I would love to eat antelope again before I die."

This time Waya wanted to do what Ghigau asked. "I will not come back until I have antelope for you. Also, I wonder if you would be more comfortable in a lodge."

"Would you take me to the lodge of your future wife?"

"If you would like, or you can stay in your own lodge."

"I would rather be in my own lodge with you, Dustu, and Adahy."

Waya went back to Luyu's home. "Please ask if we can stay in the empty lodge."

Bethany wanted to help, so she volunteered. "I will go to ask."

"Mina would say yes to Tahatankohana," Ehawee suggested.

Luyu explained to her granddaughter why she was wrong. "He has lost his power over her. Her heart has found its home in the arms of Nikiata."

Roscoe offered, "I can take him over, but I do not think it will help influence her."

"I should go with Waya." Ann told them, "Mina would probably feel she should grant my request."

Tahatankohana refused to let her do it. "I am not letting you close to Mina without me."

"Mina no longer has any desire to hurt me. I think it's safe."

"I won't take a chance with you and Wambleeska."

Waya alleviated the issue. "I will go alone. Where is she?" *Later, I will ask what is between these families.*

Luyu pointed to the lodge of Nikiata.

Wakanda saw Waya go into the lodge of Chetan. He knew it would be a time of great sorrow for Waya, Dustu, and Adahy. He asked the Great Spirit to help them at this difficult time as Ghigau lived her last days on Mother Earth. In the east, west, south, and north, Wakanda had already burned the second purification herb to Father Sky and to Mother Earth. He scattered the herbs on the ground in the lodge then lit another twist of sweet grass and fanned the smoke over the meeting lodge. "Great Spirit, remove everything negative, bless the land, the buildings, and the couples who will soon join. Prepare and direct the hearts and minds of the people negotiating the hunting treaty."

To speak with Mina, Waya made his way through the clouds of sweetgrass smoke. "I have come to speak with the owner of the empty lodge."

"Welcome to my lodge," Enapay opened the door.

Everybody in Chetan's lodge tried to see through the smoke. All they saw was Waya enter the lodge. A few minutes later, he hurried away. They hoped Mina had agreed. Before long, they saw Waya and Ghigau crossing the village. At her request, he allowed her to walk with dignity to the lodge. As soon as she was inside, he picked her up and carried her to a chair beside the table.

FORTY

Ghigau's family already had several pieces of pottery on the table as well as a stack of mussel shells and a gallon of mussels in brine. Dustu and Adahy waited outside until they saw their grandfather signal then asked Mikoishe to come to the lodge.

"Mikoishe, we will complete this agreement. I propose we have Waya create four talismans. He is the husband of my daughter and has become my son. I know he will make them for us. We will use them when a hunting party goes onto the prairie. They must carry one of the talismans to hunt. Any hunting party can only have twelve people. Only two hunting parties can be on the prairie at the same time. For every antelope or deer, you must give one piece of pottery of this size and ten mussel shells." Ghigau pointed to some large jars and bowls. "For every ten rabbits, prairie chickens, or other small game you will give either one piece of pottery of the same size or two smaller pieces of this size or ten mussel shells." She pointed to a group of medium-sized vessels. "If you gather berries or plants, you must give one piece of pottery like these small pieces for a basket of this size full of plants or berries." Dustu handed Mikoishe the basket so she would know the amount for gathering plants and berries. "If you take a buffalo you must give five of the very large water jars and ten of the middle-sized pieces and twenty mussel shells. One of the middle-sized jars should be full of mussels in brine."

"The hunters cannot carry so much. We have four villages. I will agree if four hunting parties can hunt on your land at the same time if they do not hunt in the same area. Seventeen people must be allowed in each hunting party. For each buffalo, we will give twenty shells, one large water jar, and one medium-sized jar with mussels in brine for one up to ten buffalo. Another medium size jar full of mussels if we take eleven to twenty and the same for each further group of ten. We give pottery or mussel shells for plants or small game only if gathered farther away than a person traveling the road would gather."

"If we can also come to Spring River to gather mussels."

"There are too many of your people. They will take all the mussels."

"Instead of pottery or shells, if you take animals, the first trade per village is to harvest mussels. That way, each village can only come once per year."

"We would give a talisman for permission to come and get mussels. How would we trade these things?"

Waya spoke up. "May I say something?"

"Go ahead," Ghigau replied.

"I have seen a way to divide the land. I can bring somebody to show you."

"Is this person a female?" Ghigau asked.

Mikoishe thought about suggesting her own daughter, Mikakh, but she guessed what Waya was thinking. *It would be best to have one of Chetan's women. It is their system. They know it best.* "This person can be Hanataywee."

Ghigau was surprised Mikoishe thought that girl would be useful. "The woman Dustu will marry?"

"Yes."

"Dustu, bring her here," Ghigau ordered.

He left his grandmother then stood at the door of his future wife. "Dustu stands at your door. I would like to speak with Hanataywee."

Chetan opened the door. "Welcome to our lodge."

"Mikoishe and Ghigau are coming to an agreement about hunting, and they need to work out a way to trade. Waya suggested they use the system your family uses to map the land. They want Hanataywee to show them."

Chetan wanted Hanataywee to present the best plan possible. He asked Dustu to share information. "Before she goes, tell us what they are considering."

Dustu explained the trade. Hanataywee stated her idea. "This is what I suggest. Divide the land into sections of one day's walk. We take the pottery, shells, mussels, or the talisman to gather mussels to the village in the section where we kill the animals or take the plants. We try to not go to the same section all the time unless something can only be found in one place."

Chetan praised his daughter. "That would be good. Go have the honor of helping our people."

"Thank you, father." Hanataywee left with Dustu, who was very proud that the woman who would be his wife was part of this very important negotiation.

"I bring Hanataywee," Dustu stated when they entered the lodge.

"Thank you for the honor of helping." Hanataywee laid out the sheets of papers she had brought. "Each paper is a walk of one day, both ways across the land." She lay out seven sheets of paper in a row. "From Osage land to Fort Gibson." She drew on the paper a half sun and one vertical line, on the second paper the half sun and two lines, on the third page half sun and three lines all the way to the half sun with seven lines, then she lay out the second row of seven sheets of papers to the west. "Two days walk to the west of Military Road." She marked them with the half sun, one horizontal, and one vertical line, on the second page the half sun two horizontal lines and one vertical line, then the half sun three horizontal lines and one vertical line down to the half sun seven horizontal lines and one vertical line. She started to lay out the next set of papers. "Three days to the west."

Ghigau intervened. "Stop. No more than two days west of the road."

Hanataywee moved the papers to the east of the river. "On the east of the road to the river, anybody can hunt or gather who travels the road, so we do not have to trade unless it is buffalo. On the east of the river, if we take anything, we trade just like on the west." She drew a full sun and one vertical line to a full sun with eight vertical lines going one day south beyond Fort Gibson. Beside that row, she laid out and labeled the sheets for the rest of the land east of the road. "Show the places of your villages."

As Ghigau marked the locations, she saw the value of the system. "When your people take animals or plants, you will give the trade goods to the people in that area." She pointed to a sheet containing more than one designation. "Two should not be in the same section, but the people in these villages will not want to move."

"They could divide between them," Mikoishe suggested.

Ghigau tapped the edge of the paper. "One is the village of war woman, Kangee. She will not share."

Hanataywee said, "Then divide the section in half. If we take something, our trade will go to the village in that half."

Ghigau knew the woman. "Kangee will not take a smaller section."

"Then we divide every section in half." Mikoishe thought, *that will solve the problem.*

Ghigau pointed out why it would not. "There would be sections with no village."

"What is in this section that makes them not want to move?" Hanataywee inquired.

"Bear Creek."

Mikoishe thought one creek was normally as good as any other. "What is in the creek?"

"Fish and water."

Hanataywee asked, "Where does it run?"

Ghigau drew Bear Creek on the map. "Not exactly here, but this is close."

Hanataywee studied the map. "Which one is Kangee's village?"

"This one." Ghigau pointed.

Mikoishe said, "If the other village moved up here, it would only be a short way, and they would still have the creek."

"They could, but I don't know if they will."

Mikoishe countered, "Tell them move or have half the land, or we will never hunt in this area."

"I will not be able to tell them anything," Ghigau reminded her.

Mikoishe respectfully replied, "I am sorry, Grandmother. I wish you could."

Ghigau didn't want her life to end, but she knew it would. She wanted to leave a legacy behind. "I do too. One of the other women will tell them."

Hanataywee pointed out another issue, "We have no extra pottery, but we need to hunt now. We will gather the harvest soon. Would your people trade for seeds?"

"I see your fields. What is ready?"

Mikoishe took over. "We have beans, peas, peppers, watermelons, squash, parsnips, turnips, sunflowers, cantaloupes, and onions. If you let us hunt on your land now, we will give your village the seeds of all the plants we eat while you are here, also a sunflower head and a large basket of beans and peas. Every antelope or deer or for ten rabbits, prairie chickens or other small game in the trading sections, we will also give you the ten mussel shells. Each basket of berries or plants we gather, we will give two shells. For every buffalo, we will give twenty mussel shells, ten corn seeds, ten tobacco seeds, ten flax seeds, and ten cottonseeds. We will bring you the seeds when they are ready."

"I also want ten fresh pumpkins, ten fresh yellow squash, and ten fresh butternut squash all with the seeds inside, ten parsnips and ten turnips with their seed-laden tops for the first trade per village this year." Ghigau thought, *this will be even better than the pottery. Next spring the people can plant the seeds then harvest the plants to eat, save some of the seeds of those plants, and have the plants forever.*

Mikoishe counter suggested. "We trade the produce and seeds no matter what year we first trade with a village."

Ghigau thought it was a good trade for both sides. "Agreed."

Mikoishe made another suggestion. "I mean no disrespect to Waya, but I think all eight talismans should not be made by us. It needs to be something that cannot be imitated."

Ghigau liked the idea. "You are right, but I do not know of anything that would serve our purpose."

"I have something. I will get them." Hanataywee went to her lodge. She got her white stones with shiny gray crystals shaped like cubes growing out of them. She put the stones on the table.

Ghigau examined the rocks. "How many of these do you have?"

"This is all I have ever found."

"There are only six."

Mikoishe suggested a solution. "We can break the two biggest ones."

Hanataywee did not want to ruin the stones. She picked them up to protect them in case the others did not agree. "We need tools. We do not want to shatter them. We can get my brother and the tools."

Ghigau ordered her grandson, "Adahy, get him."

Adahy left immediately. Soon he returned with Tahatankohana, a chisel, and a hammer.

Ghigau informed Tahatankohana of the task. "We have only six stones, but we need eight. We need to break two of them in half."

"I need to look at them," Tahatankohana informed the women.

"Go ahead," Mikoishe told him.

One at a time, he carefully inspected the stones.

"I think I can cleanly break these two." He knew the stones belonged to his sister. He looked at her. "Is this what you want me to do?"

"Yes, please."

Hanataywee followed Tahatankohana out of the lodge. He dug a hole in the ground then placed one of the stones inside. He packed the dirt tightly around it to hold it at the angle he wanted. He put the chisel in the crevasse he thought would allow for the proper break and then made one hard, sharp tap with the hammer. The stone popped into two pieces. He dug it up and handed the two parts to Hanataywee.

"Perfect." She handed him the other stone. He performed the same procedure, then handed her the pieces.

"Thank you, brother." She hugged him.

He hugged her back, "I'm glad to help," then returned home.

Hanataywee went back into the lodge where Ghigau waited with Mikoishe. She put the four pieces on the table with the other four stones.

Mikoishe pushed to complete the negotiations. "Are we in agreement on everything?"

"I have to ask the other women," Ghigau told her.

"I will talk to my people too." Mikoishe turned to Hanataywee. "Thank you for showing us your plan."

Ghigau did the same. "Thank you, Hanataywee. I am pleased. Dustu did well to pick you."

"It has been my honor." She left with Mikoishe but very discreetly blew a kiss to Dustu as she passed him.

Dustu was very proud of Hanataywee. Not only was she sweet and very beautiful, but she was also intelligent. He wished he could have followed her and kissed her lips of honey.

Ghigau spoke to Waya, Dustu, and Adahy after the women were gone. "I am also pleased with my family. I know I have been hard on you. I wanted all of you to be everything you can be, but I want you to know that I am proud of you, and I love you. You may not have thought so, but in my heart, I have. I also love my daughter, my granddaughter, and her husband. I will be happy to see them again, so do not be sad for me."

Waya kissed Ghigau on the forehead. "I love you too, even though you have been very mean."

"I am sorry for the way I treated you. Even after my daughter died, you always kept yourself under control. You could have broken me in half or thrown me into the woods, but you always took care of me. Thank you."

Earlier, Waya didn't think that he would be sad for Ghigau to be gone, but he was. "I will still take care of you. I will get that antelope for you now."

Ghigau requested that Dustu and Adahy continue to help her. "Ask the elders of our village to come here."

The twins went to each elder and asked her to go to the lodge.

Mikoishe went to her lodge and told Ppahiska everything that she, Ghigau, and Hanataywee had discussed. Ppahiska called together all the men, women, and children.

Before the sun had set, everybody had agreed. The Cherokee would get seeds, pottery, mussel shells, and mussels in brine. Once per year, they could gather mussels in Spring River. The Quapaw would make and give pottery, give up mussels, shells, produce, and seeds, and do the hunting. Animals and plants would sacrifice their lives so the people could live. The Quapaw would offer thanks and tobacco to their spirits.

All the people went to sleep happy. The following day they would smoke the peace pipe.

FORTY ONE

Early in the morning, Capa sounded the alarm. Adahy, being the fastest sprinter, was first to get to Capa. "What's happening?"

"A Cherokee war party approaches from the south."

"Let me use your spyglass," Adahy requested.

"No, I told the others you people were going to rob us. Now your war party is coming."

Adahy ran to the lodge of Ehawee. "Adahy is at your door. I need to talk to you now!" Inside they had already heard Capa's alarm. Chetan and Tahatankohana opened the door prepared to fight. "Let me use a spyglass," Adahy requested.

"I will get some," Tahatankohana gathered spyglasses. He, Chetan, Roscoe, and Adahy dashed to the lookout.

"That is what I thought. Kangee comes. Ghigau is not well enough. Let me take one of our other women to talk with her."

"Go," Chetan told him.

Adahy raced down the rise to the teepee of Wasa and his wife. "Hota, Kangee comes wearing her war bonnet. Please come with me to talk to her."

Wasa stated what all three of them already knew. "If Kangee comes in a war bonnet, she is planning to fight. She has never lost a battle."

Hota stood. "I will go." Her husband, Wasa, took an arrow from his quiver, broke it over his knee, and handed it to his wife. Hota and Adahy hurried to the field, jumped onto their horses, and galloped away. Wasa went to tell everybody in the village to prepare for battle.

Hota and Adahy intercepted the forward scout. Hota held out the broken arrow. The scout saw the woman signal that she came in peace. He let the two riders approach.

Hota spoke, "Why do you come dressed for war?"

Washta replied, "Kangee heard Ghigau is planning to give permission to the whole Quapaw Nation to hunt on Cherokee land."

"You come to attack these people?" Hota asked.

"No, we come to stop this agreement."

Hota did not understand why Kangee was upset. "Ghigau asked for permission from the villages, including the village of Kangee."

"She was not there when the messenger came. Others spoke out of place," Washta explained.

"Tell Kangee to take off her war bonnet, come in peace, and talk."

Washta was not going to tell Kangee she was wrong. "You tell her."

Hota feared too, but she could not allow Kangee

to come against people who had done nothing wrong. "Adahy, go get the people ready to fight. If I do not ride with Kangee and she still wears the war bonnet, I will be dead, and it will be war." Hota urged her horse into a run.

Adahy did the same in the opposite direction. On his horse, he raced across the creek and straight into the village. "Hide the women and children. Kangee comes. Get ready to defend yourselves."

The Quapaw women gathered their children and hurried down the trail through the woods along the base of the cliff. The Cherokee women and children fled with them.

Sally felt hands in hers. Kimimela and Takoda walked beside her. Metea and Zitkala came just behind.

"I am too afraid to go to the cave." Takoda needed to be with the two people who felt like him.

Kimimela told them, "I am afraid to go into the cave, and I am afraid not to."

"Me too." Sally's stomach felt like it was in her throat.

Takoda stated his other concern. "Father may be killed. No way for me to help."

Sally held tightly to their hands. She tried to assure them and herself. "It helps them if we are safe. We have to do this."

"Less danger is in the cave than in the village." Kimimela tried to convince herself she could go into the cave.

Takoda said, "I do not know if I can." They continued to hurry away from the village with the others. Metea and Zitkala felt very grateful that Sally was there. They knew she was helping the children. Metea thought they were probably helping Sally too. She hoped that together they would be able to go into the cave.

Mikoishe, however, had a different thought. *We cannot go to the cave. The Cherokee will see everything we are hiding.*

Her daughter, Mikakh, thought the same thing and quietly said, "We should go up the ravine."

A small stream had cut a narrow crevasse in the mountain as it made its way to Five Mile Creek. They turned and walked beside the stream until they came to a waterfall and could go no farther. The Quapaw and Cherokee hid together in the deep ravine behind the falling water.

Sally, Ann, Bethany, Luyu, and Algoma's family joined to pray. Metea's family already huddled beside Sally. Sally prayed, "Holy Father in heaven, do not let anybody be hurt. Show them the way to resolve the problem."

Mina approached the group next to Luyu. She stayed away from Ann, so none of them would think she was trying to hurt her. "May I join you? I am very worried. I just found Nikiata. I do not want him to be killed."

"Of course," Ann told her.

As the five women prayed, Sally's other friends

joined. Even though they did not understand the language well, the girls knew Sally's family was calling for the power and protection of the divine. They wanted to do the same. Ann told Luyu, "Pray in Quapaw. It is not good for the other women and children around us to wonder if we are planning something against them. Also, they will hear the one true God of Heaven raised up before them."

Luyu prayed as all the people, joined by fear and worry, hid in the mountain overflowed by the waterfall. Soon, each spoke their prayer in their own way, in their own language, and all at the same time. A jumble of noise rose to heaven, where God clearly heard every individual word.

"Who is Kangee?" Ppahiska demanded to know.

Oukonunaka explained. "She is a War Woman. She is very fierce and mighty in battle." He turned to Adahy. "Why does she want to attack us?"

"She didn't give her agreement to let the Quapaw people hunt on our land. She wants to prevent it. Hota said to look for Kangee to take off her war bonnet and for Hota to ride with her. If not, be ready to fight."

The Quapaw men planned to stop the battle long before anybody got close to their village. They didn't want any Cherokee in the village to be able to attack them when they saw their people slain as easily as the buffalo. They separated from the Cherokee and took their positions with rifles in hand.

Oukonunaka had seen the power of the Quapaw

rifles. Kangee would lose this battle before she even knew it had started. He did not want Kangee and her people killed. He did not want to fight against his Quapaw friends either. Oukonunaka didn't know if the Cherokee people in the village would fight against other Cherokee or turn against the Quapaw who had welcomed them into their village. With great concern, Oukonunaka prayed silently. *Great Spirit,do not let Kangee come here to fight.*

The men looked at each other. Without saying a word, they all knew what was on all their minds. Ppahiska, Oukonunaka, and Adahy made their way to the lookout post as quickly as they could.

FORTY TWO

Holding a broken arrow over her head, Hota rode toward likely death.

Kangee called out, "Halt and speak."

"Why do you come in your war bonnet? Ghigau asked for permission to negotiate."

"I did not give this permission. We cannot let a whole nation hunt on our land."

"They are only four hundred and thirty-four people. Besides, Ghigau and these Quapaw people did not know the agreement did not come from you. They have not meant to offend you. Take off your war bonnet. Come, hear, and speak in peace."

"That few. They must have lost many when they were driven out of their land to this place." Kangee removed her war bonnet. "I will come peacefully and hear. If they agree not to hunt on our land, I will also leave in peace."

"Thank you. You are strong, brave, and wise."

Kangee told the men in her war party, "We go in peace. Be prepared for that to change."

Through their spyglasses, Oukonunaka, Ppahiska, and Adahy saw Kangee take off her war bonnet. They all breathed a heavy sigh of relief. Oukonunaka told the young man from his village.

"Hota is very brave. Adahy, you did well to pick her for this."

Ppahiska added, "And very wise. She changed your war woman's mind." The men watched and prayed the bonnet did not return to Kangee's head. When she got to Five Mile Creek, two men stood side-by-side on the village side of the water.

"Do you come in peace?" Oukonunaka inquired, believing she would not lie to one of her own people.

"If the Quapaw people will not hunt on the prairie unless I agree, we have peace."

"Then welcome to our village." Ppahiska knew they would never again hunt on the prairie if this woman told them not to do so, and he definitely would not tell any of them they had already taken ten buffalo before those that Oukonunaka had allowed them to take.

Kangee felt slighted. "Why is Ghigau not here to greet me?"

Hota explained, "She is dying. She is drowning herself."

"How can she drown herself?"

"You will see. It is because she is so old."

Kangee went into the village with her warriors, Hota, Oukonunaka, and Ppahiska.

When Kangee entered her lodge, Ghigau ordered the others out. "I will speak with War Woman Kangee privately." She would be dead in a few days. She had no fear. "Kangee, how dare you dishonor me and our people by riding across the land in your war bonnet, planning to attack innocent people. And some of them your own!"

"Be respectful, old woman."

"Or what? You will kill me. I am already dead."

"Hota told me, but you should be sure of your information."

"How would I know you would not be pleased after what the people in your village told my messenger? Your people should have said they could not tell me an answer. Everybody else trusts me to make a wise decision except you. How do you know I did not tell these people absolutely no Quapaw can hunt on our land?"

"Because you are here, you have said yes. There is no other reason for you to come."

"Kangee, you should be sure of your information. Seven of our men are marrying women of this village. That is why I came."

"Who?"

"I will introduce you, but I will tell you now that I did negotiate a deal to allow all the Quapaw people to hunt on our land. We planned to smoke the peace pipe today. Come to my table. I will tell you about the plan."

In the anxiety of the situation, Ghigau collapsed as she walked across the room. Dustu, who had stayed out of the presence of the two women, saw his grandmother collapse. He ran to her, picked her up, and carried her to Tahatankohana. Kangee followed. "Why do you take me here? Take me to Wakanda."

"No, grandmother. This is where you need to go." He said from outside the door, "Tahatankohana, grandmother collapsed to the ground."

"Bring her in."

Dustu carried Ghigau into the lodge. "Where are the women?" Ghigau asked.

"Chaska is getting them." Chetan held open the door of his home.

Ghigau asked, "You hid them?"

Chetan turned into the room. "Of course, our women and children and yours are hiding together." Kangee remained outside the lodge. "Welcome to my lodge." Chetan invited in the woman who only minutes before had it in her mind to kill all of them.

Tahatankohana said, "Make a garlic compress and the pneumonia tea."

"Be right back." Roscoe immediately went to get dried mullein leaves, dried yellow coneflower plants, rosemary, thyme, oregano, dried goldenseal root, and dried butterfly weed root to make the same tea Tahatankohana had made for him when he'd had pneumonia.

Tahatankohana got the stethoscope from his surgical toolkit. "May I listen to you breathe with this? You can hear Dustu breathe first. I will show you."

He put the stethoscope earpiece into Ghigau's ear, then placed the ivory disk attached to a wooden bell against her grandson's back behind his lung. "Do you hear the sound of the air inside his lungs?"

Ghigau was amazed. "I do!"

Kangee demanded, "Let me hear."

Tahatankohana took the earpiece away from Ghigau's ear. Dustu stepped in front of Kangee. She listened. "Do you want to hear my heart?" Dustu turned around and placed the disk over his heart.

Kangee was thrilled. "I want to hear my heart." She flexed the eighteen-inch-long silk thread covered coiled spring and placed the ivory against her chest.

Kangee ordered Tahatankohana. "Let me hear my air now."

Tahatankohana did not want his throat slit. He asked. "May I put this against your skin on your back?"

"Be respectful."

"Of course." From behind, he put the earpiece into Kangee's ear then placed the disk over Kangee's lungs.

"Let me hear Ghigau's lung." Tahatankohana showed her where to place the disk. "Her lungs do sound different." She passed the earpiece to Tahatankohana. "What's wrong with her?"

Tahatankohana listened to Ghigau. "Her parts that are called 'kidneys' are not working. What they do is make your water. Hers are not. That is why she is not passing her water. That water goes into her lungs. Soon, her lungs will be full of water."

"Turn her upside down. The water will go out," Kangee informed him.

Tahatankohana said, "I wish that would work,

but it will not. I need to hear her heart." Kangee put the disk over Ghigau's heart. Tahatankohana told the war woman, "Thank you for helping."

"Give that back to me so I can hear." Kangee listened to Ghigau's heart. "Her heart sounds like mine." She put the earpieces back into Ghigau's ears. "Listen to your heart."

"I hear it."

"Now, my heart." Kangee put the disk over her own heart. "Now, my lungs." She reached behind her back and held the disk there as Ghigau listened. "Now, your lungs." Kangee moved the stethoscope to Ghigau's back.

"I do hear it. It sounds like raspy rattling."

Roscoe walked over and handed Ghigau the garlic he had mashed into a paste. "Put this on your chest." He gave her a cup of the special tea.

"Will these things save me?"

Tahatankohana told her the truth, "No, but they will help you breathe better for a while."

Ghigau realized what had happened the day before. "This is why Wakanda asked you to bring me milk, so you could figure out what is wrong."

"He is a very good Mystery Man. This is not something anybody can fix."

Kangee asked, "Are these white man tools and knowledge?"

"Yes."

"What is this called?"

"It is a stethoscope."

"Thank you for letting me listen." Ghigau drank the tea and rubbed the garlic on her chest. After twenty minutes or so, she breathed much better. "We will go back to my lodge. Dustu, carry me."

As he carried his grandmother out the door, the women returned to the village. Dustu suggested to his grandmother, "Maybe you should have Hanataywee explain the agreement because you cannot breathe well."

When Ghigau had first met Hanataywee, she had thought the girl was not bright. Now, she knew she had been wrong. Ghigau instructed her soon-to-be-great-granddaughter-in-law. "Come, daughter. You must explain."

"What am I explaining?" Hanataywee asked as she followed them.

Dustu said, "The whole mapping system, the giving of pottery, mussel shells, mussels, and the opportunity to come harvest mussels. Show Kangee some of your pottery and explain how you will know who would get the items in trade."

Hanataywee entered Ghigau's lodge. "War Woman Kangee, it is an honor to meet you and to serve you. Elder Ghigau, thank you for finding me worthy. It is an honor to help and to serve you."

She is respectful, too, Ghigau thought.

Hanataywee laid the papers on the table and explained the proposal. She ended, "This is what we present and hope that you will agree."

"We have a problem right here." Kangee pointed

to the page with two villages on the paper. "I think this village must be where I live. One village is going to have to move for this to work."

"We saw that," Ghigau commented without making any suggestions. She wanted Kangee to have the opportunity to provide her thoughts undirected by others.

"We are close to the edge of this section, and there are no villages over here. We would still be on the creek. Maybe we should move."

"We could ask the people in the other village to move instead." Ghigau wanted to be sure that Kangee did not overlook that option.

"Yes, and they still can. But I think we will move either way."

"Are you saying you agree to let us hunt on the prairie?" Hanataywee asked, hopefully.

"First your people will help us fight the Osage."

"Absolutely not!" Hanataywee stated firmly.

"Then you must never help them fight against any Cherokee, and you must let us pass through your land to our northern section."

Hanataywee said, "If we can also hunt there with the same agreement."

"And Tahatankohana gives me the stethoscope."

"I will get him. You can ask," Dustu offered.

"Please do," Hanataywee spoke to him very sweetly.

Before they spoke many more words, Dustu and Tahatankohana arrived. Tahatankohana said, "I would like to use it for a while longer, then I will give it to you."

"He wants to use it until I die." Ghigau appreciated that he had stated the situation very respectfully.

"Agreed. You can keep it until I am ready to leave," Kangee told him.

Ghigau moved the negotiations along. "Then we should go ahead with the pipe ceremony to confirm our agreement. Now, it will be much better since you are here and also agree."

"Yes. It is a good thing I came to fix this problem with the location of my village."

On the back of Dustu, Ghigau went with Kangee. Hanataywee went with her brother to speak with Ppahiska. "We have an agreement. Kangee and Ghigau are ready to smoke the Calumet with us."

Ppahiska stated his dilemma, "We will need too much of the kinnickinnick for everybody to smoke the pipe, but I think every person should participate."

"I agree, including the young. They will continue the agreement in the future. It will be best if they commit from the beginning. I would like to offer cedar, tobacco, sweetgrass, and red willow bark."

That was what Ppahiska had hoped Tahatankohana would do. He accepted and called a meeting in the community building. Kangee gathered the Cherokee people in the field beside their teepees. Each of them explained the plan.

Wakanda departed to get the village's ceremonial buffalo skull. He situated it in the meeting lodge then propped the smudging bowl that he had used to purify the land into its horns.

Kangee instructed her people, "We are in agreement, make your way to the community lodge."

FORTY THREE

Cherokee and Quapaw—young and old alike—sat in the meeting lodge. The medicine bag containing the plants of power that would seal the treaty hung across Wakanda's chest. He reached into the bag then threw a hand full of the herb mixture into the fire. Fragrant smoke rose into the air. Symbolizing their relationship, the open shells of a large mussel lay in the bowl in the buffalo skull's horns. Wakanda dropped an ember from the fire into the shell he had filled with the plants of power. His gentle breath on the ember ignited the herbs. The powers of water, earth, fire, and air joined. With an eagle feather fan, Wakanda wafted billows of smoke. He perfumed the air and purified the hearts of the people in the open building.

Pointing it to the east, Wakanda raised the village's sacred ceremonial pipe stem that had lain on the plate of his smudging pottery. He picked up the pipe bowl that had rested on the other side. So that everybody could see, Wakanda joined the two parts high above his head and created the Calumet. He raised the peace pipe to God; the Great Creator in Father Sky then lowered it toward Mother Earth.

"The pipe stem reaches into Father Sky. Our feet rest on Mother Earth. We are the bridge between the sacred above and the sacred below. Earth, sky, two-legged and four-legged ones, winged ones, trees, and all other plants are one. The pipe binds us together."

At each position, the Mystery Man sprinkled herbs on mother earth and put a pinch of them into the pipe bowl then raised the pipe and spoke. "East, we thank you that you bring the sun and give us another day to walk on Mother Earth to learn." Circling the flames in the center of the lodge, he chanted. "South, we thank you for strength, for healing, and for new life in the spring." He moved on. "West, we thank you for spiritual wisdom and the spirit helpers. Connect us to the spirit world and the Great Mystery." With the pipe held high, he spoke in the fourth and final directional position. "North, we thank you for endurance and health." He left more of the herbs of power on the ground then returned to the place where he had begun. "The circle is complete."

Wakanda placed the Calumet into the hand of Ppahiska who took a stick from the fire and lit it. "Great Spirit, direct our hearts and minds with your power. Make all our intentions pure as we confirm our acceptance of this agreement to trade pottery, mussel meat, and shells, and give permission to take mussels from Spring River and to hunt and gather plants in the prairie lands assigned to our neighbors, the Cherokee."

Kangee accepted the pipe. "Let the bonds forged here today be strong and go beyond this agreement to share what Mother Earth has allowed us to use." She drew the smoke from the pipe into her lungs then exhaled it to carry her prayer to the Great Spirit.

Ghigau struggled to get enough air to speak her long prayer. "Let the last things I do as I walk on Mother Earth be good for the Quapaw and for the Cherokee people. Let them walk together in peace. Bring Waya, Dustu, Adahy, Luyu, Hanataywee, and Ehawee together as a symbol of the bonds we forge today. Make the bonds of love, respect, and help be strong and unbroken. Let the good brought by my current actions erase the actions of my past that were unkind and hurtful. I pray that love and hope will fill each and every being on Mother Earth and in Father Sky." Almost at the end of her life, she barely puffed the pipe to send the desires of her heart to her Creator on the smoke of the Calumet.

Ghigau passed the pipe to Mikoishe. The ritual of the pipe continued. Person after person smoked the pipe and spoke a prayer. Time after time, Wakanda refilled the bowl with herbs until every person had their turn. As the agreement was sealed, the smoke saturated the land and completed another phase of purification. The land was almost ready for the joining of the nine couples.

FORTY FOUR

The fifth day after the Cherokee people had come to Ppahiska's village, Ghigau knew she would not live to the end of the day. She fought to ask the Great Spirit, "Let me see Waya before I die if he has an antelope or not." Dustu went to get Tahatankohana. "We made the tea. It is not helping. Please come."

Tahatankohana carried his stethoscope with him. He entered the lodge. "Good morning, Grandmother."

Ghigau asked for the most important thing on her mind, "Everybody, pray to Tahatankohana's God. Ask Him to forgive me, to take me to my ancestors, to allow me to see Waya and my grandsons be married and to bring Waya home while I can still talk."

"May I listen to your lungs?" Tahatankohana asked.

"Not until you pray for what I asked."

Tahatankohana prayed, "Great God of Heaven, creator of the universe, sustainer of everything, see this woman who asks for forgiveness. Forgive her of anything she may have done wrong during her life.

Let all her family surround her with love as she passes to the spirit world. Bring her to the next stage of existence, and give her a peaceful life with the ancestors. Bring Waya home so she may speak with him one more time. Let her see our families become one as Waya, Dustu, and Adahy marry Luyu, Hanataywee, and Ehawee. We ask for these things in the name of Your son, Jesus."

Everybody heard, "Amen," at the door where Waya stood with an antelope over each shoulder. He dropped them to the floor, walked quickly across the room, and knelt beside the bed of his mother-in-law. "I am here, mother."

"You have been a good son. I say that and not son-in-law because you have been better to me than many other women's sons have been to their mothers. I love you. Thank you for bringing me antelope meat. Please, ask if they can be from all the grooms to all the brides of this village as their wedding offering for the ceremony. I want you to roast them and get married while I still live. Ask the rest of my family to come to me."

"I will, Mother." Waya kissed her forehead and then both cheeks before he left the lodge. He motioned for everybody to follow him. He looked at Dustu. "Get all of Luyu's family and take them to your grandmother. Tell them what is happening on the way. After they have spoken with her, bring the brides to Wakanda's lodge." He turned to Adahy. "Tell all the grooms and other brides to come to Wakanda's lodge."

He motioned to Tahatankohana. "We better go tell Wakanda what is happening. He can tell us what we need to do."

Adahy kissed his grandmother. "I love you. I wish I could have you for many more years. Watch over us from the spirit world and help us."

"I will always be attentive to you from the beyond."

Waya stood outside Wakanda's lodge. "Waya and Tahatankohana need the holy man."

Weayaya opened the door, "Welcome."

The men stepped inside. Wakanda inquired, "Has Ghigau passed to the spirit world?"

Waya replied, "No, but she will soon." He explained what Ghigau wanted.

"I can complete the purification this morning with tobacco."

Tahatankohana made a suggestion. "If all the grooms and brides agree, we could make a new ceremony."

Wakanda had already been thinking about how to marry all the couples at the same time. "I have no ceremony for marrying several people at the same time. Weayaya, go get them."

Dustu went to the lodge that would soon be his home. He walked right in. Yesterday, Luyu had told him if he came to their lodge, to just come in because it was his home. "Ghigau will not be in this world much longer and asks for all of you to go see her. We want to roast the antelopes that grandfather brought home this morning, and she wants everybody to accept it as the wedding meat offering, so we can all marry today before she passes." Dustu believed all four of the women of his new family would be glad to do so, and if they did, the others would agree too.

Everybody rose except Roscoe. Ann told him, "You're part of our family. You must come."

He stood up, walked to Ann, and hugged her. "Thank you for thinking so."

Luyu offered her opinion as they walked to Ghigau's temporary lodge. "We don't have a ceremony for marrying so many people at one time. I think we can do it any way we want."

Dustu told Ghigau, "Grandmother, I brought the rest of our family."

"Thank you for coming at the request of an arrogant old woman. I came here and spoke with all of you in a very haughty manner. You were all very gracious. Some of you I completely disregarded. Now that I know you, I am very glad to have my children join this family. I am sure they will be happy and loved. Thank you for every good thing you will give them. I believe they will give much to you as well. Please agree to whatever ceremony is suggested. I want to see my men safely in the arms of this family."

Luyu told her, "I will, my Mother. Thank you for allowing me to have Waya as my husband. I will do my best to make him happy and to honor you." She kissed Ghigau's forehead.

Hanataywee said, "I will too, Grandmother, and I thank you for the good man you raised." She held Dustu's hand as she kissed Ghigau's forehead.

Dustu kissed her too. "I love you, Grandmother. I will do what you told me."

Ehawee stepped to the dying woman. "I am sorry to lose you so soon. There is so much I could have learned from you beyond this lesson you give us now."

"What have you learned from me, Ehawee?"

"I have learned not to see what is on the surface but to look for what is really in a person's heart. When it is my time to pass to the spirits, I hope to be as brave and gracious as you."

As Ehawee kissed her, Ghigau said, "Thank you, Ehawee." She turned to the others. "Chetan, Bethany, Ann, Sally, Ke, Chumani, and Roscoe, I know you are not marrying one of my children, but they will be your family. I know you will be a wonderful family for them. Thank you."

"Just as they are wonderful," Bethany replied.

Each of them kissed Ghigau's forehead. "Me now!" Chumani called out in Quapaw. Bethany raised her smallest one. Chumani kissed Ghigau and told the old woman everybody obviously loved, "Love you."

Dustu stepped over. "Grandmother, we need to go to Wakanda. I will be home again soon."

"Go on," she told them. Dustu, Hanataywee, Ehawee, Ann, and Luyu hurried to Wakanda's lodge.

Luyu told those already there, "Sorry we are late."

Wakanda comforted the late arrivers. "There is no need to be sorry. We know you were speaking with Ghigau. We did not wait to talk. We believe the Great Spirit sent Waya for the venison. He went to a place he never before saw antelope because it is much closer. As soon as he got there, he saw several and shot two of them before they ran away. He brought them straight back.

Now, we will have time to cook them and have the wedding while Ghigau lives. She is very old, and we should honor her last request. We are asking for all of you men to offer the two antelopes as a group for the ceremony and that you women will accept them. The men will all work to skin the animals then the women will roast them and prepare their other food to offer to the men during the ceremony. Will this be acceptable to you?"

"Of course!" they all agreed.

Wakanda released them. "Then go prepare for the ceremony. As soon as you men have skinned the antelope, come back to my lodge."

Tatonga walked into the lodge. "Petang has not paid the bride price. He cannot marry Zitkala."

Zitkala turned to Petang. "I thought you gave father the horses."

"He does not want horses. He wants a loom for your mother."

Zitkala snapped at her father, "Where would he

get a loom? You want to ruin my life." She ran out of the lodge.

Petang respectfully asked Tatonga, "May the two of us speak alone?"

Tatonga walked out of the building.

"The rest of you men, meet at the community lodge. Start skinning those antelope. Women, stay here a while longer."

Tatonga strode toward the mountain.

Petang walked beside him. "I promise I will make a loom. I will climb to the trees above and get the wood to make it." Petang showed Tatonga the plans for the loom. They arrived at the crack in the side of the mountain. Petang demonstrated how he could climb. He went several yards up the crack then came back down. "I will build a basket to go up and down, but not right here. I will only be able to do these things if I marry Zitkala. If I do not, I will have to leave."

"Petang, I believe you. It is not that I do not want you to ever marry my daughter. My sister died having a child because she was small, like Zitkala. I do not want my daughter to die. If it takes you a few years to find a loom, and she is older, then it may not be a problem anymore."

"I do not want that to happen either. Can we ask the medicine man if he thinks she would have a problem? If he says she will and somebody will let me live with them, I will build the looms and the basket and wait until she is ready."

"We will ask Wakanda."

Both of them planned to ask Tahatankohana secretly. When they returned, tobacco smoke enshrouded the village as thick as a cloud. Wakanda fanned the air with the eagle feathers. The smoke refused to move away. Petang suggested, "We should not bother Wakanda while he is purifying the land. We could ask Tahatankohana his opinion while we wait."

Tatonga thought, *this young man is wise. I believe he honestly wants to protect Zitkala.* "Only because we should not bother the Mystery Man at this time. We still need to ask him later."

"Absolutely," Petang affirmed Tatonga's reasoning. Both of them understood exactly what they were doing. They made their way through the thick smoke to the men skinning the antelopes. "Just in case, would you mind if I helped skin the antelope? Maybe we could ask Tahatankohana to let me take his place, and you can speak with him while he is free."

"Good idea." They stepped out of the smoke, seemingly materializing beside the men skinning the antelopes.

As Petang stood beside him, Tatonga asked, "Tahatankohana, would you let Petang take your place for a moment?"

Tahatankohana quickly realized that the two were working together to speak with him. He assumed it was about the plan to build the loom or the basket. He handed Petang his knife. "I will go out of this smoke, so I can get fresh air." He walked away from the other men. Tatonga followed him to the higher ground closer to the mountain. Through the thick smoke, neither of the men noticed Zitkala following with her mind and heart full of anger.

In the lodge, Petang started a conversation with the men skinning the carcasses. "Since we may all be having children soon, what do you think about any of these women dying having our babies?"

You should be thinking about making those babies, not your wife dying," Zhawe told him.

"I am thinking about that, but Zitkala is a small person, and I want her for many years."

Nikiata thought about the question. "The baby could get out of her. Her hips are wide like her mother's."

Petang was relieved. "So she will have no problem?"

"You can never know for sure, but I do not think she has any more of a chance of having a problem than any of the other women," answered Nikiata.

"Are you sure? I could wait to get married."

Nikiata knew how deeply you love when you wait years for your mate. *Zitkala will have a good marriage. All of us should have been thinking about this. Most men would not be willing to delay experiencing the pleasures of a wife.*

Nikiata told him, "You can put your seed on the ground and not inside her."

Zhawe informed the group, "Not me. I am not doing that."

"I do not think any of us have to do that. I say this because Petang wants to know."

"Thank you, Nikiata. You are a good Mystery Man. You thought about more than one part of this."

Maybe I will be a good Mystery Man. The comment affirmed Nikiata's decision to learn everything he could.

As Tatonga and Tahatankohana walked out of the smoke, Tatonga explained, "We want to ask your opinion about Zitkala."

"Sally knows her better than I do."

"This is a medical question. Zitkala is a small person. I have fear. Maybe she will not be able to pass a baby."

Not far away and still shrouded by smoke, Zitkala heard the concern of her father. Instantly, she forgave him. He was not trying to destroy her life. He was trying to protect her. She wanted to run through the smoke and throw her arms around him. She did not. Even more, she wanted to hear the answer to the question.

Tahatankohana thought about the girl. Her wide hips already gave her a shapely figure. "The important thing is that the baby can pass through the space between the hips. If it cannot get through, the woman usually dies. Zitkala has wide hips. I do not believe it would be a problem, but another year would be safer. Also, I can show Nikiata how to get the baby out by cutting here." With his finger, he drew a line across his stomach just above the pelvic bone. "It would be good for all the women if he knows how to do this."

"A woman can live after you cut her open like that?"

"The medicine man would sew her together again, and she would heal."

"I will also ask Wakanda and Nikiata what they think about her. Will you find out if Nikiata is willing to learn how to do this?"

"I will. Go find Wakanda. Do not tell him you already spoke with me. You must hear his very valuable, uninfluenced opinion."

Both men went to do as they had agreed.

Zitkala followed her father. She didn't want to die. She wanted all the information she could get about this possibility.

Zitkala heard her father. "So you do not think this is a problem?"

Wakanda said, "First, I am glad to know that is why you asked for a loom. Her hips are wide like Metea's hips. She should be able to have a baby."

"Thank you for your knowledge. I will tell Petang and Zitkala."

For the first time, Zitkala was happy about her hips. She quickly went back to her lodge then, so nobody would know she had followed her father, sat outside the building.

Tatonga came out of the purifying tobacco

smoke and saw his daughter sitting against the side of the lodge. *She looks miserable.* He sat beside her and leaned against the lodge. "It is not Petang. The more I know him, the more I like him. I was afraid that you would die like my sister, Kimimela. She died when trying to have a baby. Your body is small like hers, but I spoke with Wakanda. He says you have wide hips. He says you will not have that problem. It is good that you are like your mother. I have always liked the shape of your mother. Now, I know why. What I am saying is that you can marry Petang. He can do what he promised me after you get married."

"Thank you, Father." Zitkala hugged his neck. "I love you. Please go tell Petang? I have to get ready."

"I love you too, my daughter. I will tell him now."

Zitkala ran to Wakanda's lodge. *Men like this shape. I am very glad to know this.* "Father is going to let me get married. What do I need to do?" she asked.

Wakanda passed on the information she needed to know. Zitkala hurried away to do as instructed. When she entered her lodge, her mother was already making the traditional corn dish that brides present to their grooms. "How did you know Father would change his mind?"

"Because I know he loves you, and he does not want to upset you. I know you can have a baby. You have wide hips like me. It is just that he never forgets his sister dying. He is worried about you."

"Thank you, Mother. I did not know how I was going to make this in time. They must be almost finished skinning the antelope."

Ke ran past. "Brides, come to the community lodge."

When all the women were there, they worked together to attach strings to the antelope hides between the lodge poles but left the hides in a heap on the ground.

The people walked on the tobacco sprinkled on the ground as they entered the lodge. Ghigau arrived on the back of a captured Osage slave, who Kangee had named The'-ha, meaning soles, because he was lower than the soles of the feet of the people who had captured him. However, it was The'-ha's feet that touched the sacred tobacco, not Ghigau's feet.

FORTY FIVE

Every soul in the village was in his or her place inside the lodge. Ann, Luyu, Hanataywee, Ehawee, Mina, Dowanhowee, Mache, Zitkala, and Weayaya stood before Wakanda. He asked the brides, "What do you provide for this union?

Every bride carried a basket lined with cedar and a piece of red cloth. Inside were two ears of corn, buffalo jerky, one squash, a handful of beans, one tobacco twist, and two apples. Each woman handed her basket to her chosen one, all of whom were still bloody from skinning the antelopes. The brides then walked to the hides, pulled tight some of the attached strings, and then fastened them to the poles of the meeting house. "I provide these things for my husband and our home as a symbol of my continual care and love."

Wakanda asked the grooms, "What do you provide for this union of marriage?"

The two skinless antelope carcasses lay on reed mats before the men. Tahatankohana, Waya, Dustu, Adahy, Nikiata, Zhawe, Ishtasapa, Petang, and Tizhu had also brought a basket like those carried by the women. They held their offering baskets before them as they spoke their vows, "I provide these for my wife as a symbol that I will provide, love, and protect our family always." Together the grooms chanted, "O' my beloved, our love has become firm by your walking with me the first step. Together we will share the responsibilities of the lodge, food, and children. May the Creator bless us with noble children to share. May we live long."

The brides replied, "This is my commitment to you, my husband. Together we will share the responsibility of the home, food, and children. I promise that I shall discharge all my share of the responsibilities for the welfare of the family and the children."

Wakanda spoke the wedding blessing. "Now you will feel no rain, for you will be a shelter for each other. Now you will feel no cold, for each of you will be warmth to the other. Now there is no more loneliness, for each of you will be a companion to the other. Now you are two bodies, but there is only one life before you. You will go to your resting place, to enter into the days of your togetherness. May your days be good and long upon the earth."

The people watched the brides skewer the antelopes before their grooms then place them on spits over the fire. Wakanda spoke to all. "Brides and grooms, go and prepare for the second step."

The brides and grooms went to wash and dress in their wedding garments. While the couples got ready, Wakanda created the wedding circle. "Father

Sky, be the roof over our heads. Mother Earth, hold us. Trees and plants, surround and embrace us. We give tobacco to the grandfathers & grandmothers of the plants and to the stone people. Thank you for allowing us to have this ceremony in your space." He sprinkled tobacco on the ground in the shape of a circle large enough for all the people to fit inside. He then lit a bundle of sage and waved the smoke into the wedding circle. "Purify this space and remove all malice."

With the eagle feather fan, Wakanda smudged each guest with sage as he or she entered the wedding circle. "Be cleansed and purified." After them, he waved the sage smoke over the brides and grooms as they entered. Wakanda came in last. He stood before the couples, who faced each other holding hands.

Wakanda spoke to them. "Above you are the stars, below you the stones. As time passes, remember; like a star, your love should be constant. Like a stone, your love firm. Be close, yet not too close. Possess one another, yet be understanding. Have patience with the other; for storms will come, but they will go quickly. Be free in the giving of affection and warmth. Make love often, and be sensuous to one another. Have no fear, and let not the ways or words of the unenlightened give you unease. For the Great Spirit is with you, now and always."

The men spoke to their chosen one, "O' my

beloved; now you have walked with me the second step. May the Creator bless you. I will love you and you alone as my wife. I will fill your heart with strength and courage: this is my commitment and my pledge to you. May God protect the lodge and our children."

The women replied, "My husband, at all times I shall fill your heart with courage and strength. In your happiness, I shall rejoice. May God bless you and our honorable lodge."

Wakanda instructed the families of those marrying, "Family members, come give your couple a kiss and speak a blessing." The families took many minutes to speak their blessing to each person in their family and then return to their place in the wedding circle.

Wakanda asked, "Will you take another step?"

Together, the grooms and brides stepped forward in their march around the circle. The grooms said, "O my beloved since you have walked three steps with me, our wealth and prosperity will grow. May God bless us. May we teach our children well and may they live long."

The brides replied, "My husband, I love you with single-minded devotion as my husband. I will treat all other men as my brothers. My devotion to you is pure. You are my joy. This is my commitment and pledge to you."

Wakanda explained the state of marriage. "When you leave this circle, you will be reborn as a married person – not just to each other, but their family and the community are also joined to you. Will you take another step?"

All the grooms chose to take another step into the lives of the women who held their hands. "O' my beloved, it is a great blessing that you have now walked four steps with me. May the Creator bless you. You have brought favor and sacredness in my life."

The brides walked one pace forward around the circle. "O' my husband, in all acts of righteousness, in material prosperity, in every form of enjoyment, and in those divine acts such as fire sacrifice, worship, and charity, I promise you that I shall participate, and I will always be with you."

Wakanda invited the community to affirm their joining of the couples. "Anybody who would like to welcome these into the community may come forward and speak to these brides and grooms." For two hours, the people moved about freely to speak to any or all of the couples. When it seemed that everybody had welcomed anybody they had a mind to speak with, Wakanda signaled to Chaska. He beat the drum one stroke and wondered what it would be like if he walked the seven steps with Sally. Everybody returned to his or her place in the circle.

"Will you take another step?" Wakanda asked.

Once again, the couples took a step. The grooms spoke. "O' my beloved, now you have walked five steps with me. May the Creator make us prosperous. May the Creator bless us."

Every bride spoke to her love. "O my husband, I will share both in your joys and sorrows. Your love will make me very happy."

Chetan, Sally, Roscoe, and Ke carried four sets of blue blankets to the wedding couples. Roscoe covered Tahatankohana and Ann each with a separate blue blanket. Chetan covered Luyu and Waya with blue blankets. Sally did the same for Hanataywee and Dustu. Ke covered Adahy and Ehawee. Enapay draped blue blankets over Nikiata and Mina. Petang's older brother with the crooked feet covered him and Zitkala. Zhawe's sister wrapped him and Dowanhowee each in their separate blue blanket. Ishtasapa's sister draped the blankets over him and Mache. Tizhu's sister covered Weayaya and her brother.

After the family members of the couples had draped them with the blankets, Wakanda continued. "Before you met, you were halves un-joined except in the wide rivers of your minds. You were each other's distant shore, the opposite wings of a bird, the other half of a mussel shell. You did not know the other then, did not know your determination to keep alive the cry of one riverbank to the other. You were apart, yet connected in your ignorance of each other, like two apples sharing a common tree. You knew the other existed long before you understood the other's desire to join their freedom to yours. Remember this time when your paths collided long enough for your indecision to be swallowed up by the greater need of love. When you came to each other, the sun surged toward the earth and the moon escaped from darkness to bless the union of two spirits, so alike that the creator designed them for life's endless circle. Be beloved partners, keepers of the odd secrets of each other's hearts. Be clothed in summer blossoms, so the icy hand of winter never touches you. Thank each other for patience. Your joining is like a tree to earth, or a cloud to the sky and even more. You are the reason the world can laugh on its battlefields and rise from the ashes of its selfishness to say, in this time, this place, this way - I loved you best of all.* Will you take another step?"

Every groom took the next step. "O' my beloved, by walking six steps with me, you have filled my heart with happiness. Time and time again, may I fill your heart with great joy and peace. May the Creator bless you."

The brides all joined their husbands. "My husband, The Creator blesses you. May I fill your heart with great joy and peace. I promise that I will always be with you."

The'-ha helped Ghigau to Waya and Luyu. She placed her hand on each blue blanket as The'-ha removed them then draped a single large white blanket over Waya and Luyu together.

Bethany removed the individual blankets from all three of her children. She handed them to Sally who returned white blankets, one at a time, to cover and join each couple together. Anpaytoo did the same for Nikiata and Mina. Onida replaced the blues with the white blanket over Weayaya and Tizhu. Metea brought Zitkala and Petang together under the one blanket. With the help of her daughter Mi, Algoma did the same for her two oldest daughters and their grooms.

"Will you take the last step and be joined?" Wakanda inquired of the men.

Each groom took the final step forward and committed his life to the woman holding his hands. "O' my beloved goddess, as you have walked the seven steps with me, our love and friendship have become inseparable and firm. We have experienced spiritual union in God. Now you have become completely mine. I offer my total self to you. May our marriage last forever."

The brides joined their husbands in their decision to join in marriage. "My husband, by the law of the Creator, and the spirits of our honorable ancestors, I have become your wife. Every promise I gave you I have spoken with a pure heart. All the spirits are witnesses to this fact. I shall never deceive you, nor will I let you down. I shall love you forever."

Wakanda walked to the first couple, removed the white blanket, and spread it on the ground before them as he spoke. "For the moment that brought Waya and Luyu together, we give heartfelt thanks to Father Sky, Mother Earth, and the Great Creator, nurturer of all life. You have consented to join together and have pledged your faith to each other before your family and community. You are now husband and wife." He did the same for each couple before Chaska began the beating of the drums.

Before they returned to the edge of the group, the people danced seven circles, placing gifts on the blanket before every couple they desired to bless. When the last person had returned to the outer wedding ring, the drums stopped.

As a symbol of their union and the beginning of their two lives together, the bride and groom tied the blanket closed. The mothers or sisters of the brides picked up the blankets and took them out of the wedding circle to a safe place where the blankets would not touch the ground nor could the couple have them until the marriage had been consummated.

The newly married couples left the wedding circle, followed by the remainder of the people. Everybody joined in the community lodge to celebrate with roasted antelope, the wedding corn dish prepared by the brides, and a banquet of other food and drinks. On September 13th, the same day Noah had married Ann the previous year, he had again married her as Tahatankohana.

FORTY SIX

Waya carved slices of meat from the roasted antelope and scooped out wedding corn. He filled three bowls. "Luyu, my love, would you mind if we sat with Ghigau?"

"Of course not." They walked to Waya's mother-in-law. Luyu asked, "May we sit here?"

"Please do," Ghigau replied.

The two women sat side by side, Waya handed each woman a bowl. "As I promised you both. I have brought you antelope."

"By your hand, I have eaten well for many years. Thank you for bringing me antelope one more time," Ghigau replied.

Luyu told him, "Just as I thought, you are a strong wolf providing for his family. Thank you for bringing me antelope for the first time."

"It pleases me very much to provide this for both of you." He sat between the two women. As the three of them savored the meal, Waya spoke about the many good days of life in Ghigau's home that he remembered. He realized he not only loved Luyu, but he loved Ghigau too. It made Ghigau happy to remember the days of which Waya spoke. Mostly, it pleased her to know that her son-in-law remembered good things about her. Even so, it was not long before Ghigau went to her lodge carried on the back of The'-ha.

Ghigau wanted another good deed to her credit before she met Maya Owichapaha. She feared the evaluator of souls would not find her worthy. She told the man who had carried her while they had prepared for the weddings, "I will ask Kangee to let you go."

The'-ha declined. "I do not want to go away from her."

"Do you not want to return to your people?"

"I have nobody. Kangee is good to me. I do not want to leave her."

"But you are a slave," she told him.

The'-ha gently placed Ghigau on her palette. "May I tell you why I am happy?"

"Please tell me."

"The Osage and Cherokee have fought many battles since we came to this land. Kangee came to punish us for a Cherokee village we had burned. Many of the Osage and Cherokee lay dead in both villages. The last of the Osage in my village were gathered. Kangee came to each of us. She asked, 'If you could do one thing before you die, what would you want?' Some said, 'slit your throat' or 'kill you.' Others said, 'Kiss my wife or husband or child.' I was young. I had never known a woman. I thought Kangee was glorious and powerful. I told her, 'I would lie in your arms and become a man.' She continued until she had asked every one of us her question.

"Those that had asked to say farewell she allowed to do so then put all her captives back together. 'Kill them all, except that one.' She pointed to me. 'I claim him as my slave.' I watched her warriors kill every person in my village. She tied me and threw me over her horse like a sack of corn then rode back to her village, victorious.

"When we got to her teepee, she asked me, 'Do you still want to become a man with the woman who killed your family?' I believed she would kill me either way. I said, 'Yes.' She granted my request. Ferociously, with a knife at my throat, she made me a man.

"After she had as much as she wanted, she raised then plunged the knife toward me. I did not flinch. I was prepared to meet Wakan Tanka. The knife sunk into the ground beside my head. Something had changed her mind. Maybe it was because I had been brave. She tied my hands and feet to stakes, cleaned and bandaged my wounds, and then slept through the night with her head on my shoulder. She hadn't needed to bind me. I had not wanted to kill her. I have never wanted to leave her. I do everything she asks. I am happy to please her. She has captured me completely."

"Love comes in many ways," Ghigau remarked.

"May Wakan Tanka accept you into his arms."

Of his own free will, The'-ha went back to the woman who would never walk the seven steps with him.

Ghigau contemplated, *"What else can I do to tip the scales of my life?"*

Dustu didn't want his grandmother to be alone at her last moment. Dustu and Hanataywee went to Ghigau's lodge for their wedding night. The celebration continued long after the last couple had gone to their wedding chamber.

Late in the night, Ghigau saw the reaper at her side. "You cannot take me yet. Their wedding day will not be the day of my death." Ghigau gasped for breath. When the first ray of light entered the lodge, she knew death would wait no longer. "Dustu," she whispered.

Dustu immediately went to her side. He knew she would not speak another word. He held her in his arms as Hanataywee ran to her parent's lodge. "Ghigau is breathing her last. Come quickly."

Waya and Adahy sat beside Ghigau. They held her hands as Dustu rocked her. Ghigau looked at Waya, tightened her grip ever so slightly, then closed her eyes and breathed no more. Waya, Dustu, and Adahy began keening softly. Their new family joined them. Others in the village united with them to lament. That day, Quapaw and Cherokee alike mourned.

Waya told Luyu, "I will take Ghigau to our burial grounds."

"I can come with you."

"Will it upset you if only Dustu, Adahy, and I take her home? We will lament properly then return."

"Go, but come back to me."

Waya knew his new wife was afraid that he would do what Chetan's father had done so many years before. "I promise I will return. I take only my horse, blanket, knife, bow, and arrows. I leave everything else of mine here with you."

Waya and his grandsons wrapped Ghigau in her burial shroud then lay her over her horse and left.

FORTY SEVEN

At first light, Cherokee runners left to tell the other impacted Cherokee villages the terms of the treaty. When they woke, the newly married men and their wives opened their white blankets and looked at their gifts. Not long afterward, as instructed by Capa, Mantu, and Paytah, seventeen men from each of the other Quapaw villages arrived with produce and seeds.

It was decided that the first hunting expedition of two of the Quapaw villages would be in the new location of Kangee's village. As the new leader of Ghigau's village, Hota agreed to allow the other two villages to hunt in the section assigned to her. Kangee and Hota left the Quapaw village with two sets of produce and seeds, and the many mussels their people had dug from Spring River. Kangee also carried the stethoscope in her medicine bag. Untethered and on his own horse, The'-ha rode beside her.

Even though each Quapaw hunting party rode with a Cherokee guide, they brought their white stones with cube-shaped crystals of Galena.

Enapay, Capa, Mantu, and Paytah led the

hunting parties escorted by Oukonunaka and Wasa onto the land assigned to Hota's village.

Other Cherokee men, Washta and Shangke, went to Kangee's land with the hunting parties headed up by Wakanda, Chetan, Tatonga, and Ppahiska.

All four Quapaw groups carried large quantities of shells and slips of paper representing sets of ten seeds of corn, tobacco, cotton, and flax. Unknown to the Cherokee, the papers had a hidden mark so the Quapaw would know they were legitimate.

James and Sally left the village with those going to Kangee's land. Their ways separated when Sally and James stayed on the road to Fort Gibson. They would continue beyond the fort to Harmony. Sally hoped she could convince Stephanie, Eli, and Tom to immediately return to Indian Territory.

FORTY EIGHT

When James and Wakanda left, Roscoe asked Tahatankohana, "Would you help Nikiata and me tomorrow."

"I'd be happy to."

Tahatankohana translated Nikiata's words. "Wakanda told Nikiata that I want to make you my relative. You will need somebody to go on a vision quest to find your new name. Nikiata wants to do that for you. In exchange, he wants a copy of your folder about plants."

"I'd be honored for him to find my name. I'm glad to make a copy, but it's going to be written in English."

Tahatankohana told Nikiata what Roscoe thought would make the information useless. Nikiata replied, "I will learn English. The papers will help me learn the language and the plants. I will study what the plant book says until I know both."

Tahatankohana passed the message on.

"I'll make it," agreed Roscoe, "and tell him 'thank you.'"

Nikiata was happy. His plan had worked. He would get a copy of the plant book. The three men studied and copied the plant pages for the remainder of the day.

The light of early morning illuminated Tahatankohana and Petang's climb up the mountain. Once on the plateau, they searched for the best place to build the lift and also kept an eye open for good trees to make looms. "How should we build the lift?" Petang asked.

"We need to look at what is here before we can decide what we need to do."

After searching all along the cliff top, they found two large trees next to the edge that were close enough together. The two devised their plan. "Are you ready to go down?" Petang asked after they had cleared the area.

"We need to fell the tree. You can get it ready while I bring up King and Hector. They are the biggest mules we have. I have gone the long way before. It will take three days."

"We will have to go down after dark," Petang pointed out.

"I know, but the moon will be very bright, and I will go first."

"I will be too tired after cutting down the tree."

"I want us to get down safely. We will go down now."

They waited until the next day, climbed up, and sawed down the tree. Before they went back to their wives they cut out the sections they planned to use. Tahatankohana started up the valley the same evening. He brought King and Hector to the slope they would climb then stopped for the night. The following two days, they ascended the mountain. The third day, Tahatankohana and the mules walked the plateau to the tree they needed to pull.

Each of those days, Petang had climbed the crack in the cliff. He had cut all the extraneous branches off the felled tree. When Tahatankohana arrived, they hooked the two mules to the log with only the five very large and extremely strong branches they needed still attached. The mules drew the log from which they planned to hang the basket. Once in position, they rotated the felled tree until two of the branches locked behind the selected anchor trees. Two other limbs projected straight out for six feet. The third extended beyond the cliff at an upward diagonal.

Once they had the tree properly wedged into position, Tahatankohana left Petang to keep watch over the mules. He descended the cliff alone, went into his home, and swept Ann into his arms. "My wife, I've missed you." He kissed her sweet lips.

She managed to say, "I've missed you too," between kisses.

Tahatankohana stayed with Ann until he had only enough time to get back up and allow Petang time to come down while the sun still lit the way. As soon as he was on the plateau, Tahatankohana started home with the mules. He hated to be away from Ann. Since he had arrived at her farm in March of 1839, he hadn't been away from her except when they had been forced to separate after they had built the ferry at Cadron Creek.

Noah not only missed Ann; he worried that something would happen to her or the baby growing inside while he was away. During the days Tahatankohana traveled home, Petang built the deck across the two lower logs extending into the air. He also drilled the hole for the rope that would suspend the pulley and lift. The four cross-sections of the tree they needed to make the pulleys rode down on King and Hector.

Tahatankohana arrived home and again took Ann into his arms. He couldn't hold her close enough. That night he told her, "I hate to be away from you. Even though I know I'll see you again in only a short time, I miss you so much."

"I missed you too, my husband. Stay here tomorrow."

"I will," he promised.

When the rest of their family went out to the fields the next day, they stayed in the lodge and shared their love.

FORTY NINE

Waya, Dustu, and Adahy rode back into their Quapaw village with three antelope.

Ke ran into the lodge. "They came back."

Luyu, Hanataywee, and Ehawee met their husbands at the door. Luyu threw her arms around Waya. "You came back."

Waya assured her, "I meant every promise I made before we married, all I made during our wedding, and everything I have told you since."

Hanataywee and Ehawee also welcomed their husbands. After a long kiss, Dustu stated, "We saw ropes hanging from the mountain."

Ann looked up from the shirt she was beading, "Tahatankohana and Petang are making a way to the top."

"Nobody can climb a rope that far," Adahy informed them.

Dustu looked through the window at the dangling hundred-foot hemp ropes Tahatankohana had given up. "How did they get them up there?"

"You can ask Tahatankohana when he comes home tonight," said Ehawee.

Ke jumped up from the mattress on which he reclined. "I can show you right now."

Bethany opened the lodge door. "Show us."

The family followed Ke to the crevasse in the mountain. He pointed up.

The people on the ground watched as the two tiny figures far above descended. Repeatedly Ann told herself, *don't watch; leave.* She forced herself to remain.

When the two were close enough to hear, Dustu called up, "I want to go with you the next time."

Adahy echoed the desire, "I do too."

"Be there soon," Tahatankohana called down. When his feet were on the ground, the first thing he did was hug Ann. "How is Wambleeska?"

"Scared, and he wasn't even watching, but I told him you can do it," Ann replied.

"Thank you for telling him his father is strong, brave, and capable." Tahatankohana turned to his brothers-in-law. "You have to be tested, you have to practice, and you have to do everything exactly as I tell you."

"I will," the twins vowed at the same time.

"How are you building the lift?" Waya asked.

Petang explained as they walked home. Once in the village, they quickly said goodbye then hurried home to enjoy their families. That night, the men made sure their wives knew how much they adored them. The next morning, none of them hurried away.

When the four young men finally gathered, Zhawe, Ishtasapa, Tizhu, Chaska, and Kanizhika came out of their lodges. "What are you doing?" Chaska asked.

Petang looked at Tahatankohana.

"This is your plan," Tahatankohana told him.

Petang again explained his idea about the basket lift.

Chaska requested, "Let us help."

Tahatankohana stated the rules. All the young men agreed to the requirements, then went to learn how to climb the mountain behind their village. Petang went first. He climbed straight up, so he could gather grapevines to build a basket able to carry people and tools. Tahatankohana taught the others using the same procedure he had used to teach Petang. When the afternoon was almost over, Petang started his descent, and the rest of the men knew how to climb a fourth of the way to the top.

"How did it go?" Tahatankohana asked Petang.

"I have a large supply but not enough. How was the training?"

"Like you, they are natural climbers."

During supper, Luyu suggested, "You should throw all the grapevines down here. We women can weave the basket. Toss some strong, long, straight branches down too."

Tahatankohana told her, "It's Petang's project. I'll tell him what you suggest."

The sun came up. Petang again went straight up to the plateau. He pushed the huge tangle of grapevines he had already gathered over the edge before he went in search of more. Far below, Tahatankohana taught his brother's-in-law and friends how to ascend all the way to the ledge.

FIFTY

Zitkala knocked at all the lodges. "They threw down the vines."

The women and children gathered. First, they picked all the dried wild grapes and gathered up those that had popped loose when the vines had slammed into the ground. Once all the raisins had been gathered, so the creek wouldn't carry them away while the water softened them, they shoved the vines in front of the fish weir in Five Mile Creek.

Luyu instructed the other women, "Get all your knives, mallets, and axes."

In a few minutes, the women had the tools at the base of the mountain. Luyu held a branch. "Chop them this size. We need four with a strong double crotch to hold the branches at the corners. Ann, don't try to chop any branches, just drag the small ones we will not use to the village."

The women searched and chopped until all the branches they needed lay in a pile. Algoma informed the group, "We are ready to get the vines."

Once they had the vines back at the cliff, they struggled to stretch them out. "Should we end them at different positions?" Zitkala asked.

Anpaytoo finally got a vine untangled. "We can adjust them after we get them all laid out."

As they stretched and placed twenty-four very long, thick vines, Weayaya spoke of something that was troubling her. "I wonder why our husbands want to go to the mountain every day. Why don't they want to stay with us?"

Zitkala stated the reason she thought Petang was on the mountain, and why she didn't mind him going. "Petang is a man of his word. He is doing what he promised my father."

Ann related what she thought was her husband's reason. "Tahatankohana agreed to help Petang. He always wants to help people. However, he also loves doing things like climbing that cliff using nothing but his own power and skill."

Mina said, "Tahatankohana is very brave and skilled. That was one reason why I used to like him, but Nikiata is too. Nikiata has always been a good friend to me, and he is the one who loves me."

Anpaytoo said, "I know you love my son because you were afraid for him, and you went to help him when he was trapped with the buffalo."

Mina agreed. "I was very afraid for him. I could not live without him in my life. I never felt that way about anybody else."

Bethany believed the other women didn't accept her as part of the village. Therefore, she rarely spoke to them. On this day, she went ahead and voiced her feeling about her man. "I think Chetan is very exciting. The day he found me, I rode with him on his horse. He saw the herd of antelope he had been hunting. He used my dresses, tied me to him, and then raced in every direction, shooting antelope. I held on so tight and tried not to get in his way. He was completely thrilling. I knew I would be safe with him. I wanted him so much. I still feel that way."

Ann thought about Noah. *It's hard for me to let Noah do dangerous things because I don't want him to die or be hurt, but I also don't want to lose him in his heart by not allowing him to be himself. Besides, he only does the things he believes he can do, and he is very strong and very skilled.* She remembered how marvelous she had thought Noah was when she had watched him spear a sturgeon in the Arkansas River. She had felt that way ever since. She realized seeing Noah do those things did bring out her desire for him.

Mikoishe added what she thought. "Ppahiska is not only a very great warrior and hunter; he is also very good at leading us. He cares very much about all of us. This is what I will tell you about our men; they need to be strong and capable. Not only because we need them to provide for us, but also because they will be happier if you let them and you appreciate them. If your husband is happier, you will be happier."

All the women married a long time agreed.

"Thank you for your advice," Weayaya told the other women.

The vines were in position. Luyu pointed. "You

twelve hold two vines each. Hold down the one in your right hand and hold up the other one. You twelve do the same at the other end but hold up or down the opposite way.

"Algoma you get on that side. I will pass a vine to you. Pull it all the way across then all of you change the vines to the opposite of how you just held them. I will pass another vine across, and then we will squeeze them together. We do the same repeatedly until we get twenty-four vines woven across these twenty-four. That is how we can make the floor."

Each person got into position. They wove the twenty-four vines in only a few minutes. With ropes, they pulled them together as tightly as they could. Onida looked at the floor. "I think that is big enough."

"What next, mother?" Bethany asked Luyu.

Wichahpi suggested, "The vines are drying. We should take the rest of them back to the creek."

"All right," Luyu agreed.

As they dragged the rest of the tangled mass back toward the fish weir, Luyu explained what she thought they should do next. "We should stake down the long ends of our floor. Some of us can drive the tall uprights into the ground at the edges of our floor. To keep it from falling in, we will have to place branches from top to bottom diagonally across inside the frame while we build it. When the frame is in position, we will temporarily hold it together with ropes. Next, we can raise up the free ends of the floor vines and start weaving the sides from the bottom up."

Ojinjintka, Paytah's wife, thought of something. "It will need an opening to get in and out. That will make the basket better."

Mikakh said, "We could make three sides go all the way up to protect from arrows from the ground but leave one side open."

Mikoishe expanded on her daughter's idea. "It would be weak if we left a whole side open. Maybe just an opening large enough to get in and out but the rest woven closed."

Algoma warned, "Somebody could try to shoot into the basket from the cliff. We need to have it protected on all sides."

Tatonga's wife, Metea, stated her idea. "So we make a door after about two feet up. We make the opening two feet wide and center it in the side facing the cliff. We can make it swing open or closed and be latched shut."

"If we go all the way around again for a hand's span or two at the top, it will be perfect," Zitkala pushed the vines into the creek.

The others all agreed. They walked back to their basket, placed the branches of the frame into position, pulled the vines up and over the top of the frame, and then back down again. With the skeleton in place, they could start weaving the sides when the vines had again softened.

FIFTY ONE

With Tahatankohana's guidance, the young Cherokee men, along with the sons of the Quapaw village chief, climbed to the plateau and joined Petang. Together they looked for animal sign and trees of wood hard enough to make looms.

Chaska squatted beside hoof prints. "Deer came this way."

It's nice to be with people who know how to see what's around them. Everybody else was unfamiliar with the lay of the land. Tahatankohana informed them, "The tracks go toward the spring."

Ishtasapa suggested, "Let's go shoot some."

Tahatankohana followed the tracks. "They will not go there until dusk. Your first climb down should not be in the dark."

Ishtasapa followed the man he had agreed to obey while learning how to go up and down the mountain cleft. "Can we stay overnight and go down tomorrow before it gets dark?"

"I would rather not spend the night and two whole days away from Hanataywee," Dustu replied.

Tahatankohana stood by the spring and imparted his wisdom. "Give your woman food but not your love, and she will never be happy. Ann would starve to be with me, and I would starve to be with her. I make sure she knows how much I love her. As a man married a whole year, I say, your wife will be happier if she knows that you want to be around her. If your wife is happier, you will be happier."

During the wedding, Ishtasapa had promised to provide meat. "Tomorrow, we can spend the day with our wives then leave late but get here on time."

Kanizhika went down on one knee. "If we come at dusk tomorrow then stay up here and get more at dawn, then you could go home. I don't have a wife. I will stay and lower the deer with the rope." He scooped water in his cupped hands and took a drink.

"Dowanhowee must see that I love her. I will go home now." Zhawe started to walk away.

Petang stopped him. "First, we send down the trees we have cut."

They pulled one dogwood and six ironwood trees to the cliff. When they had lowered the last tree to the ground, the men signaled. Their wives waved back and then hauled the trees to the village.

After navigating the narrow crack to the river valley, Petang walked to the village. "After we kill the deer, we should stay on the mountain until we get enough trees. Then there would be no need to go up again before the basket is ready."

"I want to practice. I will climb up and look for trees," Dustu informed them.

"I will go with you," his brother replied.

Tahatankohana felt he should go with his sisters' husbands until he was sure they knew the climb well. "Me too."

FIFTY TWO

On the prairie, the older Quapaw men loaded the latest batch of buffalo parts. When the travoises were full, the mules, horses, and donkeys began the work of pulling bones, meat, horns, hooves, internal organs, and skins. Each man brought home two buffalo, and each village owed either Kangee's or Hota's village three hundred and forty seeds of cotton, corn, tobacco, and flax.

When Tatonga and Ppahiska rode back into the village, Petang's promised way to the plateau dangled on a rope. Petang hoped his new father-in-law would be glad he had allowed him to marry Zitkala. "The door is still being made." He stepped into the grapevine basket then proudly invited Ppahiska and Tatonga to join him.

There was just enough space for the three men to stand without touching. The four pulleys allowed Petang to raise the three of them without help. He fastened the rope to the tie-down-stick, stepped onto the platform, and then walked to the land. As if placed by God to symbolize the hunting grounds now readily available, a bear walked through the trees before them. Since they already had the buffalo meat to process, they allowed it to stroll away.

FIFTY THREE

Two weeks after he had left the village and twenty-three years after he had left Harmony, James stepped into Yates Mercantile. Sally entered before him. The man running the store saw her. "Greetings, Sally. Who is this with you?"

The man with Sally introduced himself. "James Williams."

"As in The James Williams?"

Sally informed him, "Yes, Earl, The James Williams. How are you doing?"

"Leg is still about the same."

Stephanie heard the voice. She ran into the store and threw her arms around her sister. "You came! I've missed you so much. Is Ann's baby all right?"

"I've missed you too. As far as we can tell, the baby is fine."

"Thank you, God. I've been praying and praying. It's been so long since Eli went to Fort Gibson. I didn't think you were coming."

"I couldn't leave until after the weddings."

"Weddings?" Lola asked as she joined her friends in the store.

"Noah's sisters."

"Come in and tell us everything." Stephanie turned to James. "I heard you tell Earl you're James. It's so nice to meet you, Uncle James."

"You too, Stephanie." James turned to the just-arrived young woman. "You must be Lola De La Cruz."

Sally asked her sister, "How is your little one growing in there?"

"Doing fine." An older woman joined them. "Meet Eli's grandmother, Helen. This is my sister Sally and my Uncle James."

"Pleased to meet you." Helen held out her hand.

James shook her hand. "Pleased to meet you too."

James and Sally clomped across the wooden floor in their dusty boots, which they removed before they left the store through the side door. They went into the kitchen of the Yates family home. Sally asked, "Where are Eli, Sebastian, and Tom?"

"They're helping Zachariah at the farm. We should go out there. You should see how far they've gotten!"

Sally requested, "Let's go tomorrow. I want to spend the rest of this day not riding."

"All right. We have plenty of time."

Sally didn't want to bring it up yet. *That's something I'll talk to you about later.*

They made their way to the sitting room then heard a knock at the door. Stephanie went into a room that hadn't existed when Sally had left Harmony that spring.

The new room projected onto the boardwalk. Stephanie pulled out the peek-hole plug and viewed whoever was knocking. She went back into the sitting room and opened the front door. "Come in."

Minnie Eggleston and Mara Wyman came into the house with their babies. "We came to say hello. We thought you would want to see Smithfield Wyman Junior and Zachariah Eggleston Junior."

Sally hugged both women. "It's so nice to see you. Come in and let me hold those babies." She sat on the sofa and took both babies in her lap. "I'm going to have to be able to cuddle two babies."

Stephanie introduced her uncle, "This is my Uncle James."

Mara turned to James and shook his hand. "My husband has told me about you. It's very nice to meet you."

"I'd love to speak with him," James replied.

"Do you want me to take you, or can you go down the road to the livery?"

"You stay here with Smitty Junior. I'll go." James left the women to enjoy each other and the babies.

Minnie said, "We heard Ann is pregnant and that a woman attacked her over Noah and that she may lose the baby."

"Ann is fine, except for a long scar right here," Sally traced a line across her collarbone. "She didn't lose the baby. We think he's fine, but we don't really know. Ann was about to stab the woman, who was trying to kill her, but then the men got there. Noah hollered for her to stop. She did. Then the woman tried to throw a knife into Ann's back."

Mara said, "Ann did all that while she was pregnant but didn't lose the baby. That is a miracle."

"I think so too." Sally knew the Holy Spirit had intervened but didn't tell them about the sweat lodge or the spirit world. Instead, Sally told them about her birthday at Fort Gibson. "Then Lieutenant Jackson jumped up and said I had stolen the necklace and the dress. I thought he would rip them right off my body!"

"I would have been scared to death!" Helen exclaimed.

"I had to give up the necklace on my birthday. It was the worst birthday ever, but Noah had read his law books. He thought he knew a way that I might keep the necklace. Colonel Howland agreed and told Lieutenant Jackson to write me ownership papers for the necklace and the dress. If Lieutenant Jackson could have shot arrows from his eyes, I would be dead. He even refused to do it. They took him to the stockade. The colonel had a different soldier write out the papers."

Stephanie remarked, "So, in the end, it was a great birthday because now you legally own the necklace and the dress."

"And with your real name," Lola added.

Helen redirected the conversation, "I heard you say you had to stay for weddings."

Sally told the women about the lack of food in

the village, the men shooting the buffalo, and then the women going to help butcher. She drew a yellow hide from her bag and handed it to Stephanie. "I got this yellow one then many more. The Cherokee men wanted to talk with us women, but the chief's son wouldn't let any of them talk with me."

After Stephanie had passed the buffalo hide to Helen, Sally handed her the white buckskin moccasins. Sally whispered to Stephanie, "I'll tell you what these are for later." She continued her story. "By the time all the buffalo were butchered, seven of our women and seven of the Cherokee men had fallen in love. Noah's grandmother, his two sisters, and Uncle James' two daughters were five of them. Two of my friends were the other two."

Minnie stroked the hide. "It's beautiful. Do you like the chief's son?"

Sally confessed, "I like him. He's handsome and strong, but there is nothing between us. He'll be their leader someday. He already thinks very carefully about what he does. He would never start a relationship casually. We just talk. Anyway, along with those seven couples, Noah married Ann again, and Mina married Nikiata in the same big wedding. It was a very beautiful ceremony."

Minnie stroked the buffalo fur. "That woman who attacked Ann over Noah married somebody else just like that?"

"I guess it seems that it was just like that, but really it wasn't. Mina and Nikiata had been friends their whole lives. Nikiata is the right man for her. Everybody knew it. They finally did too, and they love each other. It was right and good."

As Sally related all the Indian Territory news, Eli, Tom, their friends Sebastian De La Cruz, and Zachariah Eggleston finished the day's work of cementing stones together to rebuild the house. It was their third day at the farm, and the day they were to return home. When they got everything put away and locked in the new barn, they rode back to Harmony.

A few hours after dark, Eli, Tom, and Sebastian put the horses into the stall at the back of the store. Tom knocked three times with a long pause between each knock so the women would know who was at the door and that everything was safe. Sally put her fingers around the edge of the door, signaling to the men that all was well in the house. She opened the door but remained on the other side of it. When Eli came through, she jumped from behind the door, "Surprise."

The men were startled. They had just seen the signal that all was well and were anticipating a normal entry into the house. They quickly realized who was in the house. Eli hugged his sister-in-law and swung her around. "You came! This means so much to us." He put her down.

Sebastian hugged her too. "Hello, Sally. Welcome home to Harmony."

Tom also hugged Sally. As they walked into the sitting room, he asked, "Did you come alone?"

A man stood as they entered. "Hello, Tom. It's been a long time."

Tom thought the man looked like his friend who had left many years before, and he had arrived at the same time as Sally. "James?"

"In the flesh."

Tom walked across the room and shook James's hand firmly and vigorously. "Welcome back to Harmony and my home. How is Algoma?"

"Algoma is as beautiful and wonderful as ever."

"Have you spoken to anybody in town?"

"Everybody."

Stephanie said, "Go clean up, so we can eat."

Soon they were eating and happily talking. Sally listened for any signs that indicated how they felt about going to Indian Territory before winter. After the meal, Sally and James walked across the street to the saloon to stay in the rooms they had rented earlier in the day. Sally got out the white pants and the beads. She spent an hour sewing the tiny colored spheres in an intricate design on the bottom of one leg.

In the morning, the Yates, the Egglestons, the De La Cruz's, James, and Sally went to see the farm. As they approached, they saw the stones built to half the height of the original house. The corn and tobacco fields had already been harvested, but workers were still bringing in the cotton. "You're using so much more of the land than we ever did," Sally commented.

James looked at the partially built house and remarked to Clyde and Tom. "It's a shame the house we built is gone."

Zachariah replied, "I hate what happened, but Gus did clear all the land and fertilized it with the fire. I had a very good harvest. The people in Harmony helped me buy seeds, and hire the first workers to plow and plant this spring. When I sold the corn, I paid our people back double their investment. I also paid the hired workers for their help and had the barn built. When I sold the tobacco, I paid those hired hands and repaid Smitty the money I borrowed to buy the land.

"I still have enough to pay the men bringing in the cotton. Everything I get for the cotton will be Minnie's and mine. I've also kept enough seeds to plant all the fields in the spring. I'm using the stones from the land to build the house. I hope to get the walls up before winter. Next year I'll have enough money to buy materials for the roof and the inside of the house."

Sally praised him, "You've done very well. It makes me very happy to see the farm is still alive."

So her husband would know how much she appreciated him, Minnie told her child, "See how wonderful your father is. He's making you a house." She rocked Junior in her arms. "Let's go inside."

Zachariah held out his arms. "Let me take my son into the home where he'll be raised."

Minnie put the child into his arms. Zachariah

lovingly held his son against his chest. As his son slept in his arms, Zachariah explained how they put together the stones to build the walls. "…and I plan to build the inside exactly like it was before. It was a very good design, James."

James replied, "Thank you for the compliment. It's nice to see all the fields planted and harvested. I hope you won't be upset, but I will forever be sad that the house I built was destroyed. I'll tell you some secrets about the house nobody may have known."

"I'm not upset at all. I know I'd be upset if the house I'm building gets destroyed. I know how much work and love you must have put into that house because I know how much I'm putting into this one."

Sally took James by the hand. "Come see your brother's grave. Father was a very good man. It's too bad you left home when he was so young. You would have liked each other."

Stephanie walked with them. "Zachariah has promised to take care of the graves. He's going to make this area into a graveyard for anybody who lived here."

James told Zachariah, "Thank you."

Sally and Stephanie spoke to the stone markers, then James did as well. "I'm glad you took the farm, Chris. I'm sorry you and Emma died. I would have liked to have known you better. You have wonderful daughters. I'm glad I get to know them."

The whole group strolled around the farm. At the creek, they ate the dinner they had brought. If trees had still grown there, they would have been displaying their beautiful fall colors. James, Stephanie, Sally, and Eli remembered the creek reflecting that beauty back to the world. Now, only fields surrounded them for a hundred acres.

After they ate, they packed up and went back to Harmony. Stephanie rode beside Sally, "The moccasins look like they're made out of that white buckskin Noah earned in Little Rock."

"They are." Sally then explained why she had given Stephanie the shoes.

"Show me the pants, so I can make the shoes match."

The next day, Stephanie went to Sally's room at Joe's Saloon and looked at the pants.

"This is very beautiful. I'll buy the beads and such from the store. I'll also ask Eli to make another ceremonial knife."

James knocked on the door. "You two ready?"

"Coming." Sally folded the pants and put them in her bag.

FIFTY FOUR

James, with his nieces and Tom with his son and mother, rode out of Harmony to visit Rock House Cave. Many decades earlier, a tribe of Indians had lived in the enormous indentation in the cliff. With an open front so large that Sally felt smaller than a flea, she rode in with no fear. While the others explored the tunnels going out the back of the cave, Sally spent the day drawing replicas of the ancient wall painting in the main area.

The following day, Sally refused to go near the smaller cave containing the Indian skeleton. It was the very cave in which she had lost her lantern in a pitch-black tunnel at the rear. She stayed in town with Lola and Sebastian.

All the years that James had lived on the farm, he had never known about Indian Skeleton Cave. He was excited to experience something new about the land he had given to his brother.

All of those on the excursion enjoyed the walk on the ledge that encircled the large but shallow central pool. They admired the formations by the light of their lanterns as they strolled around the lip at the edge of the large hollow bubble in the mountain.

At the rear, Eli, Tom, and James crawled through the crack that opened on the right into a dark pit in the mountain. Once all three had made it to the far side, they hollered, "We're through, take the rope."

Stephanie and Helen pulled the line back and carried it out the way they had walked over. Meanwhile, the men completed the circuit around the outer circumference of the cave.

That night, not long before they would be going to their rooms, Sally brought up the topic that had been consuming her since Noah had first told her that Stephanie wanted her to return to Harmony.

"I don't see any reason why we can't go to Indian Territory this fall. We should be together when Ann has the baby, and we'll still be together when Stephanie has hers."

Eli immediately nixed the plan. "I think Stephanie should stay here until after the baby is born."

"Is there a problem with the baby?" Sally asked.

Eli resisted. "It's safer here."

"What about the next one? Will you come back here for every baby?" Sally persisted.

"Of course not."

"It's as safe there as here. Indian women have babies in their villages all the time. The lodges are well built, and we have plenty of food."

"Darling, I think we should go. If we go now, I'll make the trip fine, and it will be better for the baby if it doesn't have to travel when it's very small. I want to be with Ann when she has her baby. I don't want to miss it."

Tom and Helen stayed out of the conversation. They wanted Eli to decide for his wife and child. "I'll think about it," Eli told his sister-in-law.

"Thank you for considering the possibility."

Eli knew he hadn't heard the last of it. Sally was going to press the request until she was sure there was no hope. He steeled himself against the upcoming battering. The tension in the room felt as suffocating to Sally as being in a cave. "I'm going to my room. See you tomorrow." As Sally walked across the dirt street, anxiety made her heart beat wildly and her chest constrict. Just as when confronted with caves, she felt she wasn't getting enough air.

James enjoyed being with his birth family. However, he didn't want to be in the middle of the conflict. "I'll do the same. Goodnight, family." He decided he would visit with his friends the following day.

That night, Stephanie lay next to Eli. "Please, don't keep me from seeing my nephew's birth. Something may go wrong with either of us but especially Ann. If she dies and I never see her again, it will be horrible. Please, darling."

"I'll think about it. I love all of you. You know that, don't you?"

"I do, and we all love you."

Eli lay in the bed after Stephanie fell asleep and

fretted over the subject. He knew she was right about Ann. Noah had told him she had been badly injured when she was pregnant. It was very likely that something would go wrong. He thought maybe they should go, but he was afraid for Stephanie. This was her first child, women died giving birth, and he didn't want to lose her.

When he finally fell asleep, he dreamed Ann's baby came into the world. It ripped apart Ann's insides, and then pulled them out. As Ann died, her shredded flesh lay on the bed around the child. He woke up screaming.

Stephanie did just what she had done when Eli had been injured coming down the hill out of Little Rock. She stroked his hair. "It's all right. It was just a dream. Go back to sleep."

Eli informed his wife, "We'll leave as soon as everybody is ready."

"What happened?"

"I had a horrible dream about Ann dying when the baby is born."

"James probably wants to visit for a while, but we can start getting ready. Thank you, darling."

"You know it's just that I want you to be safe."

"I know my darling. I love you for that."

The next day, they told the family, "We're ready to go if you're also willing to leave now."

James answered, "Let's stay a while longer. I want to visit, ride around, and enjoy remembering."

Sally hugged her brother-in-law. "Thank you,

Eli." They spent several days sorting out the goods in Yates Mercantile. They packed part of what they were taking into the wagon that Noah had left in Harmony. Eli bought a second prairie wagon from Clyde. Tom's horse, Spirit, pulled it to the back of the store.

Sally joined Eli and Tom in the natural cave under his backyard that he had made into a cold storage area. Tom and Eli had been the only two people who had known of the cave's existence until the Butterfield Gang Trial. That was when Tom had taken all the townsmen through the hidden entrance in his kitchen then down the stairs. The smoked meats, smoked cheeses, seeds, tools, cloth, raisins, apricots, dried peaches, canned peaches, fresh apples from Mara's trees, and other foods of all kinds were emptied into the wagons or moved into the store.

They packed plenty of winter coats, leather gloves, wool gloves, scarves, wool socks, pants, shirts, and extra walking shoes for everybody, including their family in Indian Territory.

They loaded packages of vegetable and crop seeds, fishhooks, fish lines, poles, knives, and blankets. They also took needles, awls, scissors, threads, and yarn, along with bolts of calico and other types of cloth.

The items that would be useful to anybody were taken to trade when they crossed the prairie. Tom still left the store fully stocked and the shed behind the store full of seeds. Yates Mercantile passed from the hands of Tom to Earl and Clara Carpenter.

Sebastian and Lola De La Cruz, the Yates, the Carpenters, and the Egglestons packed. They moved the personal belongings of Tom, Eli, Stephanie, and Helen into the wagons. Tom sold the furniture left in the house to Sebastian and Lola.

Since all of them had read every book from the Butterfield house, Ann had decided to let Sally and James bring them to Harmony and give them to Betsy for the school. Sally had given her the books shortly after returning to Harmony. From Earl's store, Sally bought books they had not read, all the leather binders, paper, pencils, and erasers he had in stock, and the two jars of peppermint sticks. To replace the ropes that were part of the lift Petang was building, she bought the longest hemp ropes he had. Sally also bought a stethoscope from Doctor Gridley along with a book about midwifery.

James had seen something he wanted when visiting his friends. He went to speak with Clyde. "The spinning wheel and loom you built are very nice. Would you sell them?" *If they will, I'll give the smaller loom and spinning wheel I have at home to our village.*

Patty told Clyde, "Let him buy them. After all, you are a carpenter, and James is a customer. You can make me a new set. Take these apart so they'll take up less space in the wagon."

Tom and Eli paid Smitty to shoe their mules and horses. They also bought several additional sets of shoes as well as lots of nails and a set of furrier tools.

From Mara, Stephanie bought dozens of seeds of the best apples any of them had ever tasted. From Betsy, she bought a dozen embroidered, fine linen handkerchiefs. From Clara, she bought every one of her jars of honey.

Once the wagons were loaded, all the townsfolk joined for the great house exchange. First, they filled the wooden boardwalk from the store all the way to the other end with everything the De La Cruz's had bought from the Yates.

When nothing but empty rooms remained in the house attached to the store, they started on Earl's home. The beds came out of his home then into the home attached to the side of the store. They carried the dressers, chairs, sofa, and tables across the dirt road and positioned them in the house that would still be the home of the storeowners. Now, however, the store was Carpenter's Mercantile.

Eli and Stephanie paid Joe to make dinner for everybody to thank the people who would have gladly helped for nothing. Because Joe was a great cook, they all accepted the meal. They ate together in the saloon then finished moving all the possessions of the Carpenters.

Moving heavy furniture was something Earl would never have been able to do with his leg that had been shattered when his horse had fallen on it. He appreciated the help. Therefore, he paid Joe to prepare supper for all the folks, grown and young alike. They blessed the food and prayed that it wouldn't rain during the night. Everybody that would soon be leaving Harmony stayed at Joe's Saloon for the night.

The following day, they moved the belonging of the Egglestons from the house they had sold to the De La Cruzes into the now empty house that still belonged to Earl and Clara. Earl had agreed to let Clyde, Patty, Zachariah, Minnie, and Junior stay there until they moved to the farm. By the time Joe had the midday meal ready, the home of Earl and Clara was full of the possessions of the Egglestons. Zachariah paid Joe for dinner for all the townsfolk.

The latter half of the day, they moved everything sold to Sebastian and Lola from the boardwalk into the house they had bought from the Egglestons. To thank the folks for helping them, that night Sebastian and Lola bought everybody supper at Joe's Saloon.

Thus, all the people of Harmony benefited from legitimate transactions. Nobody received a free handout, but everybody in town had much more money. Even though it had come a year and a half later, the horrible events caused by the Butterfield Gang ended up being a blessing to the folks of Harmony.

Eli attached the two mules belonging to him and Stephanie, the two James and Sally had ridden to Harmony, and the two mules left by Ann and Noah, to the prairie wagon left by Noah. Tom hitched his and Eli's horses, the two horses of his mother and father that Helen had brought west, and two more horses purchased from Horace into one of the three six-animal harnesses he bought from Horace. They packed the four-mule harnesses they already owned with the two new harnesses they planned to use with Roscoe's wagons when they went west.

Everybody gathered to bid farewell to the Yates and the Williams family. Tears flowed as hugs were exchanged. Doc Gridley's daughter, Laura, made sure she talked with Stephanie and Sally. "I want you to know that I think you're fine people. I apologize for anything unkind I ever said to you and for the way I treated you. Thank you for helping me understand the true value of people by persevering. Please tell Ann and Noah the same."

Stephanie hugged Laura. "Thank you, Laura. We'll tell them. You have become a fine person, as well."

The Williams and the Yates were glad the waiting was over and that they were finally on their way to their new lives. At the same time, they were sad to end their lives in Harmony.

FIFTY FIVE

Beside Spadra Creek, they rode south out of Harmony toward the Arkansas River. Just like when they were transporting the prisoners, Gus, Ben, and Roy, the Shagbark Hickories were loaded with nuts. They gathered then dropped the small, green pumpkin-shaped nuts into the leather pouches that hung on the sides of the wagons. Stephanie told the others, "We should cast away our past. We need completely new names."

"Who would you like to be Grams?" Eli asked Helen.

"I knew a woman named Blanche Kennedy. When I was young, I wanted to be her."

"Then we'll be the Kennedys." Tom told her, "I'll be your son Phillip."

Remembering the people of Fletcher Creek, Eli informed his family, "Call me Fletcher."

James said, "I've always liked the name Royal."

Sally laughed. "Royal you shall be, Your Highness. I'm Prudence."

"How about Sarah for me?" Stephanie stated her chosen name. "But let's keep all the family relationships the same." That night, they secured rooms in Spadra as the Kennedy family.

The following day, they were almost at the town of Horsehead Post Office when they saw a wagon train heading their way. Through her spyglasses, Sally examined the people approaching. "Oh, no! That's Russell French."

"Is it too late to hide?" Eli asked.

Sally waved. "He's already seen us. Besides, he would recognize Beauty."

All of the family had been told about the man who had bought Bacon's Trading Post. Even though Russell didn't know their real names, he knew they were connected to Dr. Luke Smith, and Judge Daniel Hall knew Dr. Luke Smith was an alias of Noah Swift Hawk. Still, Eli didn't want to give the man any more information than he already knew. He quickly reminded his family, "I'm James Bacon. Sally is Nancy Bacon, my sister, and Roscoe Bacon is our uncle." Eli spoke as James Bacon when they came together. "How goes the trading business, Russell?"

"Well enough, but Arnold was some trader. I miss him."

"How are Arnold and the trading post?" Sally asked, "Did Arnold change its name? How are the injured mules Arnold kept?"

"Arnold is doing very well. He married that woman. It seems to agree with him. So many people know it as Bacon's Trading Post, that Arnold kept the name. All his mules are doing fine. Is that Mule 17?"

Sally straightened him out. "Her name is Beauty."

Russell was surprised. "I was sure she would die."

"Lots of Nancy's care and love saved her." Eli stroked the mule's neck.

"What about the rest of them?" Russell inquired.

Sally reported the condition of the other mules injured in the blizzard. "All the mules we have are fine except Dollie. She still doesn't see well with her right eye."

When they heard that Mule 17 was alive, Russell's men walked to the front of the wagon train to look. They gathered around the mule. Will, the man who had attempted to have his way with Sally, approached. *Nancy is a remarkably beautiful woman.* He stood beside her and rubbed the mule's side. "She feels lumpy." Will glanced at her brother.

Eli put his hand on the gun, strapped to his hip. "Hello, Will."

"I see you. Don't worry. I'm not a complete idiot. I'm glad she didn't die. I hope you're doing well too, Nancy."

"I'm well, and you?"

"I'm fine." *I don't want James to think he needs to protect his sister with that gun.* "I'll just be going back to my wagon." He walked away

Russell inquired, "How's Roscoe? Is he close to here? I would love to visit if he's not too far."

"He's fine, but he's far away," Sally informed him.

Russell asked, "What are you doing here?"

Tom quickly offered what he thought was a plausible need that could only be satisfied by going west. "I'm going to Fort Smith to get fruit for my store. They're helping me."

"I have apples and limes," Russell informed him.

Tom was astounded. *I wish I had known of this trader years ago.* "How many?"

"Four barrels of apples and ten bushels of limes."

"How much?"

"Eight dollars for the apples out of the barrels and twenty dollars for the limes out of the baskets."

Yates mercantile didn't have some of the things we'll need, and the cost of the goods at Fort Gibson is ridiculously high. Eli had an idea. "How about tin dinner sets and green goggles?"

Before Russell answered, Sally asked, "Do you have garlic?"

"Why don't you make a list of everything you want? I'll see if I have it and give you a price."

Tom said, "Be right back." He led his family to the back of one of their wagons. He wrote: We want all four barrels of apples in the barrels and all the limes in the baskets.

Their Uncle James informed them, "You should get goggles, india rubber ponchos, ground cloths, and water mattresses for everybody."

Sally took the paper. She wrote how many adult and child sizes of each of the items James mentioned then wrote on the list: twelve india rubber canteens, twelve tin plate, cup, knife, fork and spoon sets, one sheet metal stove, garlic, paper binders, paper, pencils, and erasers.

"I have all of this. How much paper and how many pencils and erasers?"

Nancy replied, "Ten binders, ten reams of paper, two gross of pencils, and five dozen erasers."

"Are you sure you want all ten bushels of limes?" Russell had picked up the limes from stores that had not sold them. He thought he would never resell them. "I also have dried fruit: cranberries, currants, peaches, and apricots."

"We only have so much room. The apples and limes will take up a lot of space," Tom replied.

Russell offered a suggestion that would allow him to sell more items. "You could put the limes in ten-gallon washtubs and attach them under the wagons."

Stephanie looked under a wagon. "How?"

Helen suggested, "Tie a rope through the handles."

"They'll tip over or bounce out," Tom scratched his head and looked into the distance.

Uncle James offered a possibility. "What if you attach a net under the wagons then put a wagon cover inside and poured in the limes."

Eli asked, "Do you have any india rubber wagon covers?"

Russell replied, "I do, but you don't want to put something that expensive under a wagon."

Sally spoke up, "Give me all the limes, eight ten-gallon washtubs, two cargo nets, two india rubber wagon covers, twenty pounds of garlic, ten sets of snowshoes for adults, and one for a child. We'll take the dried fruit too. Do we need anything else for the store?" she looked at Tom.

"Not unless you have full powder horns, ammunition, and wadding. Would you be interested in buying harnesses?"

I didn't have a very good year. If I don't have to buy anything and I sell everything James and Nancy want, I'll have enough to recover all my expenses, pay the men, and have a small profit. "I only sell this time of year." Russell calculated the cost. "Three hundred and seventy-three dollars."

"It's safer to carry supplies than money." Eli handed over the money.

"I have fireproof steel boxes."

Sally wanted a safe place to protect her paper of ownership of the necklace and the dress. "I'll take one."

"Two dollars and fifty cents," Russell told her. Sally gave him the money.

"It's been a pleasure seeing you again, James and Nancy, and meeting the rest of you. Give Roscoe my regards."

"It's been nice to see you too, Russell. We'll tell Uncle Roscoe," Eli replied.

Russell called out, "Forward ho," then left Sally, Eli, the real James, Tom, Stephanie, and Helen to figure out how to get everything loaded.

Everything fit into the back, the wagons seats, and floorboards except the barrels and baskets of fruit. Therefore, Eli and Stephanie stayed behind with the limes and the wagons while Helen, Sally, James, and Tom rolled the barrels of apples down the dirt road.

They entered the town of Horsehead Post Office as Helen sang "Amazing Grace." At the inn, Tom rented rooms. They rolled the fruit down the hall and emptied the apples onto the floor of their rooms.

Helen sang, "The Old Rugged Cross" on the way back to the wagons. Once there, they filled the empty barrels with the limes and rolled them just as they had with the first batch of fruit.

In town, they secured the wagons, barrels of limes, mules, and horses in the stable then went to the inn. They bought supper before sleeping in rooms filled with the pleasant aroma of apples.

Before leaving town the next day, they installed the india rubber covers over the canvas wagon covers. They tied the nets under the wagons and then loaded the items that wouldn't go through the webbing or be ruined riding below. To minimize damage from bouncing, they carefully packed then loaded the fruit into the wagons.

The sun shone through the yellow, red, and orange leaves of the hickory and oak trees as Stephanie walked beside the wagons. "God really took care of us."

Sally held her sister's hand. "I agree. What was

the chance that would happen? I can't believe Russell had all the things we needed."

Eli pointed out the negative side of the encounter. "Except now if anybody asks, Russell will know we were here this fall. Somebody could put it all together."

"That won't happen. What are the chances that two things so unlikely will both occur? Don't worry." Helen then sang her feeling about God.

"God is so good. God is so good. God is so good. He's so good to me!

God answers prayer. God answers prayer. God answers prayer. He's so good to me!

He cares for me. He cares for me. He cares for me. He's so good to me!

I love Him so. I love Him so. I love Him so. He's so good to me!

I'll do His will. I'll do His will. I'll do His will. He's so good to me!

I praise His name. I praise His name. I praise His name. He's so good to me!"

They collected more hickory nuts until the bags were filled. When they let the animals rest at mid-day, they roasted all of them as they enjoyed hymns sung by Helen.

Every night, they stayed at an inn or boarding house in the towns spaced just far enough to reach in one day. After leaving Pleasant Hill, Sally cut the mid-day stop short. "We need to hurry. So far, we've been very blessed with good weather. If it rains, Frog Bayou could hold us up for days."

When they stood beside Frog Bayou, Helen commented, "I'm glad we got here before dark."

Eli completed his examination of the bayou. "The water doesn't look too deep."

James, however, wasn't happy. "It's a lot deeper than when we crossed going to Harmony."

Sally told them what had happened the first time she had crossed Frog Bayou. "I crossed when the water was much higher than this. Although we did ride the ferry. Even so, Ann and Noah barely survived the final ride across. You know what we learned; if you can, always cross the waterways when you get to them."

"She's right," James agreed.

"Then let me drive the first wagon across alone," Eli requested.

Helen pointed out the problem. "We can't fit five in the second wagon."

Eli didn't give in. "The men will go first. I want to make sure Stephanie will be safe."

Helen didn't know much about Sally or Stephanie's ability to survive in the wilds. She automatically believed the men could keep them safe. "If all of you die, the three of us women will be alone."

James had an idea. "Then Tom and I will ride across on the first wagon. Eli, if we get across without any problems, you ride that big mule of yours at the front of your team. The three women can ride in the wagon seat."

"You mean for me to ride Glory?" Eli asked.

"Yes."

"All right. Go on and try it out."

Stephanie stopped them. "First, we pray. Heavenly Father, You parted the Red Sea, and You made Balaam's donkey talk. We know You can control both water and animals, so control them both and get us safely across this stream of water."

They all said, "Amen."

The six horses easily pulled the wagon carrying Tom and James across the ford of Frog Bayou.

Eli sat on Glory where he wouldn't press the harness into her back. "Mules are stronger than horses. We shouldn't have a problem." He called out, "Forward ho," as he squeezed his legs together and gave the mule a second signal to go.

Their wagon was lighter than the first. It floated at the deepest part of the river. The thick layers of pitch on the outside and inside kept it watertight for the few minutes it was a boat pulled by six mules, blessedly able to keep their feet firmly on the riverbed. As soon as they came out of the water, they set up camp. They spent the night sleeping on cedar boughs they cut from the forest.

After the first night that Helen had ever slept on the ground, she told her family. "The cedar branches made the ground soft, and they smell so nice." Before

Tom had come home, Helen had spent her life being a respectable city woman married to Tom's father. She thought her new life in the wild western frontier sleeping on branches was exciting. She had loved her husband very much, she was sad that he had died, and she missed him deeply, but Helen was glad she was free to go with her family. She would never have been able to do anything like this if he had still been alive. It made his passing more bearable.

Seven days after leaving Harmony, the Fort Gibson guard inspected the family's wagons as Helen sang Charles Wesley's hymn, "Jesus, Lover of my Soul."

Just before nightfall, the soldier told them, "Go on in."

They parked their wagons where instructed, and set up the tent Tom had brought from his store. Luckily, the soldiers at the gate hadn't recognized Sally. Inside the fort, she stayed crammed in the wagon until the tent was erected then quickly moved inside and out of view. She hoped she would not encounter the young officer, Lieutenant Jackson, who had wanted to take her necklace and give it back to its previous owner. Nor did she want to see either of the privates who had spent two days carrying heavy sacks of rocks because they had touched her and Ann.

As they set up camp, the smell of baking bread beckoned them. Sally knew what had happened when she and Ann had ventured into the bakery alone, and she didn't want to affiliate James with anybody but his village, so she spoke up. "James should stay in the tent with me, Stephanie, and Helen. Eli, you and Tom go to the bakery. Get bread, éclairs, and danishes." While the two men checked out the store and went to the bakery, the women set out a meal of food they didn't need to cook.

When he rejoined the rest of their family in the tent, Eli informed them, "They were selling peach seeds. We bought some." To their meal, Eli added a loaf of the freshly baked bread along with the apple cider and danishes they bought. "The prices here are so high. It's a good thing we ran into Russell."

The next day, they took down the tent, packed it into the wagon, and then headed to the Neosho River crossing. On the far side of the river, they traveled at the edge of the prairie. They fished when the road was close to the river. When farther away, they shot prairie chickens, jackrabbits, prairie dogs, and even an antelope. James showed them where and how to gather useful plants and then demonstrated how to prepare them. When they got to the place where they had killed the buffalo, Sally took them to the field and pointed to the very place where the yellow buffalo had lain, slain by her rifle.

Eli commented, "I hope I can get one someday."

Tom agreed with the sentiment. "I do too."

"And me," Stephanie added.

They were all surprised when Helen said, "Don't leave me out."

James assured them, "I'm sure you'll come across plenty of buffalo when you cross the plains."

When they arrived at the second crossing of the Neosho River, Helen asked, "Why are we crossing back to the east? If we should be on the other side, why did we come over here?"

James explained, "The Cherokee have not given permission for people to travel in their land on the east side of the river. If we had a hunting talisman, we could be there, but we don't have one. Anybody can travel this road, and hunt and gather what's close to the road. Also, it's easier to travel on the road."

The weather had been beautiful so far. Eli knew that could change in a hurry. "Let's cross before we set up camp."

Back on the east side, James told his family, "This is where the soldiers and our people stayed while they tried to hide the buffalo we didn't have permission to kill."

Sally lay down beside the fire. "Tomorrow we'll be home." It struck her that she had thought of Noah's village as home. She had not felt that way while she had been in Harmony.

Stephanie closed her eyes. "I can't wait to see Ann's big belly."

FIFTY SIX

On guard duty, Chaska saw Sally through the spyglass. *I thought she would be in Harmony until spring.* He ran into the village. Tahatankohana was outside his home. "Sally comes with two women, two men, and James."

"She does?" Tahatankohana put down the cradleboard he was making and went with Chaska to the lookout. "It is them."

Chaska asked, "Did you think I wouldn't recognize Sally?"

That comment pointed out to Tahatankohana that he needed to keep an eye on Chaska. They walked back into the village. Tahatankohana went into his home. "Get ready to celebrate. The wait is over. "

Ann stood up. "I need to be at the creek."

Tahatankohana told her, "We have time to start getting things ready."

Chaska offered, "I'll watch and tell you when it's time."

When he came back, the whole village was ready to welcome home the travelers. As the travelers neared, James looked through his looking tube. He saw the crowd on the far side of the creek. "Looks like everybody."

Ann remained on the village side of the creek and called across the water, "Get over here."

As soon as he had crossed, James jumped off the wagon. He immediately hugged his wife and children. When Stephanie and Sally crossed in the second wagon, Ann hugged them as close as she could in her condition. "I've missed you so much." Ann told the rest of her family, "Get over here." Eli, Tom, and Helen joined the group hug. Ann requested of those who had remained at home and had not realized they were included, "You too." The rest came into the hug. Ann stated, "Now we have everybody, and everything is perfect."

Tahatankohana stepped out. "Let's introduce ourselves."

Sally hugged her friends. Chaska stepped over to get a hug as well. She blushed as he gave her more than a brief hug. "Welcome home. I'm glad you're back," Chaska whispered into her ear.

Each person told his or her name as they started across the field. They put the wagons beside the lodge, unharnessed the mules and horses, and then let them into the field with the other animals. Even after the long separation, the mules returned to their established places in the herd. The six new horses joined the ever-increasing herd and sorted out their relationships.

The wagons remained packed while the

newcomers went to look at the lift. Petang pulled himself up a short way then lowered the basket to the ground. "Very nice," Tom commented in English. Chetan translated into Quapaw.

"Take me," Chumani spoke her first English words. She hadn't been allowed to go into the basket with her Quapaw speaking family members. She thought this new person might let her go. She had heard so much English that she had learned both languages. Nobody had realized that until she spoke to Tom.

"Chumani, I didn't know you understood English," Bethany exclaimed.

"May Eli and I take her?" Stephanie asked.

"Yes, but be very careful and keep her away from the opening." Chumani clapped as she climbed into the basket. She clapped all the way to the top and all the way back down.

The others took turns pulling themselves to the top before the people gathered in the community lodge to share food and listen to the story of the trip to Harmony.

Sally told the story in Quapaw. When she couldn't think of the Quapaw words, James helped. Ann understood most of the story. Eli, Tom, Stephanie, and Helen understood none of it. Tahatankohana, Bethany, Luyu, and Chetan sat beside them and translated. At the end of the day, they went to their lodge happy.

FIFTY SEVEN

In Little Rock, Russell drove into Martin Harrow's Livery. "You will never guess who I saw."

"You're right. I'll never guess, so just tell me," replied Martin.

"Nancy and James Bacon."

Not far from the two men, Robert, Mr. Harrow's new stable hand, pitched hay. Robert shoveled the same spot repeatedly as he focused on what the new arrival was telling Martin.

Martin didn't want to encourage Russell to give information to anybody about where he had seen them, and he surely didn't want to know. He lied, "I never cared for them."

"Really? Well, you might want to know she saved Mule 17. That's the one she calls Beauty. It was all lumpy under its fur, but it was alive and doing well."

Martin told Russell, "I'm always glad when an animal is healthy. I need to get going. Have a good stay in Little Rock," then he called out to Robert, "Get Mr. French's mules put in and fed before you go home."

Martin walked away quickly. *I got away in time. I don't know anything.*

Robert helped Mr. French park the wagons inside where they could lock them up for the night. Robert talked to Mr. French as he helped unharness the mules. "Dr. Smith helped me with my father-in-law's pig. That's why Bertha's father let us get married. Did you see him too?"

"No, I only saw James and Nancy. They bought a lot of supplies from me. If I didn't know better, I would think they were planning a long trip for ten or twelve people."

"Maybe they are. Where did you see them? When was it?"

Russell was glad to talk about the family of his old friend Roscoe Bacon. "It was two weeks ago, just west of Spadra. They bought close to four hundred dollars of supplies and all my fruit. That sale made this a good year. I wonder how they got so much money, and James said something odd. He said carrying supplies was safer than carrying money, and his sister bought a strong box. They were traveling with two older men, a young pregnant woman, and an older woman." Russell chatted on about other people he had met while traveling until they had all the mules watered and fed. "Everybody wants to get home before the end of October. We'll be moving out at sunup, so have them fed again early."

Robert assured him, "Yes, sir, they'll be ready, Mr. French." He locked the barn door. *I've finally found out. Now, I can collect the money Judge Hall promised me.*

Robert knocked on the judge's door. A servant opened it. "Mrs. Hall gives out scraps to the needy at the back door."

"I'm not one of the needy. I work for my money. Judge Hall will want to talk with me. Tell him the newsboy has arrived."

Assuring that the foul-smelling person stayed on the outside of the door, the butler shut the door then went to the library. "The newsboy is here, sir."

"He is! Thank you." A smile spread across Judge Daniel's face. *I'm going to win this one.* He opened the door and stepped onto the veranda. "What did you hear?"

"Give me the money first." Robert held out his hand.

The judge fished several silver coins from his moneybag but held them tightly in his hand. "I have the money right here. Speak then I'll give it to you."

"Russell French saw the sisters and the brother-in-law at Spadra just two weeks ago."

"Still so close to home." He dropped the coins into Robert's hands. "There's more if you find out anything else significant."

"I'll see what I can find out in the morning." Robert went home to his wife with five silver dollars.

Judge Hall could barely believe it. His wait was finally over. He stepped back into his house. *Now, they'll get what they deserve. Nobody disrespects me!*

ACKNOWLEDGMENTS

*Apache Wedding Blessing

Cover

By Happybluemo - Own work, CC BY-SA 4.0, modified, https://commons.wikimedia.org/w/index.php?curid=39607195

Chapter Headings

Image from page 174 of "Our greater country; being a standard history of the United States from the discovery of the American continent to the present time ..", modified, Northrop, Henry Davenport, Philadelphia, National pub co., 1901

Did you like this story?
Please write a review.
https://www.amazon.com/dp/1945858133

Follow me at
ChanceAndChoicesAdventures.com

Made in the USA
Columbia, SC
02 May 2021

36762412R00207